Lisa Dickenson was born in the wrong body. She was definitely meant to be Beyoncé. Despite this hardship, she grew up in Devon attempting to write her own, completely copyright-infringing versions of *Sweet Valley High*, before giving Wales a go for university, and then London a go for the celeb-spotting potential. She's now back in Devon, living beside the seaside with her husband and forcing cream teas down the mouths of anyone who'll visit. She is sadly still not Beyoncé.

Lisa is the author of *Catch Me If You Cannes*, now available as a four-part ebook, and *The Twelve Dates of Christmas*, which won the Novelicious Debut of the Year award. *You Had Me at Merlot* is her second novel.

Follow her on Twitter for all her book news and Beyoncé-related chatter: @LisaWritesStuff.

You
HAD ME
AT
Merlot

Lisa Dickenson

sphere

SPHERE

First published in Great Britain in 2016 by Sphere

1 3 5 7 9 10 8 6 4 2

A CIP catalogue record for this book
is available from the British Library.

ISBN 978-0-7515-6193-7

Typeset in Caslon by M Rules
Printed and bound in Great Britain by
Clays Ltd, St Ives plc

Papers used by Sphere are from well-managed forests
and other responsible sources.

MIX
Paper from
responsible sources
FSC
www.fsc.org   FSC® C104740

Sphere
An imprint of
Little, Brown Book Group
Carmelite House
50 Victoria Embankment
London EC4Y 0DZ

An Hachette UK Company
www.hachette.co.uk

www.littlebrown.co.uk

Dedicated to red wine
(Mmmmmmmmmmmmmmmm)

Oh, and to Emma
(who only drinks Malibu and Coke)

Part One

'I've done it!' I paced around in my little flat in my heels, slowing my breathing. 'Eight years after it came out, I've finally just perfected the "Single Ladies" dance routine.'

'Congratulations,' said Laurie down the phone. 'Does that mean you haven't left home yet?'

'I'm not getting a boyfriend now – all this hard work's not going to waste,' I warned her.

'Fine, you don't have to get a boyfriend today, but you do have to get on the Tube and get down to Wimbledon.'

'Are you there already?'

'Not far. Now take off that leotard—'

How did she know?

'—and get your smelly self into the shower.'

I put down the phone and peeled off my sweaty leotard and heels, chuffed to bits with my achievement.

I hummed and danced all the way into my lovely waterfall shower in my lovely turquoise bathroom, surrounded by only beautiful-smelling girl stuff, feeling as happy as ever to be living alone. And after I stepped out, I pulled on a dress and flung open the curtains as if I hadn't been doing anything weird.

'Hello out there,' I said to the brightly dressed people of Notting Hill. 'How's the furnace this morning?'

♡

The Tube train shuddered to a stop, allowing another heave of bodies to clamber aboard, while two more rivulets of sweat pole-danced their way down the backs of my legs. It was pretty sexy. London hadn't been this hot since the great fire in 1666 (possibly), and the residents were dropping like flies and grumbling all the way round the Circle line.

I like London in the heat – the more *scorchio* the better. I like it when tourists flock in and their preconceived idea of an England gushing with rain is carried away on a warm breeze; cloudy, bruised skies windscreen-wiped to reveal bright, royal blue.

And there's nothing a Brit loves more than sitting out in the midday sun at the first sign of summer, which was why I was joining hundreds of people on the annual pilgrimage to Wimbledon for the start of the tennis. My friend Laurie is an event photographer, which means she gets coveted seats at amazing stuff, and as I'm the only stable other half in her life I'm often along for the ride.

I lifted the hem of my maxidress off the floor, cooling my ankles. I'd seen Paris Hilton wearing a similar maxi at Coachella this year, and thought it would be perfect for Wimbledon, but looking at my fellow passengers in their Jack Wills and Ralph Lauren I felt a bit silly in my tie-dye tent.

The doors finally dragged open at Southfields, throwing up its contents upon the platform, and I followed the crowd on the fifteen-minute walk to the famed tennis courts.

As I entered the All England Lawn Tennis and Croquet Club Laurie flew at me, an excited bundle of cameras, bags, merchandise and messy black hair. 'Elle! I just saw Venus Williams coming out of the toilet!' she shouted as a greeting.

'Are you sure? I feel like she'd have her own toilet, like in a dressing room.'

Laurie considered this. 'Well, I took a photo, so we can check later on. If not, I have a photo of a stunning woman coming out of a toilet.'

'What did you buy?' Laurie's house was chock-a-block with memorabilia from everything she goes to – she's the only one I know who will buy up everything on the overpriced merchandise stalls at a concert, or will actually purchase the robes, flannels and soap dishes from a hotel gift shop rather than just stealing them from her room.

'Everything. I got us T-shirts, pencils and sweat-bands,' she said, slipping a fluffy white one on my wrist.

We made a pit stop at a strawberries stand and the bar before hauling all of Laurie's equipment over to Centre Court and positioning ourselves on the green plastic seats, blobs of cream threatening to fall off our strawberries and land with a splat upon the head of the spectator in front, and plastic beer cups splashing foam on my flip-flopped feet. It was only when I noticed the empty seat next to us that I realised someone was missing.

'Hang on, where's Tim?'

'I can't believe I forgot to tell you!' Laurie cried. 'We split up.'

'I can't believe you forgot to tell me as well!'

'Well . . . he was kind of forgettable. You just proved that yourself.'

We took a moment to mourn the loss of Tim, who was indeed forgettable, so much so that I regularly forgot his name when we were out and kept calling him m'dear.

'What happened?'

'I just couldn't see myself still with him in a couple of years, let alone growing old. He was very nice and everything, a lovely guy really, and I wish I'd felt more towards him, but it was all just a bit "meh". So I broke up with him.'

At that point the crowd shushed as the players, glistening men in crisp white shorts, took their places on opposite ends of the court. We chomped on our juicy strawberries and watched the sweating gents on either side of the net, their balls thunking back and forth, so to speak, accompanied by primal grunting, which turned my thoughts back to relationships.

'Are you sad?' I whispered.

'No. Just disappointed that it didn't work out, again.'

'The ladies aren't going to be happy about this setback,' I reprimanded her. 'The ladies' are our group of girlfriends, brought together through university, a mismatched group of opposites who all attracted. All of them, except for Laurie and me, grew up and are now in one or more of the marriage, mortgage or baby club. And they are positively, plague-infestedly itching for us to join.

'Tell me about it. When Tim and I met Jasmine for drinks a few weeks back she actually started suggesting ideas for our honeymoon. I just . . . ' Laurie trailed off and sighed heavily into her strawberries and cream. 'I just don't want to keep dating and never feeling like I'm actually getting close to anyone.'

'I know,' I soothed. I didn't know. The thought of getting close to someone, having them move into my home, having to make joint decisions on what TV to watch and what to have for dinner, knowing that if I want to work late I should let my 'other half' know just all seemed like a lot of effort.

'I don't want to feel like I'm putting on a show,' Laurie said a while later.

'No.'

'I don't want to feel like I'm always the bridesmaid.'

'But you've never been a bridesmaid. It's actually really fun. You feel super-important.'

'I just want to feel . . .'

'What?'

'Love.'

'—LOVE!' boomed the umpire down on the court.

'Leave me alone!' Laurie cried back, then hid behind her camera as about twenty people turned to shush us.

We settled back to watch the game, neon-yellow balls whizzing across the blue sky and getting thwacked back where they came from with a grunt. I was itching to give my attention back to Laurie, worried she was sat there suffering in silence, and eventually there was a break in play and the stands broke into excited chatter.

'I'm over internet dating, you know,' said Laurie, turning to me, her tongue wedged into the bottom of her bowl, licking the cream.

'Really? You're taking a break from men, joining me as a happily single lady?'

'Hell no, I'm just going to do things the old-fashioned way, and meet someone face to face.'

'Well that sounds sensible. Are you going to join a new gym or something?'

'No, no, we're not going to do that ...' Laurie smirked at me with her *I've had an idea* face. 'I've had an idea. And it's a really, really good idea that I really, really want you to join me on. I think we deserve a holiday.'

'Ooo yes! I love holidays. It's been too long. Where shall we go? Cancún? Greece? Thailand again?' I raised my eyebrows at her.

'Well actually I've already chosen the holiday, but I think you'll love it.'

'Oh.'

'Hold this.' Laurie handed me her empty, saliva-covered strawberry dish and reached down between her legs to her handbag. After some unladylike struggling she picked up her beer and gulped the remainder, handing me the empty cup as well. She then yanked out a thin, glossy brochure and placed it on her lap, laying her hands over it. On the cover, between her fingers, I saw a large, sparkling glass of wine with a sun-drenched background of a vineyard. Interesting – I do like wine and sunshine.

The crowd cheered and Laurie lifted her hands to clap, as if she knew what was going on, and my eyes caught the title of the brochure.

'"*You Had Me at Merlot" Holidays*,' I read. 'What kind of a holiday is this?'

'It's a vineyard holiday, in Italy.'

'That sounds nice. A little red, a little white, a little siesta in the sun.'

'A little smoochy smoochy with some *full-bodied* men?'

'What?'

'Nothing, I mean, except it's, like, a group trip.'

'Like a tour?'

'No, more like a get-to-know-you holiday, where you do activities with other people . . . '

I watched one of the players pour a bottle of water over himself at the side of the court, much to the swooning of one of the women in the Royal Box. 'So you *have* to mingle with the other guests?'

'It's kind of an essential.'

'But what kind of a— Is this a *singles*' holiday?' I hissed.

'Yes, but I really want to go, and I really want you to come with me.'

'No way.'

'Please, Elle. It'll be so much fun.'

'I really don't want to do this.'

'Why not?'

'Because … *You Had Me at Merlot*? It just sounds incredibly cringey.' I took the brochure from her. 'It's going to be all greasy Casanovas and titillating drinking games.' But, flipping through the pages, I saw pictures of sunrises over medieval villages, rolling vine-covered hills, delicious Italian platters and zero bondage-masked men or booze buses.

'You're always saying how much you *loooove* being single, so why wouldn't you love a singles' holiday?'

'Because the whole point of a singles' holiday is to meet potential partners!'

'I guess—'

'Or is it just to have a romp in the sunshine?'

'No, the first one. Well, maybe a bit of the second. But this isn't an eighteen-to-thirty holiday, Elle, it's a really classy affair. Just like you.' She prodded my sweaty arm and gave me a look that told me she already knew I'd agree.

'I can't leave work.'

'Yes you can. You haven't taken any holiday yet this year.'

'Can't we go to Cancún?'

'Next year, I promise.'

I sighed. 'What would I have to do on this holiday? Is there anything to occupy me while you're off sampling the . . . selection.'

'There's loads to do.' She opened the brochure at a page that showed a smiling middle-aged couple leaning against a row of Vespas, the immense terracotta frontage of Bella Notte vineyard rising behind them. 'You can pick grapes, you can go for walks, you can borrow a Vespa and explore the area. Or you can just taste-test all the wines and fall asleep in the sunshine.'

My friend is annoying. It's like she has a built-in algorithm that targets my weak points and knows exactly what to hard-sell them with. And the thought of sleep and sun and endless wine had me considering her proposal. In a way, you could say she had me at 'Merlot'. Dear God, what was I getting myself into?

♥

It was late the following week and the office was having an early-closing day due to a need for

12

fumigation following a fruit-fly invasion (thanks to some over-zealous juice dieters in Accounts). I was meeting the ladies – Jasmine, Helen, Emma and Laurie – for drinks by the water in Greenwich, and the ice was already melting in the first round by the time our final femme, Marie, arrived with squidgy little baby Daisy.

'It is so hot; my nipples will not stop lactating.'

I put down my White Russian.

'They lactate when you're hot? Is that even a thing? What about the women who live in countries like Tunisia?' asked Laurie, holding her beer bottle to her hot forehead.

'I think my body's just trying to find any possible way to cool me down. I actually had to stand in the paddling pool at midday yesterday because they were just flowing like Timotei waterfalls.' She stared at my cocktail. 'I want your alcohol.'

'By all means.' I slid the milky drink across the table.

'No!' Jasmine smacked my hand with a *you don't know ANYTHING about being a new mum* glare. 'You're doing so well; not long now.'

'I just want some wine, just four big glasses of wine.' She grappled around for her orange juice, unable to see the table thanks to her ginormous breasts. 'Gah – these things are ridiculous!'

'I think your boobs look amazing,' said Laurie jealously.

'You'll have them soon; Tim is going to baby you up in no time.'

I grabbed the White Russian back again. Here we go.

'No, Tim and I split up.'

There was a chorus of 'Oh-no's and all four heads tilted to the right. 'Why?' demanded Jasmine, personally offended. 'He was The One.'

'No he wasn't,' I said. 'She wasn't that into him.'

'But I thought you were going to get married.'

'We really hadn't been together very long.'

'He would have made a great dad, though,' Emma sighed, and the others nodded in sorrow.

'It's okay, because Elle and I have a new plan.' Laurie shuffled in her handbag and pulled out the brochure. 'We're going on a singles' holiday.'

Squeals of delight.

'A *posh* singles' holiday,' I clarified. 'To a vineyard in Tuscany, to do wine tasting and suchlike.'

'The company's called *You Had Me at Merlot*!' said Laurie with pride. The ladies sniggered.

'Can I have a little less cheese with that wine?' asked Jasmine, and Marie guffawed so hard she started spouting again and had to hand Daisy over to Emma.

'The vineyard itself is called Bella Notte.' I was

aware I was bristling, which was ridiculous, as I'd had exactly the same thoughts. But hearing them bash my first holiday in for ever smarted.

'That's pretty,' said Marie. 'I envisage you both gazing at the stars, mambo Italiano-ing with signors, utterly happy-drunk on wine. Are you gonna snog someone?' Her eyes glazed over as she transported herself into our heady, single world.

'I am.' Laurie put her hand up.

'Really? With tongues?' Helen breathed.

'Who doesn't use tongues? Isn't that standard? Do people kiss differently these days?' asked Jasmine, turning to us for answers.

'I'm not kissing anyone,' I said.

'*You have to.*' Helen slammed her wine on the table. 'I mean, wouldn't it be rude not to on a singles' holiday? What else will you have to do?'

'I don't think it's a tally-sheet, notches-on-the-bedpost type of singles' holiday. I think it's probably going to be older single people, not your eighteen-to-thirty crowd. We might be the youngest there.'

'Older men can be very hot,' said Helen, she of the younger husband. 'Think of George Clooney.'

'Hold on,' said Emma. 'George Clooney lives in Italy, and he's often single, and he's older – maybe he'll be there.'

'He's so going to be there!' cried Helen. 'You're going to marry George Clooney!'

'Nope, George is hitched now. But even if he wasn't, although I'd be willing to have a summer fling if he wanted one, I don't think either Laurie or I are going to be getting married off the back of one holiday.'

'There's something about holidays though – being in a new place and not having to do dishes—'

'And drinking carafe after carafe of wine,' added Marie.

'—it just puts you in the mood for romance. Brian proposed to me after five too many Bahama Mamas in Barbados.'

'Ellie proposed to me at the bottom of Snowdon,' said Emma.

'At the bottom?'

'We couldn't be bothered to climb it, when it came down to it. But we were still on holiday. My friend Claudia's taking Nick to New Zealand next week; they're bound to come back engaged.'

'But these are all established relationships. I have no plans to walk down the aisle any time soon.' Jasmine and Marie exchanged raised eyebrows, which irked me even more. I know myself better than they know me, and why did they think I could only be happy if I was like them? I wasn't single because no one loved me, nor because I surely must give out too many desperate vibes, nor because I won't find a man unless I stop looking, and no (Dad), not because I'm a lesbian. It's because I like my life, I like being able to come home to my own flat and be by myself and learn dance routines, and I've *chosen to be single*. And I was getting pretty fed up with having to justify myself to everyone. Of course, that little speech didn't come out as planned, and instead I grumbled like a sullen teenager: 'I'm not swapping my life for anyone else's idea of my Mr Perfect. So there.'

'I'm just glad I don't have to go on singles' holidays any more,' sighed Jasmine.

'It's not that we have to, we want to.' Laurie grinned, opening the brochure to a page with a large photograph of a girl riding on the back of a Vespa, sunglasses reflecting the Italian sunshine. 'How could you not want to go here?'

'Exactly,' I said. 'Sometimes it's nice to go on holidays without kids and couples all over the place.'

'Talking about kids' holidays,' said Jasmine, 'does anyone know where I can buy good, organic travel nappies? As you might have seen on Facebook, Max used his potty for the first time last night, and it was just the most adorable thing ever, but we're going . . . '

I'm a horrible friend, but I faded out. I looked beyond

the ladies to the baroque white architecture of the Old Royal Naval College and wondered if I'd ever fancy going back to university. Or joining the navy. Then I thought about the YouTube clip of the cat dressed as a shark, rolling around someone's house on a Roomba. *That* is the most adorable thing ever, surely? I just don't think a child weeing into a bowl compares.

The week before my holiday, work seemed even busier than usual, if that were possible. There were a million loose ends I wanted to tie up, and a million more 'little things' people wanted me to do for them before I left. I hated saying I couldn't do something, so I always said yes. But tears tickled the backs of my eyes sometimes. Not coping wasn't an option.

I'm one of three marketing managers at a PR agency in the City, and I'd been at work since seven fifteen that Thursday morning. By two thirty I needed to stretch my legs, having only gone as far as the loos and the coffee machine since I arrived. I decided to go and wander about by Donna.

Donna is our managing director, and kind of my idol, though I've never said more than a 'Hello' and a 'Yes, I *love* working here' and an 'Actually, it's Elle' to her. But she's a woman – the only woman – near the top of the company, and one day I want to be up there near her, so I need to make myself known.

I smoothed my hair, grabbed a ringbinder (no idea what was inside) and headed downstairs to her floor with a plan to pass her office.

Here's how I was hoping it would go:

I stride past Donna's office, confident and professional, and she looks up.

'Elle?'

'Oh hi,' I say, going in. 'How's your daughter?'

'She's great, thanks for asking. I've been meaning to run something by you. You're in this for the long haul, right?'

'Absolutely, I'm not going anywhere.'

'That's fantastic. You have such an admirable work ethic. I've noticed the extra hours you put in, the passion you show for the company, your drive to achieve results. Oh, and everyone absolutely loves you. There's a position opening up that you'd be perfect for. It's very high up and important, and you'd have your own office and a company credit card and a six-figure salary, and people will add you to their LinkedIn accounts.'

'Donna, how nice of you to think of me! I'd love to!'

Here's what actually happened:

I walked past her office five times; eventually Donna got up and closed the door. I had a mild panic attack that she'd think I was useless if I had enough time on my hands to be wandering about all day, and decided to put in an extra couple of hours before home-time this evening.

Ah well, I'll try the same routine tomorrow.

The rest of the day flew by in the usual blur of conference calls, marketing plans, PowerPoints and problems until my stomach let out a large growl and I glanced at the clock in the corner of my screen, which read 19:25. I looked up and there was no one else on my floor. No one at all.

Turning my chair, I used my feet to drag it and myself to the window, where I leant my forehead against the glass and gazed down at the street below. Colleagues and suited strangers spilled out of the bars and restaurants, enjoying the warm evening air that I couldn't feel now the sun had dropped below the building opposite, and the lack of life made the air-con seem all the colder.

Why did I try so much, when those people seemed to be actually having all the fun?

I decided I'd leave early for a change, and treat myself to dinner out, somewhere in the last of the sun. I rolled my chair back to my desk and went to shut down my computer when an email came through from Donna. I replied instantly, unashamedly hoping for brownie points, and then sat back and waited.

I waited fifteen minutes, just in case a message pinged back, commending me for still being at my desk, but nothing. And then the cleaner switched out the light and I was forgotten, invisible.

For a moment I just sat there, staring at the pod after pod of empty desks, which looked eerily dead in only the shaded light from outside the tinted windows. I was important to this company, wasn't I? I was needed, an asset. I was one of their best workers. Maybe they didn't always notice when I was here, but I was sure they'd notice next week when I wasn't here. Wouldn't they?

Fine, I'd bloody go home then. I'd be back in less than twelve hours anyway.

♡

The following day I was indeed back at work, my last day before my holiday, and I was slouched in the boardroom with fifteen other people, waiting for a meeting to begin.

I wondered how soon this meeting could be finished with, so I could get back to the never-ending to-do list upstairs.

Then I wondered if Dan from Accounts knew how much he looked like Anneka Rice.

Damn it, my new work shirt was gaping open at the boobs again.

As the clock ticked around to ten past the time the meeting was supposed to start, I let out a ginormous sigh with an accidental audible 'Uuurrrggghhhhhh.'

'Bet you can't wait to get out of here and start your holiday,' murmured Kath, one of my executives, who was sitting next to me, polishing off her third tepid coffee.

'There's just something so annoying about us all waiting for one person when we're all busy. Who are we even waiting for?'

'Chill out, think of all the gelato you'll be eating this time next week.'

My team knew I was going to Italy, but no more than that. I really didn't need them on my case about my single status too. Or, worse, asking me when I got back if I'd met anyone 'nice'. 'Will you be okay while I'm gone? Are you happy with everything that needs to be done on the Lush Hair account?'

'Of course, just go and have fun and stop being such a worry-arse.'

The door opened and in strode Donna, and immediately I pulled myself up, tugged my shirt closed and nearly toppled off my chair trying to look like the most professional person in the room. There was something about Donna which always made me feel I should be on my best behaviour.

'Morning all, let's begin,' she said, no nonsense. The

meeting started and I tried my hardest to look interested, confident, to ask insightful questions, which I
only fudged once when I said, 'And did you want the
full title, Prime Minister Boris Johnson?'

'No, Ellen,' said Donna, 'let's go with *Mayor* Boris
Johnson.'

'That's what I meant – ha ha ha, silly me – oh, and
it's Elle, just so . . . ' My voice was swallowed up by Dan
starting his Excel presentation.

Kath leaned over to me. 'Don't worry, I get them
mixed up all the time. Just remember this: Mayor
Mayor blondie hair.'

♥

I'd decided to take a quick trip down to the Devon seaside to visit my parents and eat a cream tea before my
Tuesday-morning flight to Italy. Although the holiday
was only for ten days, last year I got into trouble for not
taking all of my holiday allowance, so I took two full
weeks this time. I was already on edge, thinking they'd
realise they got on fine without me, didn't need me at
all and I'd be fired before I could say *arrivederci*.

So, late at night on the Friday, when I finally left
the office, I leapt on the train to Exeter where my
mum picked me up and drove me home, putting me

to snoozeville in my teenage bedroom, complete with purple walls, a blow-up chair and a big faded poster of Craig McLachlan that I won't let her take down.

I woke up to seagulls thumping on the roof, squawking loudly about the appalling lack of chips at six in the morning, and our cat, Breakaway, standing all four heavy paws on my stomach as if to say *You see how much my feet sink into you? LOSE WEIGHT.*

Mum was already up, because whereas I can't start my day without a handful of crisps and checking my work emails before I've taken off my PJs, she can't start the day without a walk along the seafront. I had a cheeky dip into a tube of Pringles and scuttled off to join her.

The sea was calm, but a cool breeze was hanging out with the clouds that had scattered themselves over the pink skies.

'Cold, isn't it?' I yawned, curling my arm around Mum's.

'These clouds'll blow away by lunchtime, I'm sure. It never rains down here, in the Fiji of England. I expect it'll be lovely and warm in Italy, won't it?'

'I hope so. My aim is to leave Laurie to it and just lie back in the sunshine with some vino, and eat every scrap of Italiano food that passes by.'

'It sounds blissful. I love Italy; I could eat antipasti for every meal of the day.'

'Then you should! Yolo, Mum.'

'Yellow?'

'Yolo. It means "you only live once".'

'So if I was at a funeral I'd say, *"Well . . . yolo"*?'

'Probably not – it's more of live-for-the-moment saying. Not a ha-ha-you're-dead saying. It's what us hashtag-cool-kids say.'

'Are you drunk now?'

'No, hashtagging is . . . never mind. Yes, antipasto is *delizioso*.'

'Did you know my first holiday with a boy was to Italy?'

'Urgh, a boy that wasn't Dad?'

Mum threw her head back and laughed. Is there anything better in the world than someone laughing? Seeing that spontaneous burst of joy take over their face, and knowing that it's the most wonderfully infectious disease in the world? 'I'm afraid so! He took me there with the intention of proposing to me at the Trevi Fountain, but just as he was about to do it I looked down at my strawberry gelato and realised I loved that more than I loved him, and that was the end of that.'

'Blimey, Mum, you heart-breaker.'

'We'd only been together a couple of months. I think his mummy was just wanting him to find a bride.'

'You've never been to Tuscany, have you? With or without potential dads from the past?'

'No, but it looks absolutely beautiful. One day I'd like to go for a month or two, and just paint pictures and—'

'Eat antipasti?'

'Eat antipasti.'

'I wish you could come on this holiday with me.'

'I'm not sure a singles' holiday's quite up my street. Plus it would be a bit mean to your dad.'

'It's not up my street either.'

We stopped to lean over the railing and watch the rolling waves, the wind blowing our hair about. Half-asleep dog walkers and early-risers with metal detectors were the only others out at this time.

Mum put her arm around me and I shuffled closer. 'Just don't be closed off, sweetheart. There's more to life than work.'

'Antipasti?'

'You know what I mean. It won't do you any harm to experience some of the other lovely things in life. Hashtag yolo.'

Late that afternoon Mum was making a cake, so I was poised at the breakfast bar with a spoon ready to eat the raw mixture. I watched her tip a pan full of melted butter and golden syrup in with the flour, sugar and eggs, and then furiously beat them together while I leant in closer and closer.

Sweet, warm, spicy smells filled the kitchen and I couldn't resist any longer, plopping my finger straight into the batter and causing her to gently thwack my hand with her wooden spoon.

'Mmmm, Mum, you should be a professional cake baker. A caker.'

'I think the Food Standards Agency might have a problem with all the sticky fingers that keep going into my bakes.'

I grinned and prodded my finger back in and out, quick as lightning. 'It's your own fault for making such yummy things.'

'This is a very easy cake.' She shook in some ginger powder. 'Do you want the recipe to take back with you?'

'I don't really ever have time to bake.'

'Maybe you should try leaving the office at a normal time at least once a week. I feel like we only ever speak when you're making the commute home in the middle of the night.'

'It's not the middle of the night.' I stuck the spoon in this time. The mixture was so delicious; all buttery and smooth. 'I never stay past nine. Besides, when I'm marketing director I'll probably just swan in and out when I please, and won't have to do any work at all.' Actually, that wasn't true. My boss, the current marketing director, was always busy, always tired-looking. 'Maybe when I'm CEO.'

To my utter heartbreak, Mum poured the mixture into the cake tin and I watched it being led away to its oven of death. Then she started making buttercream icing. Score! Spoon and I were poised.

'How is everything with your job? Is it all going well?' Mum looked at me closely.

'Yeah, it's brilliant. I really like my position, I really like the company . . . '

'But?'

'But nothing.' Mum shuffled about with the scales while she waited. 'It's just . . . I'm kind of ready for them to give me a bloomin' promotion already!' I chuckled and stole a blob of icing.

'You do seem to give them an awful lot of blood, sweat and tears.'

'Yeah, and it's tiring, but my manager does seem to be pretty happy with me so it's all helping the goal in the end.'

'The goal to run the world?'

'Yep.'

'Okay. Well, as long as you're happy. Remember they don't own you. You're always on about not wanting a boyfriend to mess up your "you" time, so don't let a job either.'

'Yes, Mum.' We both knew that was going in one ear and straight out the other. 'How's everything with you? How's the abbey?' Mum volunteered several times a week at a National Trust property.

She lit up. 'It's just marvellous. I'm outdoors all day, with the trees and plants. A school group came in last week and all the little children were giving the ducks individual names; it was the sweetest thing.'

'That sounds so nice. Not regretting retirement yet, then?'

'Not even a tiny bit. I get to organise my own time, go where I want when I want, have cream teas left, right and centre, and bake a cake in the middle of the day. How jealous are you?'

'Feel free to come up to London and bake cakes in the middle of the day at my house.'

'Will you come home from work early?'

'Will you leave me some bowl to lick?'

'Deal.'

At that point, Dad ambled in, Breakaway in his

arms, both nosing about for a snack. 'What are you two hatching?'

'Mum's coming up to London to be my personal chef.'

'Why don't you just come and live back down here, then she can be chef to both of us?' Dad was always trying to lure me back from the grip of London. He regularly sent me links to stories on the BBC News website about crime in the capital, or Tube strikes, or even weather forecasts when it looked bad.

I tried to give him and Breakaway a hug, but the cat leapt from his arms and legged it under the table. Dad slung an arm around me and poked a finger into the mixing bowl. 'Mmm. What shall we have for dinner?'

Mum dusted off her hands. 'Elle, you decide. What would you like?'

'Would you like fish and chips?' asked Dad with hope.

'Would *you* like fish and chips, Dad?'

'I would quite like fish and chips. I'll pay.'

'Crikey!' said Mum, whipping off her apron. 'Quick, Elle!'

Mum and I did a frantic dash about the house, grabbing handbags, shoes, glasses, the cat, putting the cat back down, turning the oven down low. It wasn't often Dad's wallet opened and the moths were allowed to fly out, so we had to grab this opportunity before it snapped shut again for another hundred years.

♥

Monday came too quickly, and though I was excited about Italy I was always sad to leave home. I bid farewell to Craig McLachlan and took my weekend bag downstairs. Mum and Dad waited by the door, Breakaway blocking it with a scowl.

'Look, Breakers doesn't want me to go!' I sat on the floor and scooped him up. I *knew* he loved me. He wriggled and flailed his paws, a soft grey mess. 'No, don't leave me, please, I love you.' I pushed my face into his fur and he leapt from my clutches. I looked up at my parents. 'See, consider that a sign telling me I shouldn't have a boyfriend.'

I struggled to my feet and Mum gave me a big, warm, lavendery hug. 'Have a lovely time, sweetheart.'

'Thanks, Mum, I'll text you when I get there and I'll bring you something back.'

'Ooo, thank you. Just something small. I hope this rain lets up soon and there's no problem with your flight in the morning.'

'Hey, how bad can a British summer be?' I chuckled at the sky.

'Don't let Laurie drink too much.'

'I won't.'

Mum pulled back and looked me in the eye. 'Don't do anything you don't want to do.'

'I won't.'

'Do you have the pill, or whatever?' she whispered as Dad went off to put my bag in the car, since he was dropping me at the station.

'Yes.' I blushed.

'Okay then. Remember to do whatever makes you happy. Maybe take a little time on this break to really think about what that is.'

The trouble with mums is that they are pretty much always right, which left me in limbo on how to take that advice. With a last hug, and a pang for her to come too, off I went.

♥

When I'd first turned up at the airport I was feeling ever so Cameron Diaz. I'd copied a flight outfit I'd seen her wear, right down to the big sunglasses and trilby, despite the rather crap turn the weather had taken. But after my third cappuccino I removed both hat and sunglasses, and looked anxiously at my watch. Where the hell was Laurie?

I tried to call her again. *Ring-ring, ring-ring.*

She could not be ditching me to go on a stupid singles' holiday alone, when I didn't even want to go in the first place.

Ring-ring, ring-ring.

It went to answerphone. Again. Rain pounded against the terminal windows with ferocity, as if it were hungry zombies trying to get in and infect us all. The sky was utterly grey, and inside little red 'cancelled' lights peppered the departures board. It was as though someone up there was reminding us not to get too comfy in our shorts: we were still in England.

The Tube is notorious for grinding to a halt at the hint of a change in the weather – be it too much wind, too much heat, too much cold, too many leaves, too much *rain*. I pictured Laurie stuck halfway down the Piccadilly line in a total flap, heart pounding, and eventually having a meltdown with her fellow passengers about how she was destined never to find Mr Right and would have to marry her cousin after all.

If only I knew she was even on the Tube, and therefore on her way. Check-in would close in twenty minutes, and we were seriously cutting into our duty-free time. Would I go without her, assuming she'd be on the next flight? Or would I wait at the airport, sitting on my suitcase like a forlorn loner from a Richard Curtis movie montage?

'Elle.'

I spun around, yet couldn't see Laurie.

'I'm sorry.'

Now that was definitely her voice. Had she got into some terrible accident on the way here and now her ghost was talking to me?

'*Psst*. It's me,' said a figure dressed head to toe in baggy clothing, face wrapped in a scarf, with sunglasses and a pink trucker cap.

'Laurie?'

'Yes,' she whimpered.

'Why are you dressed like a member of TLC?'

'*You're* dressed like a member of TLC.' She jumped to her own defence. Laurie lifted her sunglasses slightly to reveal bruised, puffy eyes.

'What happened to you?'

'My face went wrong.'

'Show me.'

Laurie unravelled the scarf as slowly and tenderly as she could, and it was like watching a really awkward burlesque dance. 'I did a Botox.'

Her face was blotchy and swollen, her lips huge and her forehead frozen solid.

There are times in your life when you shouldn't laugh,

when you don't even want to laugh, but the very knowledge that you don't want to laugh makes your body pull its cruellest practical joke and set you off into a hysterical giggling fit, peppered with apologies. For me, these moments include funerals, people falling over and, evidently, when my best friend has a botched Botox job.

'I must have been allergic. Will you stop bloody laughing?'

'I'm not laughing at your face.' Yes I was. 'I'm laughing at . . . your reaction. It's funny that you're so worried that it looks bad because it really doesn't.' Yes it does. 'Does it hurt?'

'Yes.'

'Why did you get Botox? You don't have any wrinkles.'

'Because I wanted to look fabulous on our holiday.'

That brought a fresh peal of laughter, which I smothered with a cough and shuffled Laurie over to the check-in desk. They seemed to ask her very carefully if she had anything sharp or flammable in her hand luggage.

'The thing is,' Laurie was saying as we eventually got through security with little more than a pat-down and an explanation of the now-inflated face from the passport photo. 'Celebrities have Botox all the time and they look fine.'

'You look fine too; maybe it just needs a couple more days to relax.'

'But we don't have a couple of days, we're meeting everyone tonight.'

'Maybe being at altitude on the plane will help it. Don't flights do something to the water inside your body and make it—' I stopped myself as I remembered that flights make your ankles swell, not shrink.

'I don't want deep-vein thrombosis in my face!'

We hit the free samples at the duty-free hard, and then Laurie gently slicked some bright red lip gloss from the Elizabeth Arden counter onto her massive mouth. 'It looks awful,' she declared. 'But at least it might distract from the rest of my face.'

We stocked up with three giant Toblerones and went to hang about the gate and pray to Cupid that our flight wasn't cancelled. When they called us to board, Laurie, gutted, stuffed two pieces of chocolate in her mouth at once – she had seen any kind of delay as bonus time for her face to deflate before Italy.

Laurie curled in next to the window, hiding herself away from the other passengers as much as she could, while I sat in the middle seat with a male model on my right, which obviously meant I was going to throw up or chuck wine down myself.

'Hello,' I said. Let's get the awkwardness out of the way now.

'They're not really going to fly this thing, are they?' he answered, panic in his eyes.

'I think they are.'

'But it's raining.'

'Maybe it's got a waterproof coat on.'

Mr Model didn't know what to make of that and stared straight ahead, tugging his seat belt tighter. The wind howled and our plane started to slowly circle the airport, on the prowl for somewhere to make a dash for it, while the flight attendants showed off their life vests and synchronised signalling. Thunder crackled overhead.

The plane came to a brief stop, took a breath and then hurtled off down the runway, bumping and grinding like a nineties backing dancer before lifting off with a whoosh and an almighty wobble that left the flight attendants with rictus grins and Mr Model clutching my chiffon scarf.

Now, I might have no desire to share my lemon-yellow boudoir with anyone's stinky man socks, but I'm not numb to the odd lusty hormone. When a total hunk is inches from my face, hands wringing my scarf and leaning against me for protection, it's not unnatural that I'd put my arms around him, surely?

'Shhh,' I comforted.

'Have you seen those clouds?' he stage-whispered. 'We're about to go right in them and probably never come out.'

Underneath us, England's soggy fields faded away as we thumped our way into the dense layer of dark grey cloud, which enveloped the plane and made me feel eerily like we might never be seen again. Turbulence shook us from side to side; the cabin remained silent, until the lights flickered off.

'*Holy crap!* What was that? *What was that?*' Mr Model yelped.

The lights came back on, and somehow he was now wearing my scarf on top of his head, gripping its flamingo-covered ends as his breathing slowed along with the turbulence. We reached our cruising altitude and I managed to prise my scarf back. At lightning speed the flight attendants served our snack lunch and then raced back to grab the teas and coffees, and finally ice lollies for everyone. It was as we were tucking into the lollies that we hit the really bad weather.

Ding went the fasten-seatbelt sign (as if anyone had unfastened), which of course meant that a woman near the front immediately had to get up for a wee.

'Madam? Madam? Madam? You need to take your

seat now, madam, because the captain's switched on the fasten-seatbelt sign. Madam?'

'But I need to go to the toilet.'

The plane shuddered horribly and the woman wobbled in the aisle. Mr Model was back under my scarf. 'Why don't you just wee in the sea once we've crashed?' he cried out.

'Madam, please take a seat right now.'

Who knows how, but Laurie, though she hadn't left her seat, nor made eye contact with any attendant, had stocked up on miniatures and was glugging whisky.

'London Gin or Bombay Sapphire?' she offered. 'The Southern Comfort's mine.'

'London, please, and can I take one for my hunky wet-wipe?'

I offered Mr Model the Bombay Sapphire, which he downed in one. The plane lurched again, causing gasps around the cabin. Laurie clutched my hand. Mr Model clutched my hair. He looked over and started, as if noticing Laurie for the first time. 'Why are you wearing that?'

'Why are *you* wearing *that*?' she retorted.

A long, groaning rattle began, and suddenly the plane dropped several feet. My stomach heaved. I'm a good flier, but for the first time I actually felt scared. This couldn't be it. I'd never loved anyone. Don't let this be it.

A violent lurch to the left squashed me into Laurie, whose eyes I met through her sunglasses, her fear mirroring mine. Oxygen masks dropped from the ceiling.

'Ladies and gentlemen, can I have your attention?' yelled an attendant over the intercom. 'Do not put the oxygen masks on – we're not losing cabin pressure, this is just because of the panels becoming loose in the turbulence. I repeat, there is no need to put your masks on.'

I yanked the mask off Mr Model's face as the plane rumbled on and I tried not to throw up, or cry.

'This is YOUR fault,' he screamed past me at Laurie.

'*Why?*'

'Because there's something very dodgy-looking about you! You're dressed like a gang member!'

'That's right, pretty boy. My gang are out there kicking the shit out of this plane – it's not turbulence at all. Idiot. Now, how about you apologise and we make out?'

'No!'

'Fine, if we die, don't say I didn't offer you one final moment of pleasure.'

'We'll shortly be making our descent into Pisa International Airport, ladies and gentlemen. We hope you enjoyed your flight with us today,' said a shaky-voiced captain.

A bright burst of lightning illuminated the cabin, and the plane jerked away from the storm once and for all. Several rows ahead, a plentifully licked ice lolly took flight and spun back down the plane, splatting itself onto my Cameron Diaz-styled lap.

♥

We exited the airport and entered a hot, still Italy. Laurie took a breath and leant against me. 'Thank Vodka it's not raining. I'm so over storms. I literally thought the Botox was going to fall right out of my face.'

I couldn't quite talk yet, my stomach still queasy, which wasn't helped by the thought of globules of Botox plopping out of Laurie's nose.

'I feel sick,' I mumbled and grabbed a Toblerone out of my bag, stuffing a triangle into my mouth before it melted all over my hands. Laurie was watching me. 'But sugar helps. Maybe. Well, chocolate helps anything. Want some?'

She shook her head, and then reached for it anyway. Within five minutes we'd hailed a taxi, devoured the whole Toblerone and were feeling much brighter – thoughts of turbulence, storms and that half-eaten ice lolly landing in my lap far away.

The sun was high in the sky as the taxi took us out of Pisa and into the burnt green of the Tuscan countryside. Tall, thin cypresses rushed past, and fields scattered with red roofed buildings filled the landscape. Next to me, Laurie was wincing as she dabbed Touche Éclat on the purple bruises under her eyes.

'You know what'll help you stop worrying?'

'If one of the other guests is a really short-sighted hunk.'

'A glass of wine.'

'You know, that would help.'

The taxi turned on to a long, dusty track that curled around an olive grove, fat green olives hanging from the trees. It climbed a hill and the trees turned to row upon row of neat, but rustic vines.

'I could just get out and eat those right now,' I said, pointing at dusty blue grapes dangling in bunches.

'No, don't do that, seeds very bitter to eat,' said the driver. I squinted against the sun and saw the shape of someone hunched over in the distance, halfway down one of the rows, a brown fuzzy blob of a dog leaping about beside them. I felt a huge need to climb out of the car and join them, pick some grapes, lie back among the vines and while away the summer.

We came to a stop outside a building that felt so Italian, so removed from everything I knew in London, that the worries and stresses I hadn't even known were there dripped away from me like olive oil.

Before us was a large house of peach-pink stone, with a typically Tuscan red-tiled roof and burnt-red shutters. *Bella Notte* was carefully scribed in large, black calligraphy over the doorway, and stone steps led off from the side into the expanse of vineyard above and below. The rosy walls and emerald fields gave everything such a warm glow in the sunlight it was like I was looking through the Valencia filter on Instagram.

'Italia . . .' I breathed, smelling wine and tranquillity in the air. Laurie and I stood by the car, hot sunshine stroking our skin, crunchy pale yellow dust beneath our feet, and the sounds of birds and distant farm machinery music to our ears.

'*Buongiorno!*' Out of the doors leapt a man, oak-barrel aged with suntanned skin and curly brown hair. Joyful wrinkles encircled his dark eyes and a voluptuous woman with lustrous black hair and the same happy wrinkles bounded out from behind him. 'Welcome to Bella Notte!'

He was Australian! 'You're Australian! I mean, hello.'

'*Si*, I'm Sebastian, and this is my beautiful *bella bella bella* wife, Sofia.'

'I'm Laurie,' stepped forward my oddly dressed friend.

'Lorry? Like, broom-broom?' Sofia mimed driving and honking a horn.

'No, more *law* – like a court of law – *ree.*'

'Lawyer-y?'

'Um, let's stick to Lorry, that's close enough.'

'I'm Elle.'

'*Bella* Ella: beautiful name, beautiful girl. *Mamma mia*, what is it about English girls? Sofia, I married the wrong nationality – it's over between us,' he teased.

'*Bene!* You think I started *You Had Me at Merlot Holidays* to help *other* women find a new man?'

They smiled at each other and Sebastian grabbed my hand. 'There you have it, *bella*, we have my wife's blessing. Just two minutes here and you have found love, and we will be together for ever.'

I laughed. 'Actually, I'm not here to find love. I'm just here for the wine. My friend's the one ready for romance.'

Sebastian tilted his head at me. 'You're human, you're always ready for romance. It's in your genes, *bella.*' Something about the way he said it made a blush creep over my face. He turned to Laurie. 'I'm sure you're beautiful too, Laurie, underneath all that scarf.'

'You are not hot? Or are you saving your beauty for this evening? Keeping the men guessing,' Sofia said.

'I'm just a little sensitive to the sun, and I don't have any lotion on yet. Are there many men booked in?'

'Oh yes, we always make sure there are roughly the same number of men and women.'

'Are the men . . . '

'Yes?'

'Tasty?'

'Tasty?'

'Yummy. Delicious, like good wine.'

'Well, much like wine, there's a different flavour to suit everyone.'

Laurie gave me a thumbs-up. I turned back to Sebastian. 'How long have you lived in Italy?' I asked with jealousy.

'I came here in my early twenties, straight from my folks' vineyard in Margaret River. Cockily thought I'd teach the Italians how it's done. But they hit me straight with their best weapon – this one – and I surrendered. Been here ever since. You guys are from England right, guv'nor?'

'Yep, on a very important mission from the Queen to make sure you don't steal all our eligible bachelors.'

Sebastian guffawed. 'Fair play, Her Maj!'

'Ladies,' beckoned Sofia. 'Follow me and I'll show you your rooms.' Our rooms, plural? How lovely! Then a thought occurred to me: *Ew, is that so we can have sex with people?* Well no one's having sex with me; joke's on them.

♥

Sofia led us through the large oak doors, past a communal lounge with huge wooden furniture that she called the wine-tasting room, and up a staircase completely covered in bright blue, green and red mosaic tiles.

'If you wear heels here, hold the banister – especially after you've had wine. Otherwise, whoosh!' Sofia tinkled with laughter, presumably at memories of past guests sloshed and splatted at the bottom of the stairs. We were in adjoining rooms, and Sofia left us outside with our keys, great chunky ironmongery.

'Everything's just lovely and rustic, isn't it?' I grinned happily at Laurie, and then we went into our respective rooms.

My bedroom was beautiful – wide and white-washed, with low ceilings and big red shutters that opened out to a spectacular view across the stripes of the sun-drenched vineyard. I was leaning my head out of the window, breathing in the fresh Italian air, when I glanced sideways to see Laurie doing the same.

'*Ciao!*' I called.

'*Ciao, Bella Ella!*'

'Is that going to be my name this whole trip, do you think?'

'And back home. I think it has a lovely ring. Better than Laurie the Lorry.'

'Broom-broom. Hey, did you see we have free wine in our rooms? Three bottles.'

'What? Favouritism!' Laurie ducked back inside for a moment, then popped back out. 'Don't panic, I found mine.'

We turned back to the view and I closed my eyes behind my sunglasses. It was nice to shut my eyes for a reason other than just because it was finally bedtime. After a while I found enough energy to open my mouth again. 'Can we just forget London and move out here and own a vineyard and live happily ever after?'

'That escalated quickly, considering you didn't even want to meet anyone on this holiday.'

'I'm not saying we have to find men; why don't we do it? Me and you.'

'Okay, darling,' said Laurie, basking in the sunshine. 'But I think if I made wine I'd drink all the stock.'

'Maybe you could take stunning photos of gorgeous Tuscan scenery and sell them for thousands of pounds, and I'll make the wine.'

'I think you'd drink the stock too.'

'But how happy we would be ... My tummy is

growling, I hope there's food at the meet-and-greet tonight.'

'Urgh, don't remind me,' groaned Laurie.

'How am I more excited about this than you?'

'Because my face is massive.'

There was no arguing with that. I leant my head against the window frame and considered having a nap standing up.

Laurie ruined my peace and quiet by shouting, 'Do you want to stop ruining the peace and quiet with our shouting, and come to my room and get one of these bottles open?'

'I'll be right there.' I discarded my flip-flops and pulled my hair back into a high ponytail. I never wear my hair up at home. It was nice being out of London, not caring about having perfect tresses or fancy shoes.

I padded barefoot down the hall, past a large mural of fat purple grapes, and walked straight into Laurie's nearly identical room. She was standing in the cool of the inside, in front of the mirror, her sunglasses and scarf finally discarded.

She turned to me, and for the first time I saw the full extent of her pains: big bruised bags under her eyes, a bumpy forehead, swollen cheeks and red blotches down her neck. She looked so sad. 'My face hurts.'

'I know,' I soothed, giving her a gentle hug. She let out a huge, shaky sigh.

'I'm such an idiot.'

'No, you're not; you didn't know this would happen.'

'I just wanted to look amazing, like a Real Housewife of Beverly Hills, and then have an amazing holiday.'

'This'll pass in no time; we'll still have an amazing time.'

'But now I'm going to be known here as "the girl with the botched Botox", and everyone will think I'm some shallow princess who does this kind of thing all the time, and I don't, I just—' She sobbed, and tried to squeeze her eyes closed. I grabbed the bottle of white wine from the ice-filled cooler and held the cold glass up to her face. Laurie tried to steady her breathing, leaning her hot cheeks against the bottle. But she was too far gone, and with a sharp intake of Italian air choked out a sob. 'I'm just tired of being lonely.'

'Oh, Laurie.' My heart broke for her. 'This is nothing. We'll fix your face up and no one will even notice. And don't you realise you're always one of the most stunning women in the room? Not just because of your bloody lovely face, but because you're like human sunshine.'

'Then why doesn't anyone love me enough to marry me and start a family with me?'

'But lots of men want to, they just haven't been the right ones, and you've broken up with them.'

'I'm so stupid.'

'No, that's not what I meant. This is just the beginning of our "start a family" era – there's plenty of time. I know some of our friends are already there, but don't you think the grass is always greener? You want to be in their position, with love and security and babies, and they want to be in yours, with freedom and less responsibility.'

'Please just help me make the most of this holiday, Elle. I don't know where to go after here.'

'Okay, I will be your wing-woman. This won't be a wasted trip. Well' – I smiled, picking up the white wine and pouring two large glasses – 'maybe a little wasted. Now come on, the meet-and-greet is in two hours, so let's sort out your face. Come with me.'

I grabbed the wine cooler and marched into the en-suite bathroom, dumping all of the ice into the bidet. 'Put your face in there.'

'In the bidet?'

'Yes.'

'Um . . .'

'Put your face in the bidet.'

Laurie knelt on the floor and timidly pushed her face into the pile of ice.

'Hang on, let's add some water.' I nudged her aside and we watched silently as the upward-facing hose spurted a cool fountain of water over the ice. We tried not to think where that water usually went. When a mini ice bath had been created, Laurie dunked her face back in. I sat on the toilet (with the seat down, we're not *that* close) while she repeated the face-dunking several times and admired the bathroom. A large roll-top freestanding bath with cast iron feet sat under a window offering a panoramic of the vineyard, and opposite was a vanity table with soft lighting and scented candles. The walls were light peach, with vines hand-painted along the tops.

After a while, Laurie looked up at me between dunks. 'This does feel good, you're a genius. Just please don't tell anyone here I did this. I don't want to be the botched-Botox-bidet-facial girl.'

'Of course I won't.' I sipped my wine. Oh my, it was delicious. I'm not a big fan of white wine – I think it often tastes like sick – but with one sip I realised I'd just been drinking the wrong kind. This one was icy cool and nearly transparent, with just a honey-gold hue. It had a tiny dash of sweetness and – perhaps this was also influenced by my view of a vineyard and being in Italy – it immediately made me want to eat a large plate of pasta, al fresco, and clink my glass with a lovely man. Now, where did *that* come from?

At that moment Laurie came up for air again and asked, 'Do you ever feel lonely?'

'No,' I said, not meaning for a hint of defensiveness to come out. But Laurie was baring her soul for me, even putting her face in a bottom-cleaner for me, so she deserved a more rounded answer. 'I mean, I've never been in love. Maybe I just don't know what I'm missing, but when I think about meeting someone and having to move in together and share space, not being able to decorate exactly how I want, or watch what I want on TV, that freaks me out a bit. And I'm busy all the time anyway, with work.'

'You're *always* busy with work.'

'It's going to pay off in the long run: I'm doing well there.'

'But you're never lonely?'

Was I lonely? No, I was fine. I had plenty of time to meet someone when I'm done having 'me' time, if that's even what I want to happen. I can't be the only thirty-year-old out there who doesn't know what they want to do with their life.

'Well . . . I have a double bed which I only ever sleep on one side of. And sometimes I stand in the doorways of my house just looking into the room and wishing I had someone to talk to. So yeah, I guess I get lonely too.' I took another big gulp of wine; we didn't need me starting waterworks too. Laurie put a soggy hand on my knee.

'What a great conversation to start ten days in Italia. Shall we try to get out of this funk and find a way to fix my face? That should provide some laughs.'

'I have an idea. How tender is your skin? Can you put make-up on?'

'Yeah, that'll be fine, though we might use up all our make-up with one application, since my face is the size of a beach ball.'

'Okay, back in a mo.' I stepped out of Laurie's door and turned to head down the corridor back to my room when I smacked nose-first into a rather hard chest. *Oof.* I looked up at a tall man with dark hair and familiar dark eyes. He steadied me with his hands on my arms.

'Hello,' he said. '*Ciao, hola, konnichiwa*, g'day.'

'Hello,' I laughed.

'Hello.'

'Hello. I'm so sorry – *scusi*.'

'It's okay, are you hurt?' He smiled at me, concerned yet amused, speaking in English but with a local accent. He reached up to touch my face at the exact moment I glanced down to check my boobs hadn't leapt out of my dress and my nose got another thwack. 'Oh, I'm sorry!' He cupped my face in horror, and my eyes trailed his bare forearms and the neck of his crumpled pale blue shirt. '*Benvenuti in Italia*, please don't sue me.' He gave me a melting grin, like a schoolboy who'd been caught eating your Mini Eggs.

'I'm fine, completely fine. Did my nose hurt your, um, chest?'

'No.'

'Or your hand?'

'These old things? No, they're quite . . . how do you say it . . . ?'

'Manly?' Idiot.

'I was going to say drawable.'

'Drawable? Well yes, I guess they are.'

'You know, they are tough from working hard.'

'Oh, durable!'

'Durable – gah! But thank you for saying they're manly.' He dropped his hands from my face and we stepped back from one another.

'You're welcome.' Um. 'Are you—'

'Can I—' he started at the same time. We chuckled and paused.

'I'm—'

'Did—' The old chuckle and pause repeated itself.

'Well, I must dash,' I said formally, as if I was some kind of lady-in-waiting. Then followed the excruciating awkward dance, where you shuffle from side to side to pass the other person, always moving to the same direction they're moving to. Eventually I yelped 'Bye' and raced past, my head ducked, and into my room. Well that was strange. Obviously I'm just feeling a bit fluttery because of our conversation and the wine, I'm not that easily won over, *You Had Me at Merlot*.

I grabbed my make-up bag and my iPad, but before leaving my room stopped to look at myself in the mirror. Loose dress, hair up, flushed cheeks – I looked kind of pretty. I looked carefree. Which was strange for me, because usually I think I look a little frazzled. Maybe I really did need this holiday, and maybe I should keep a bit more of an open mind.

'You're so drunk,' I scolded myself.

Back in Laurie's room I laid the entire contents of both of our make-up bags out on the writing table by the window. I then scrolled through YouTube.

'My idea is this: one of the things I like to do as a happy singleton is experiment with YouTube beauty tutorials for hours on end, and I've seen one on contouring. I think I could do this on your face using your darker foundation and concealer and my lighter ones. I think it'll make a huge difference to the appearance of the puffiness and will add your cheekbones back in. Look.' I showed her before and after images of a pretty girl whose face had been transformed by some simple contouring tricks with make-up.

'Let's do it,' said Laurie, leaning back in her chair. 'Let me know if you need me to put down my wine.'

I started the video tutorial, and using Laurie's concealer stick started to draw lines on her cheeks, nose and forehead. She winced a little, but was very brave. I then scribbled my lighter concealer under her eyes and at the top of her cheeks, between her brows and down the centre of her nose.

'Finished!' I said, and Laurie opened her eyes in surprise.

'How do I look?'

'Perfect.'

Laurie tottered to the bathroom and giggled. 'I've never looked better. It's like I'm going into a very girly war.'

She resumed her position and I picked up her foundation brush to start blending all the stripes together. 'How are you feeling now?'

'Better, thank you. Can I just marry you instead?'

'Sure.'

'I'm a little nervous about the meet-and-greet. Are you?'

'A bit. I don't really like talking to new people.'

'Ah-ha! That's why you're single.'

I laughed. 'Maybe you're right – it's a deep, psychological fear, and it's a lot easier to just watch the *Twilight* movies over and over again and pretend Jacob Black is my boyfriend. You know what's good about this holiday, though?'

'The wine?'

'Yes, but unlike when you go on a date with someone at work, or a friend of a friend, no one knows us here.'

'You're right! We can be whoever we want!'

'Remember, you want someone to know you afterwards, so best not to lie and say you're Victoria Beckham's sister or anything. But you can be whatever version of you you want to present.'

'That's true. No one needs to know that I think my stomach is too big or that I pick my toenails.'

'I don't have to talk about work, which is what I talk about almost all day every day, unless it's the weekend or if I'm on the phone to Mum when I get home late.'

'No one needs to know that I'm jealous of people with babies.'

'Or that I pee with my bathroom door open so I don't miss any of *Keeping Up with the Kardashians*.'

'But hang on, isn't this hiding the real us?'

'Not at all, I'm not saying we keep it secret, I'm just saying it's going to be nice that we're starting with a clean slate and can get to know people at our own pace. Well, you can.'

'As can you. Don't be closed off.'

I smiled, but didn't answer. Wasn't that the advice of the moment? First Mum, now Laurie. I'd never thought of myself as closed off – quite the opposite. Without a partner or babies I was always willing to socialise and to be the one who travelled about to visit others. When I had time and wasn't working, of course. I finished blending and stepped back to admire my work. Not bad. Laurie definitely looked like a woman who liked to wear a lot of make-up, but there's nothing wrong with that, and you couldn't see any blotchiness or swelling now, and the darkness under her eyes was almost entirely gone – you wouldn't even notice in low evening light.

Laurie looked at herself in the mirror for a long time, tilting her head this way and that. I sat back, my face to the sun, and let out the most enormous sigh.

'Are you okay?'

'I was just thinking about how far away from the office I am now.'

'You're not missing work are you?'

'Not at all. I mean, you know I love it – I love all the craziness and business, I love knowing I'm getting better and better at something and that I'm respected, I love knowing I'm building a career, but my oh my, it's nice to step away.'

'That's the spirit!'

'I think I could sit on the veranda looking at the view for the whole holiday and be perfectly content.'

'You're going to join in with all the activities though, aren't you?'

'Absolutely, I'm going to do everything. I just mean it's a refreshing feeling not having to be "on" or "professional" or having anyone watching my every move. And I don't think I realised I needed refreshing until I got here.'

We sat side by side, reclining in the sunshine, for some time, eyes closed and listening to the silence. Eventually, I put down my empty glass and stood up. 'We've had some very third-glass-of-wine conversations already this holiday, and we're only on our first one. I'm going to leave you to get dressed now and I'll come back and get you just before the meet-and-greet. Don't go down without me.'

Laurie stood and wrapped me in a hug, tilting her work-of-art face away from mine. 'Thanks, Elle, you're brilliant.'

'No problem, it's nice to play make-up artist on someone else's face for a change.'

'But thanks also for coming to Tuscany with me. I know it wouldn't have been your first choice.'

'You're my first choice, you big weirdo.'

'Love you too.'

I left her room with a smile and dawdled in the corridor for a while, looking up and down at the doors. I wondered which room that man was in ... I walked slowly, in the hope of another encounter, but then I realised the doors had spy holes and became paranoid that everyone was peering at me and thinking I was a pervert, so I scampered inside my room.

♡

I wasn't dressing to impress that evening (*no I wasn't*, I told the part of my brain that immediately thought of yummy hallway man) but it was still baking at six o'clock, and because of that I was putting on a dress. Just a floaty turquoise number that was a little less travel-crumpled and sweat-smelling than the one I'd been wearing since leaving the UK. Very casual. And the thirty minutes I took pulling my hair back, taking it down, pulling it back, teasing out tendrils – that was all so I looked super-casual as well.

I knocked on Laurie's door and was greeted by a bombshell. She'd done her eye make-up with dramatic smokiness, which balanced out the heavy face paint quite well. Her hair was in big, loose waves and her maxidress was violet ombré, the colour of unpicked grapes, with a plunging neckline.

'Okay, I've tried all the wines,' she said, grabbing my hand and pulling me inside. 'And I think I'm now just merry enough to be an absolute charmball at the meet-and-greet. Do I look like an extra from *Dallas*?'

'Do you . . . want to look like an extra from *Dallas*?' I asked carefully, not sure of the right answer.

'No. I'm going for fabulous, exotic, intriguing English rose.'

'Then you look perfect.'

'Thank you! You look stunning too; how are you so naturally delish? You look like you should be in an Abercrombie and Fitch advert.'

I laughed. She really was a bit tipsy. We linked arms and headed down towards the wine-tasting room, which was where the do was taking place. As we reached the bottom of the stairs faint chatter got louder, indicating the party was already beginning to grow. Laurie stopped me to take a breath and then, head held high, plunged us around the corner.

Everyone turned to look when we entered – not because we were the most beautiful creatures to grace the room with our presence but because, if we're honest, everyone wanted to see everyone as quickly as possible to see if they should be on their radar. Although conversations didn't stop I felt exposed, like when I have to give a presentation at work. The women, who on first glance ranged from a couple of girls in their mid-twenties through to a rosy-cheeked grey-haired lady, smiled and nodded as we caught their eyes. We saw each of them casting a quick eye over us, like opponents in battle, looking for our weaknesses and our flaws. But there was also a sense of stoic camaraderie. The men (I'd say mid-thirties and up) looked surprisingly bashful. I'd been expecting bravado and cockiness – maybe that would come later – because right now they all seemed amusingly out of their depth.

My mistake: the bravado and cockiness had just been sucked out of the room and into one man, who marched straight up to me, all chinos and tan, crinkled his eyes and said, 'Missy, missy, missy – what a dress!' He grabbed my hand and tried to twirl me, but I've never been twirled before and didn't know what he was doing so our arms just went up in the air and bent awkwardly before we dropped them.

Laurie handed me a glass of red that she'd acquired from somewhere, and with a wink waltzed off.

'Hello,' I said to the man. He was looking me up and down and nodding.

'You are *beautiful*. Badabing, badaboom!'

I can be pretty in good lighting, and I have an *okay* body, and *okay* hair, but let's not pretend I'm 'badabing, badaboom' material. This man's falseness was already putting me off. But he was trying to be nice, and I'd made nice with annoying corporate weirdos at work before, so I could handle this ageing Lothario.

'Thank you. Where are you from?'

'The Sunshine State – Florida, USA. Have you ever been?'

'Not really. I've connected flights in Miami and I've done some East Coast but never got as far down as Florida to do it properly. I'd love to go.'

'Oh, it's beautiful, you'd fit right in.' He was smooth. 'That settles it then. Let's end this holiday here and you come back with me. I don't need to meet any other girls now I've seen you, baby.'

'You don't know anything about me yet. I might be a total psychopath.'

'So might I.'

'Well that wouldn't surprise me all that much.'

'You gotta take risks in life, baby.' He tried to hold my hand again but I grabbed a passing appetiser, which turned out to be such a delicious mini bruschetta, with sweet, olive oil-soaked sun-blushed tomatoes and fresh basil leaves, that I nearly believed *You Had Me at Merlot*'s claim to be able to make people fall in love. Me + bruschetta 4EVA.

Oh yes, the American. 'Let's just move past the

"baby" thing to begin with; would you like to know my name?'

'Your name, your number, your breakfast of choice ...'

'Oh my God.'

'I'm kidding, I'm kidding. I'm George; what do you go by?'

'This is Bella Ella!' cried Sebastian, appearing behind me and topping up my wine from a dark, dust-covered bottle that I imagined had sat in the Bella Notte wine cellar for years, ageing to perfection.

'It's actually Elle,' I told George, before he also limpeted on to the nickname. I turned to Sebastian, thankful for the distraction. 'This place is beautiful, I love the bedrooms.'

'That's good to hear. All decorated by my son.'

'Your son?'

'Yep, it's a proper family business. Excuse me, Bella, I'd better just get the intros started.' He walked to the centre of the room and tapped the side of his glass. A hush fell over everyone, and Sofia appeared in the doorway and danced her way over, slotting in under his arm like they were two parts of a puzzle.

'Welcome, everyone,' he grinned, 'to Bella Notte vineyard, and your *You Had Me at Merlot* vacation. Everyone ready for romance?' There were some awkward titters and one 'woo-hoooo' from one of the younger girls. Sebastian continued, 'Glad to hear it. Now, the whole point of these holidays is for you to relax, drink some great wine – if we do say so ourselves – get to know some like-minded people and to open your hearts. For most of you I expect this'll be your first vineyard stay, and for that reason we hope the setting, the activities and the booze will loosen you up and help new experiences become shared experiences. Bloody hell, that should have gone in the brochure.' Sofia smiled up at him. 'We think it's too easy to get bogged down in real life, and work, and the closed little circle of people you meet up with to moan about work. And that's why we wanted to bring people together in this beautiful slice of the Chianti countryside, to have some bloody fun!'

'Stop saying "bloody",' scolded Sofia.

'My potty-mouthed wife here is the one to blame for the activities she's going to make you do over the next ten days. I'll hand you over to her.'

'Hello, everyone.' Sofia's beautiful face showed little sign of age, and though she was quieter than Sebastian one immediately warmed to her. I wanted to walk over and squeeze her, but that might have been the wine. 'We have lots of fun things planned for the next ten days, but also lots of free time for you to spend on your own, or getting to know people. There are plenty of walks near by, and you are welcome to roam free around the vineyard. The building near the gate has a range of Vespas you may borrow, and our son Jamie can give you a lesson if needs be. We'll put on cold breakfast and lunch buffets every day – you can come and go as you please – and a nightly dinner. Tomorrow morning we'll all take a walking tour of the vineyard and cellars, and I'll tell you a little more of what you'll be drinking while you're here, then we'll have a wine tasting in the afternoon.'

There were murmurs of appreciation, and across the room Laurie caught my eye and raised her glass.

'But it has a difference,' said Sofia. The wine tasting will be blindfolded.'

This caused giggles, but all I could think was *I'm not standing anywhere near George with a blindfold on.*

'Every night at dinner we'll give you the plan for the next day, and you can decide if you want to take part or not. The things we have planned are romantic and sultry and heady and we hope to create many happy couples.'

'Oh yeah!' cried George, looking directly at me.

Sebastian boomed with laughter. 'Steady there, Sofia love, these lot have already sloshed half the wine in their rooms – they won't need much encouragement from you. Shall we go around, and everyone can say their name and a little about themselves?'

Communal groan.

George stepped forward, full on confidence. 'I'm George, I'm from Florida, USA, and I came here because I wanted to know what European women were really like. And boy oh boy, am I impressed so far!'

The twenty-somethings linked arms and stepped into the middle next, giggling and conferring in hushed Bristolian accents.

'I'm Vicky.'

'And I'm Jane.'

'And we're here because we love wine.'

'And we hate English boys.'

'They're all so stupid.'

'And they all go on eighteen-to-thirty holidays to Ibiza, so we didn't want to go there.'

'And I like older men.'

'And I like continental men. Is that the right word? Continental?'

'Yeah, like continental breakfast.'

'Cool.'

They scuttled off, and the older woman came into the centre of the room. 'I'm Bridget, and I'm from Scotland, and I just wanted some sunshine where everyone wasn't already couples, or there weren't children around. I just want to talk to people when I go on holiday.'

She and I were going to be friends.

A shy-looking man of about our age went next. I noticed Laurie snap to attention, as if she'd spotted him across the room but hadn't had a chance to meet him yet and was curious who he was. I liked her like this: hopeful, energetic, optimistic.

'*Buonasera*, I'm Marco.' He did a little bow and then looked embarrassed. 'I am actually a journalist for a travel magazine here in Italy and my editor wanted to do a piece on these, um, singles' holidays. I won't write about any of you, don't worry. But also, I am single, and I don't want to be any more, so I put my hand up and said, "Pick me, pick me!"'

Laurie was melting, utterly ready to pick Marco. She swooped in to the centre after him.

'Hi, everyone, pleasure to meet you. I'm Laurie, and I'm here with my gorgeous best friend Elle, and back in London I'm an event photographer.' She caught Marco's eye and grinned, forming a media-types bond with him. 'And I'm here because I've tried all sorts of dating – I've tried them all – and I'm just tired of it and ready to be finally swept off my feet.'

I was impressed – that was surprisingly honest. It was nice to feel you could be somewhere where you could actually lay your cards out and say what you wanted, rather than have to act cool.

'I mean,' continued Laurie, 'I don't mean to sound like I've been out with millions of guys, I'm not a lady of the night or anything HAHAHA – Elle, your turn.'

'Okay. Um, I'm Elle, I'm also from the UK, of course . . . ' What to say, what to say? I nearly explained my job, but I stopped – I didn't want to think about work. I didn't want anyone to ask me about work. 'I'm actually more here for the wine and the sunshine, and because I've never been to Italy before.' I crinkled my nose and began to back out of the circle.

'But she is single,' declared Sebastian with a grin.

'Yes I am, but I'm okay with that right now.'

When I got back to the edge of the circle, Sebastian leaned over and whispered in my ear, 'I need to talk to you at the end. I've had the most fantastic idea.'

One by one, the remaining people went up and introduced themselves, while the rest of us watched, nodded, smiled, laughed and grazed on crostini and pâté, and tiny Italian chocolates. There were probably twenty to thirty of us altogether, which must mean the bedrooms spilt away from the main house and into the outbuildings that dotted the vineyard.

Where was my man?

My man! What a cheek! First of all, we didn't even

know each other's names, and second of all I am not here to find a man.

There, that was me told off.

The group broke up, and immediately the atmosphere relaxed, people moving around to get to know those they thought sounded interesting a little better. I was about to make a beeline for Bridget when Sebastian jumped in front of me.

'Bella Ella.'

'Sebastian. Thank you for saving me from George earlier.'

'No problem. You just tell me to back off if you change your mind about him and don't want saving.'

'Ha ha, unlikely.'

'I don't know; I didn't believe his "I want to see what European chicks are like" act. I think something else made him make the decision to come here.' He leant in close. 'And I'm going to find out. But first, I've been thinking about you and what you said. And I don't think these men are right for you.'

'You don't?' Good.

'Well, they're all looking for romance, but you're not.'

'Nope.'

'You're happily single.'

'Yep.'

'Miss Independent.'

'That's me.'

'So if you won't have them, and you won't have me, I think you need to be introduced to someone else who claims to be happily single and seems to find being in love such a chore. My son.'

'How's that going to help anything?'

'Because you're both so bloody-minded that maybe stars will collide against your thick heads – *JAMIE!*'

And then my man – I mean *the* man – from the hall-way slunk around the corner from the kitchen, glaring at his dad, wearing the same blue shirt and with a tea towel thrown over his shoulder. The other women turned like they'd heard a bang and gave him lusty stares, which he seemed to edge away from. I couldn't keep the smile from my face, and when he saw me his scowl finally changed to a smile.

'Hello again,' he said.

'Hellumunum.' I'm not sure what I replied with.

'You've met?' asked Sebastian.

'Briefly, in the hallway,' said Jamie. 'How's your nose?'

'Fine, thank you. How's your hand and your, um . . .' I waved at his pecs.

'Look at this, you guys are like a house on fire.' Sebastian took the tea towel from Jamie's shoulder and ushered us closer together.

'Dad.' A slight blush tinted his olive skin.

'Relax – she's not here for romance. She doesn't want *you*, she's being wing-woman to her friend. You can both be grumps together.' His eyes twinkled at me – dark eyes that were the same as his son's – and off he scampered.

Jamie wasn't here to try to find a girlfriend. It dawned on me that this was a good thing. Talking to anyone else would always feel laced with an agenda, whereas neither of us had one. Though my heart had protested with a little flap when Sebastian had told Jamie I didn't want him.

'I will try and introduce myself without causing you an injury. I'm Jamie,' he said, in his light accent.

'I'm Elle.'

'Ahh, the "Bella Ella" my dad's been talking about.'

'Your dad is lovely, but kind of embarrassing!' What had he been saying about me?

Jamie laughed and held up his hands. 'You are preaching to the chair, sister.' I smothered a chuckle. No one likes to be corrected all the time. And at the risk of sounding like a patronising idiot, his little mistakes were just a smidge attractive.

'Listen, I'm sorry about earlier, with the corridor and the bashing.' I placed my hand on his warm, hard chest briefly – just to demonstrate – and my heart lurched with a *bloody hell, you fancy him!* 'It's so quiet here you forget there are even other people around. I should watch where I'm going. No more zooming out of doors like I'm queen of the castle!' I babbled.

'It's okay, I really didn't mind. I shouldn't really have been wandering about in the guest corridor anyway, I just remembered a bit of paintwork that had become chipped and was checking to see if it was very noticeable.'

'Your dad said you decorated all the rooms; does that include the murals in the bathrooms and the corridors?'

'Yep, do you like them?'

'Yeah, they're gorgeous, you're like Michelangelo.' And I was like a teenager swooning over a boyband member. But he looked really, genuinely pleased – maybe the guests are normally too enamoured with each other to notice his artwork – so I saw no harm in throwing a few compliments. 'So you work here?'

'Yes. Bella Notte will always be a family business. And while those two are matchmaking, I'm getting on with the wine.'

'Ah, the important bit.'

He broke out into the biggest grin. 'I think so. I can't wait for you to try more of the selection.'

'It was you I saw down in the vineyard when our taxi arrived earlier?'

'Yes, that would have been me. I like your voice, where are you from?'

I like your face. 'I live in London, have you been?'

'No. One day.'

'Well it's amazing, but it's also crowded and fumy and no one quite has the time to just relax. Being here is like being in a different world.'

'Dad said you weren't here for romance. You came on a singles' holiday but you're not single?'

'No, I am single, really, really single. I've been single for years. It's gone too far now, I don't need someone coming in and learning all about my nasty habits, like—' No, *please* shut up. 'And how about you?'

'No, no girlfriend.'

'I guess you must have a lot of women to choose from working here.' He shot me a strange look, sort of weariness mixed with confusion. Well, I did just basically call him an opportunistic man-whore. *Stupid Elle.* 'Not to suggest—'

'No, I don't actually have all that much to do with the guests. You won't see me very much.' He ran his hand through his hair, and I felt mighty jealous of that hand. 'I have to go. Good luck while you're here, I hope you get whatever you want out of it. It was really nice meeting you.'

He touched my arm lightly as he left and I wasn't

sure what had happened. I was convinced we'd had a connection, but he suddenly seemed sad. Hmm.

I wandered back over towards Laurie, feeling a little unsure of myself, but not really in the mood to meet anyone else that night and just wanting Jamie to come back so we could chat some more. But he was long gone down the dark corridor and probably back to his room, where he'd change into loose cotton pyjamas and no top, and lie on his bed alone, staring out through his open bedroom window at the stars, wondering what I was doing and whether I too had gone to bed to look at the stars . . .

'Elle! Gentlemen, this is Elle.' Laurie pulled me in close to her and glanced around the room. I could tell she was itching to find Marco before someone else got their claws into him. I was pulled out of my strange, very un-Elle-like fantasy. My aim was now to nod and smile and listen to Laurie and the two suitors who were clamouring for her attention, and big her up at opportune moments with vast quantities of 'Laurie's an expert *this*,' and 'Laurie is the best person to talk to about *that*.' 'Elle, this is Pierre and Jon. I was just telling them about my exhibition at the Portrait Gallery last year.'

I spluttered into my wine and she widened her eyes at me. The not-actually-lying plan was evidently out the window, then.

'You say Victoria Beckham bought one of your photos?' asked Pierre, entranced. Laurie side-eyed me.

'Yes she did,' I jumped in. 'Well you know Vic – Spice Girls, Girl Power, et cetera. She's very supportive of strong females and their work.' The men were nodding with respect, and Laurie squeezed my hand.

All of a sudden the tranquillity, polite chatter and gentle sounds of teeth clanking against wine glasses were interrupted by a car skidding to a stop outside, and the door slamming.

A woman's piercing voice shattered the air as she hurled a slew of abuse at the driver, who was reeling off apologies in Italian.

'I *told* you the flight was delayed, I called ahead, I did everything to make sure I could get off that awful plane and immediately be brought here. It was a shambles. A *shambles*. An hour and a half I was waiting at the airport.'

'I think you said Florence airport, not Pisa.'

'*I knew which airport I was flying into.* Do you have any idea what I've been through? Have you ever travelled in a storm? Have you ever thought you were going to die a horrible death in the middle of the sea, if lightning doesn't get you first in a cataclysmic fireball? And then – *then* – you drive like a maniac and nearly kill us both. Why don't you look both ways? Why did you want me dead? Because I'm a strong woman?'

'No – no – *mi dispiace, signora.*'

'I just want to go to my room and have a bath, is that too much to ask? Why's it so dark out here? Could you not install a light? Why does it smell all musty? HOW DO I OPEN THIS BASTARD DOOR?'

There was thunderous rattling; Sofia's hostess instinct suddenly kicked in and she ran to open it. In burst a woman, hair like rats' tails, cheeks as red as Merlot, tights torn and a bitter snarl on her face. She was beyond the stage of needing a stiff drink – she looked like if she was given one she'd hurl it into the poor bugger's face.

'*Bueno*-shitting-*sera* everybody,' she screeched. 'Your dream date has arrived!'

And with that, my break from work, my peace and quiet, my relaxation and not having to put on a show was poured down the sink. Because stood before me was the woman in charge of my future, my managing director, Donna.

Part Two

While chaos whirled around me like a hot tornado, I was frozen to the spot. Sofia was apologising; Jamie was back in the room, swooping up Donna's bags; Sebastian was forcing a glass of wine into her hand; the other female guests were twittering about the new arrival – who they'd clearly not considered a threat until they noticed the men's looks of admiration at this bulldog-like woman and her fierce tongue.

Laurie covered her chuckling mouth with her glass and whispered to me, 'What a loon. Sounds like she's had an even worse flight than us.'

'What do I do what do I do what I do?' I rasped.

'Er, nothing, the owners are on it. Though we should help ourselves to a top-up while they're distracted.' I gripped her arm before she could leave me. 'Elle, what's wrong with your face? It looks about as blotchy as mine.'

'Her. I work with her.'

'No way. Do you know each other?'

'Not really. Sort of. She's the managing director. She's in charge of hiring and firing.'

'She's your boss?'

'She's my boss's boss.'

'Bloody hell.'

'This is going to stop me getting a promotion. You know they always say drinking leads to trouble.' I put down my glass. Then picked it straight back up again and took a large swig. 'Ohhhhh, what if one of the activities is drinking shots from each other's belly buttons?'

'This isn't *Sun, Sex and Suspicious Parents*. Calm down.'

'But this could be so embarrassing. What if I hook up with someone? What will she think of me?'

'I knew it! You *are* hoping to hook up with someone!'

'No I'm not.' My eyes flicked to Jamie, betraying me. Damn my eyes.

'So what if you have a tumble among the vines with a feisty hunk, squishing grapes underneath your naked bodies, hot Italian sun beating down on you and your hot Italian . . . anyway, what do you think she's here for?'

I glanced back over at Donna, whose face was like thunder. 'I really don't know. She got divorced years ago, before I even started—' At that point she looked up and our eyes met. Both of us turned Merlot-red, and I looked away.

Laurie aided me in taking my glass of wine back up to my lips. 'Just pretend you didn't see her for now. We'll make our excuses and duck away, and deal with it tomorrow. Or you could just act like you don't recognise her.'

'We just made eye contact for, like, four seconds. If I pretend it wasn't out of recognition my only fallback is that it was out of attraction.'

'Ellen.'

I spun around, sloshing red wine on the tiled floor; Laurie covered up the puddle with her foot. *'Donna! Hi!'* I exclaimed, inexplicably throwing my arms around her. Now she could add sexual harassment to my appraisal, along with being an alcoholic and a desperate singleton. 'Actually, it's Elle—'

'Elle – I know. My apologies. It's been a bloody awful journey.' She looked utterly crushed to see me there, which wasn't a nice feeling. I could only assume that seeing a familiar face in a place like this was the icing on her absolutely shit cake.

'This is my friend Laurie,' I mumbled. 'Laurie, this is my . . . Donna.'

'Howdy.' Laurie jumped over my fumbled introduction. 'Good old British weather; sent us all off with a fanfare today, didn't it?'

Donna nodded, the heaviness dragging her shoulders down. 'I think I'll find my room. I guess I'll see you both tomorrow.'

As soon as she'd left I slumped down onto one of the big leather armchairs, and Laurie perched on the arm next to me before the men could descend back around her.

'That wasn't so bad, was it? She seemed nice – screaming and swearing aside.'

'She's fine, it's just . . . ' Tears welled in my eyes, which was ridiculous. I held my face in my hands and Laurie rubbed my back. 'I'm so obsessed with work, all the time, it's all I think about. And being here, I was just beginning to think maybe it was okay to think about something else for a couple of weeks. And now with *her* here it's like there's a big company code of conduct sign blocking my view of the vineyard.'

'If it's any consolation, she's probably thinking exactly the same thing about you being here. Actually, that probably doesn't make you feel any better, does it? Hmm. What if I took all my make-up off? Unveiled the Botox Monster? Would that crack a smile?'

Another hand, heavier and warmer than Laurie's, gave my shoulder a soft squeeze.

'George, please can you just bugger off – oh!' I

removed my hands from my face to see Jamie crouching down beside me.

'Bugger off yourself.' He smiled, his eyes full of concern. 'Was that a friend of yours? Or maybe a long-lost enemy, because you didn't seem very happy to see her.'

'Sort of.'

'Did she hit you on the nose too?'

I blinked back the tears; there was no need for Jamie to see that I was a total wet-wipe. Absently, I reached for the cuff of his shirt and played with it between my fingers as I said, 'No, she's . . . an acquaintance. She works at my company. She nearly *runs* my company. And she'll probably have me fired if I drink too much wine.'

'She couldn't do that even if she wanted to,' said Laurie. 'And I don't think she'd even try. I bet she's up in her room now, cringing her head off at the thought of you going back to the office and telling everyone she was here.'

'Laurie, this is Jamie – he's Sebastian and Sofia's son.'

'Oh – I didn't mean any offence. It's really lovely here, it's just the stigma that comes with, you know, singles' holidays.'

'I know.' Jamie nodded, a hint of sadness in his voice. 'Nice to meet you, Laurie.'

'Likewise.' Laurie shot me a tiny look that said, *We have much to talk about.*

Jamie turned back to me, putting his other warm hand over mine, which was still fiddling with his shirt. 'Well she's gone for now, and we don't allow tears at Bella Notte unless they are the kind that come with being incredibly drunk and making a show of yourself. If you like, I'll make sure she has so much wine on this holiday she won't even remember you were here.'

I snorted unattractively, which made Laurie snort unattractively at me. Jamie stood up, stretching out his long limbs. 'I really am going now, but I'll see you both for the winery tour in the morning?'

'Definitely. Thank you, Jamie.' I watched him go and then turned to Laurie, who was fanning herself with a flatbread.

'Oh Jamie, thank you for mopping my soggy eyelashes. Thank you for being so absolutely and positively yummy that I've forgotten all about my no-men rule and remembered that I'm a lady with raging lady-hormones.'

'Shut up.' I prodded her with a finger.

'Oh Jamie, please give me a tour of your winery and also of your body – ooo, that cow in the pink dress with the eighties hair has finally left Marco alone. Will you be all right now?'

'Yes, go.' I waved her away and stood up, taking a slow sip of wine and letting it rest on my tongue, its tangy perfume filling my mouth. In front of me was a mantelpiece chock-full of chunky wooden frames containing photos of Bella Notte throughout its life. There was one in black and white, showing the main building and a gruff, moustached woman standing outside the front. Two long rows of vines stretched into the distance, but none of the other outbuildings had been erected. Another was a glimpse into the vineyard in what must have been the early eighties, with muted colours and a very tanned and short-shorted Sebastian holding a little bronzed boy upside-down by the leg, both laughing their heads off, and the boy's hands stained with purply-red grape juice. A close up of Sofia, probably taken fairly recently, showed the unmistakable gold of the evening sun on her face as she looked away from the camera, the vineyard in the background.

'Cute family, huh?' said George, appearing beside me. 'You ever want a family?'

'I have a family,' I replied, thinking of Mum and Dad, who would be falling asleep in front of *Call the Midwife* right about now.

'I mean kids of your own. Unless you already have any?'

I shook my head.

'Me neither. Never wanted them. Now I wonder if I should have.'

I didn't turn from the photos, but there was

something about the way he spoke that made me reluctant to shoot him down again right now. Perhaps Sebastian was right, and there was more to George than we realised as yet.

And then he said, 'But then young women like yourself don't want the baggage of a step-kid your own age, so I did the right thing. Gotta keep the broads happy!'

With that, and a wave to a very hair-tossy Laurie and her impatient hangers-on who were just waiting for Marco to take a loo break, I decided I was more than ready to put this day to rest and to retire to my room.

♥

Ah, my room. I loved my room. I'd forgotten to close the shutters before I fell into bed last night and now the morning sunshine filled the space like a bright cup of lemonade, bouncing off the white walls and highlighting every brushstroke of the little vine murals. The air was warm and still, and I rolled comfortably under my sheet, a smile on my face.

Perhaps I could just stay in here the whole holiday. I had everything I needed – the view, the sun, wine. No managing director.

I couldn't let it bother me. So she was here. So what, really? So I'd have to be a little careful? Well I wasn't about to get smashed and ride a Vespa naked through the vineyard anyway, was I? No, most likely not.

I ran myself a deep, cool bath scented with Sicilian lemon bath bubbles and lay back, the water cleansing my pores as I gazed out at the view. Far away in the vineyard I saw the dog again, lolloping back and forth, and then the distant figure of Jamie appeared beside him, carrying armfuls of who-knows-what as if it weighed nothing. I sat up in the bath, resting my arms on the edge, and watched. It was a bit voyeuristic, especially since I was in my birthday suit, but even if Jamie looked this way he wouldn't be able to see anything, so I was free as a bird to stare at him.

Wearing scruffy jeans and a dirt-covered once-white T-shirt, with tanned forearms pushing the sweat from his brow into his already messy hair, he could be auditioning for the next Diet Coke advert. The dog was up on its back legs, leaning against Jamie and nearly as tall; it would have probably knocked me to the ground, but Jamie just stood there, firm and strong, stroking the dog's head and taking stock of his surroundings.

Jamie did then look my way, and I ducked my head below the water, the lemon bubbles filling my hair.

I stayed under for a while, enjoying the sensation of quiet, undisturbed coolness, and then slowly brought my head up, peering crocodile-like over the edge of the tub and back outside. Jamie and his doggy friend had gone.

Clean and refreshed, but in need of some Laurie-time before the vultures descended, I quickly dressed in another loose sundress (how lovely not to be in sticky shirts and tight-waisted trousers in this heat) and left my hair in a loose plait to dry in natural waves, just like Pinterest told me to do. I left my shoes in my room and went along the corridor to knock on her door.

'Laurie,' I called softly. 'Are you alone?'

'Mmmph,' came a noise from within. I think it was female.

'Can I come in?'

'Mmmph.'

'Is that a yes?'

'Mmmph. Cumm'n.'

I poked my head around the door, giving the room a quick once-over in case it was strewn with broken men, but there was just Laurie, curled in one of the chairs, head on the windowsill, dribble making its way down the wall.

'Did you sleep in the chair?'

She lifted her head and I took her some water, which

she gulped like she had last night's wine. 'It was so hot in the night. My face was burning up. FYI, the bidet is not good to sleep in, but the windowsill is.'

'Did you have fun after I left?'

'Oh Ellephant, Marco is lovely. But I do like Jon as well. Pierre was a bit ... keen.' She hauled herself up and wandered to the bathroom to run the bath. 'How do you know Jamie?' she asked as she came back out, suddenly alert.

'We met yesterday, outside your room actually. We literally ran into each other in the corridor.'

'Had a little flirty-flirty, did you? You bloody minx.'

'No, it's not like that at all.' I laughed it off.

'Liar.'

'I'm not lying. He's just nice to talk to because he's – obviously – not here to meet anyone either.'

'Liar.'

'Shut your stupid face, it's nothing!'

'What a load of bullshiz. You may have been single for ten million years, my girl, but I remember the look you get when you fancy the heck out of someone.'

'What look? I don't get a "look".'

'It's like ... you try and keep a very still face so you don't give anything away, but you blink manically like there's a spotlight pointed at you, as if you can't quite believe a guy's actually paying you attention.'

'That is not true.' Was that true? 'And he was just seeing if I was okay.'

'You do realise you're not Lady von Uglyville? You hardly repel men left, right and centre.'

'I'm also no Jessica Alba.'

'You're right, there is no one in the world in a relationship or married, because everybody only wants to date people that look like celebrities. Everyone is single except the Hollywood elite.'

'Anyway, Sarky-Mark Wahlberg, that's beside the point. He's just a nice guy.'

'Well, just so you know, there is a strong possibility that he might fancy you. So there. Are you saying you don't fancy him even one tiny bit?'

'Would you even believe me if I said no?'

'No.'

'Well, he does have a nice chest.'

She screamed. 'And when, pray tell, did you gawp at his chest?'

'I didn't – my nose did, when we bashed into each other. But whatever, he made it pretty clear he doesn't really mix with the guests. I think he's a little disdainful of those who go on singles' holidays, to be honest.'

Laurie went back into the bathroom, leaving the door wide open, and shouted back out to me, 'Well you aren't on a singles' holiday, remember? You're on a vineyard stay which happens to be with a lot of pathetic single people. *I'm* the one on the singles' holiday.'

'Shall I go and get us some breakfast, and leave you to it?'

'Nope, I'll be just two minutes, just need to replace the stale wine smell in my pores with this lemony hoo-ha.'

'I wouldn't worry too much, something tells me the wine smell will be back on us from pretty early on today.'

'Did you know there's a spa in Japan where you can actually soak in a massive pool filled with red wine?'

'Seriously?'

'Seriously. It's a Cleopatra treatment, or something, though I always thought she just wallowed in milk. Sebastian was telling me about it.' With that she appeared, looking a lot fresher. 'But we are in Italia, so let's drink it instead! Cheers!'

♡

Downstairs, we filled our plates with yogurts, crumbly pastries, paper-thin slices of ham and bunches of cherries and grapes, and took them out to eat on the terrace in the sunshine.

'Best breakfast view ever,' I said through a mouthful

of vanilla cream. We were sat at a round wooden table overlooking the vineyard, our rooms directly overhead. The light was so clear you could see for miles across the rolling hills of the Tuscan countryside, stone towers protruding from random points and stripe after stripe of cross-hatched wine, olive and lemon groves intermixed with short red-roofed buildings. A few tables over from us were Jane and Vicky, the Bristolian girls, dressed in the most enormous sunglasses and neon butt-cheek-baring shorts.

'Morning,' Laurie called to them.

'All right?' one of them called back. 'Where are all the men this morning, eh?'

'Can't handle their drink, I guess,' I quipped, which totally must have cemented me as the 'cool older girl' in their eyes.

But, actually, by the time we all congregated outside the front door ready for the vineyard tour the men were looking sharp and dapper, a lot more beauty-slept than quite a few of us women. We greeted one another with polite hellos and a few lingering looks, and my stomach flip-flopped about while I waited for Donna to join us. Which she did, at the last minute. She gave me a curt nod, but didn't make eye contact with anyone else.

I heard Annette, the woman in the pink dress who'd

been all over Marco the night before, stage-whisper to one of the others, 'There's the crazy one,' and I winced. It wasn't often Donna was the target of someone's snide comment. Perhaps the odd 'slave-driver', but never something belittling. It didn't seem right.

Sebastian and Sofia appeared, full of smiles and charm, and went around to every guest wishing them a good morning and checking that they had slept well. Sofia was watching everyone carefully, no doubt making guesses as to who would make a good pairing with whom.

When they reached Laurie and me Sebastian had a huge, know-it-all grin on his face. 'There's my son's favourite girl, Bella!'

Sofia thwacked him. 'You take your nose out. Let them come together naturally.'

'You're one to talk; you started this whole company. Looking forward to seeing Jamie at work today, Bella?'

I laughed. 'I can't wait; he's all I can think about.'

'Talking about me again, honey?' said George, appearing out of nowhere as usual.

Sofia moved on behind me and I heard her ask Donna in hushed tones if everything was satisfactory.

Donna answered quietly, 'Yes, thank you. I'm sorry if I damaged your door at all last night, I wasn't quite myself. My flight was horrible and—'

Sofia shushed her. 'No need for an apology, as long as we can make the rest of your stay just wonderful.'

If Donna was in a better mood maybe I could relax, stop standing up poker-straight like I was about to give a presentation.

The perfect reason for me to loosen my stance then rounded the corner with Jamie – it was the big brown bear of a dog, who took off and bounded straight over to me and Laurie, tongue out and begging for a hug.

Laurie and I wrapped ourselves around the dog and he shuffled from paw to paw, unsure who to squash into the most, while we sunk our hands into his fur and pressed our faces into his ears. A shadow fell over us, and I squinted up to see Jamie beaming.

'*Ciao!* You two aren't afraid of dogs, then. Is anyone else?' he asked, turning to address the group. They shook their heads, George looking positively attention-deprived. 'This is Enzo.'

'He's cool,' I cried, not even minding that his thick fur was like a fleece blanket on my legs in this weather. 'What is he?'

'He's a Leonberger. And a menace to society. Enzo, leave these ladies alone.' Enzo obliged and went back over to wag his giant tail next to Jamie, probably causing a tidal wave somewhere in the world. '*Buongiorno,* everybody, how did you all sleep in your first night at Bella Notte?'

'It was amazing,' drooled one of the Bristolians, the one in the pink shorts. I think she was Jane. She stared at Jamie so hard he gulped and had to look away.

'*Fantastico*. Are we all wearing comfortable shoes and ready for the walking tour?' Most were in smart leather loafers, high heels or sparkly flip-flops, but no one disagreed with Jamie so off we went. I was in the sparkly flip-flop club, but in this heat I wasn't about to put trainers on, even if it would save a few scratched toes.

We followed Jamie, single file, down through the vineyard between rows of grape-gifted vines.

'You have a lot of good grapes this year,' Jon called out timidly. 'Can we help you out and pick any on the way?'

Jamie stopped and we all gathered close to him to listen, which, of course, meant George was by my side in a second and very much within my personal space. 'Thank you for the offer, but these are still growing at the moment, becoming the best grapes in Italy so Bella Notte can be the best wine.'

'So if we came back later in the summer there'd be even more?' Laurie asked. 'The vines already look like they're about to topple over.'

'There will be hundreds more, so when you stand up at the main house and look down the fields it's like there's a purple mist covering them. And as for sturdiness, you can grow a whole vineyard from one single vine, if it bears a fruit you fall in love with. They are strong. Now, turn around and look back up the hill, please.'

We all rotated on the spot and saw with surprise how much of a slope we'd walked down. The vineyard stretched back up before us, rows of vines spreading to the left and right, all basking in the morning sunshine like holidaymakers around a swimming pool, while the main house stood at the top, its terracotta roof sparkling. As far as the eye could see, the world was green and purple and red.

I glanced at Donna; she was standing with her eyes closed. To the others it probably looked like she didn't want to be there, didn't want to appreciate it, but I wondered if, like me, she was just soaking in the lack of noise from Tube trains, mobile phones, Outlook calendar alerts.

Jamie went on to explain the different vines and the wines they produce, and how soil, sunlight and the steepness of a hill can affect taste. Out here, he seemed far more animated and alive than when he'd entered the room full of guests at the meet-and-greet last night. Winemaking was his passion, and I wondered if he felt like we were all intruders.

We strolled, a slow train of people who had given

in to 'holiday time', where nothing has the need to be rushed, back up the hill where Jamie was to show us the cellars and explain more about how wine was actually made. I caught up with him, which probably made me look a bit eager, but if neither of us were here to play love games then what did it matter?

'Hey.'

'Hey to you.' His eyes crinkled at me.

'I just wanted to say thanks, and sorry, for turning into a bit of a crybaby last night.'

'It's fine. How are you feeling now?'

'Much better. It was just a shock to see her here.'

'I know. Sometimes it can be overwhelming to step away from something that feels like your whole life, even if just for a short time, and you think you're okay until something reminds you of it.'

'Do you ever feel like that?'

He walked on, thinking.

'Like, when you're in your vineyard and you look up and see a bunch of singletons trying to fondle each other among your vines?' I pressed, gently.

He looked at me in surprise, a smile forming on his lips. 'Maybe. I don't know ...'

I decided to change the subject. 'I'm looking forward to seeing those cellars and getting out of this heat for a little while.'

'The sun is strong today, huh? Are you okay?' He shielded my eyes with his hand for a moment, a warmly intimate gesture that made me feel a bubble of what it must be like to have a partner. Maybe it wasn't all bad.

'I'm okay, thanks.'

'So, have you found anyone you like?'

'No.' I intently studied the vines we were passing. 'Though the American guy, George, seems to think we're made for each other.'

'I suppose it's flattering ... but he doesn't make you smile?'

'Not intentionally.'

'I think he seems like a catch. He owns this huge company in Miami, all about ... Hmm ... hairbrushes or something.'

'Does he indeed?'

'He does. And I've seen him looking at you. It's like when Enzo wants my breakfast.'

'Ha – now that's flattering!'

'He could be your silver fox.'

'Maybe *you* should ask him on a date.'

'Maybe I will,' he laughed. 'Maybe I'll date your boss.'

'Go ahead.' Although I hoped he wouldn't. There wasn't a lot of space in between the rows of vines, and as we walked our arms kept brushing together. I folded mine across my chest, acutely aware of how my dangling hand might look like a desperate invitation to be held.

'You're really not going to fall for the charms of *You Had Me at Merlot*?'

'*Bella Notte* I'm already in love with. I'm just not that into the other guests.' I chose the word 'guests' carefully.

'Um, Jamie?' called a voice from behind. We all turned to see Vicky straggling behind, her deadly weapon Kurt Geiger heel wedged firmly into the soil. 'I think I'm stuck. Can I go back and change into some more comfortable shoes?'

♡

Once Vicky was comfortably in a pair of wedge trainers, and we'd had an alfresco lunch break and a tour of the cavernous secret cellars of Bella Notte, everybody was itching to start sampling the selection of wines.

This was Sofia's turn to shine, and she'd laid out the wine-tasting room with dozens of glittering glasses and countless bottles in all shapes, sizes and hues. The lighting was low, just enough to supplement the afternoon sunbeams that peered through the windows and the open door, and soft Italian opera played in the background. I was loving this holiday so far – boss showing up and ancient American stalker aside – because life on a Tuscan vineyard was everything I'd imagined it would be. Then I saw the stack of grape-purple velvet sleep masks and remembered the downside of the trip.

'*Ciao*, everybody, please take a mask and a glass and spread out around the room,' Sofia called. 'Don't stand near to people you want to romance, because once we start you will have no control over your own bodies.'

'I know whose body I'd like to control,' leered George, with a wink in my direction.

Do we have to do this? I thought.

'Do we have to do this?' Donna sighed, suddenly next to me.

It struck me that maybe I was coming across like her to the others, and although I'd been thinking exactly the same thing I now felt the need to distance myself. 'At least we get to try all these different wines. That's why I'm here, to be honest. I mean, just to broaden my knowledge, not to get drunk or anything.'

'You know that wine they always serve at the end-of-month drinks? As long as this is better than that I'll be happy.'

'I've never really thought about it, but I guess that's not the best wine.'

'They keep the red in the fridge. Did you go to last month's?'

'No, I was finishing up a project at my desk. I didn't really have time.' I looked back at the table of wine and at Sofia, chuckling away with Sebastian as she set everything up. That project was done, finished, and I really didn't want to think about it right now.

'The Groovy Muesli project?'

'Yes.'

'How did it go?'

'Well, thanks, the client was happy.'

'Good. Good work.' She was trying, and isn't this what I'd always wanted? Donna to notice me and my work?

'Everybody!' Sofia tapped on a wine glass, making an angelic *ting* ring out across the room. 'Put on those blindfolds and then we'll begin. The rules are simple: you smell it, you taste it, you tell us if you like it, and we will shuffle you around the room depending on your preferences. This afternoon we're working on matching up your taste in wines, and then we'll see if it is the same as your taste in each other.'

I glanced around for Jamie before putting on my mask, but he seemed to have gone. As long as I didn't end up being paired with George or Donna it wouldn't be too bad. Laurie and I had shared a fondness for

Blossom Hill since university, so maybe we'd end up being matched.

'Hold out your glasses please, our first wine is a *bianco*, best served extremely cold, and made with delicious white-skinned Vermentino grapes.'

After a moment I heard the deep slosh of wine being poured into my glass, and I lifted it to my nose. I'm not a big wine smeller, or taster, for that matter. It tends to go straight in, and if it's a goodie will be followed with an 'Mmmm, that tastes Christmassy.' But being blindfolded was definitely tuning my senses, or else I'd just always been drinking very inferior wine (highly possible) because I actually felt like I could pick out scents other than 'wine'. This was citrusy – definitely some lemon in there.

'I smell lemon,' said an unknown female voice.

'Me too!' I yelped. I guess she and I were meant to be.

'And what do you taste?' asked Sofia.

I took a sip and swished it around my mouth. 'Wine,' I sighed. And I thought I was doing so well.

'Are we supposed to be spitting?' Laurie called out.

'That's up to you, you do what you want; you get a fresh glass with each wine either way.'

I went to spit and audibly missed my glass, hearing and feeling a splat on the ground next to me. Maybe I'd just drink up from now on.

'Now tell me, do you *like* it?'

There were choruses of 'it's okay', 'mmm, hell yes!' and 'not really'. I was in the 'it's okay' group. White wine just wasn't my favourite, though I could appreciate this was a nice one. Strong hands that I guessed were Sebastian's clasped my shoulders and gently moved me a few metres to the left.

My glass was taken from my hand and a new one put in, with my helper wrapping my fingers around the stem for me.

The next taster was another white, but this time a super-sweet ice wine that Sofia explained to us was made when the grapes were frozen while still on the vine, allowing the sugars to concentrate and the flavour to intensify. It was syrupy and honeyed, and I decided I wanted to drink it all day every day, and I told her so: 'This is just yummy. I feel like I want to pour it on vanilla ice cream.'

'That's a wonderful idea. It also makes a beautiful vinaigrette for a salad of prosciutto, melon, artichoke...'

We moved onto the reds – hurrah! – sampling delicious wine after delicious wine, each with its own history, flavours, grapes and location out in the vineyard. I learnt that anything with hints of blackberry and chocolate were just fine in my books, but that grappa really wasn't my cup of tea.

We were shuffled this way and that like human chess pieces, Sebastian becoming more careful as the tasting went on and the blood alcohol levels went up. I was intrigued to see who I'd end up being matched with.

Finally, nine wines in and a lot of hazy heads later, the tasting was finished – our 'pairings' to be revealed. I removed my mask and was faced with none other than a beaming George. I turned to grumble at Sebastian, only to find Jamie behind me wearing a barely concealed smirk. He'd been the one moving me? His hands on my arms, his hand on my hand?

'Baby, we are meant to be. You can't argue with love and alcohol.' George went to caress my cheek and I backed away, eliciting a snigger from Jamie.

'Really?' I asked, then turned to Jamie. 'Really?'

'You two are the most beautiful couple here.'

'Isn't she a princess? When I first laid my eyes on her I knew I was looking at my future ex-wife.'

'Nope. No you didn't.'

'She likes you, George, I can see it in her eyes.' Jamie's eyes locked with mine. I was trying to look defiant but he could easily have beaten me in a staring contest because the longer he held my gaze the deeper I blushed. Eventually I looked away.

'George, I'm sorry, I just don't see us being a great couple.'

'That's *amore*, Bella. Love is blind,' insisted Jamie.

'You, come with me,' I said, passing my glass to my apparent future ex-husband and dragging Jamie into a corner. We stood close, and he smelled like the honey-scented ice wine, which I tried to ignore. 'I don't believe for a second that my "perfect match" just happened to be George.'

'Hey, don't blame the wines, blame the drunk people.'

'What?'

'It's not my fault you two like the same things and have everything in common.'

'You know that's not true. I don't even like his trousers.'

'But, Elle, you're not here to find love, right?' he said, his tone teasing.

'That's right.'

'So I can't take other men away from the potential loves of their lives.'

'Damn it . . . you're right. I wish I wasn't so nice.'

'It's your downfall.'

'But wait: by pushing him on to me, a rendezvous that will never happen, you're stopping George from falling in love with someone for real. Which makes you a very bad host.'

'Damn it . . . you're right. But I think it's too late for him. I hear George is besotted with you.'

'No he isn't, he's just besotted with . . . '

'With?'

'I don't know. My Englishness. Maybe he thinks I know Kate Middleton.'

'Is it so hard for you to believe he might actually find you special? Just because you don't want to be with someone doesn't mean someone doesn't want to be with you.'

He was standing close to me now, our hushed conversation causing a smile to play on his lips, which were close to my eye level.

I cleared my throat. 'I thought Sofia was the one into all this schmaltz and setting-up? Sebastian told me you find being in love a chore.'

'I don't know. I guess it's only a chore if you can't handle the work.'

'Oh, bleurgh, your lines are as bad as George's.' But, truth be told – and the last person I wanted to admit this to was my stubborn, set-in-her-ways self – I didn't mind them coming from Jamie one bit.

♡

The following day was activity-free, but we were encouraged to spend time in the communal areas, getting to know one another, and make use of the *amore*-steeped setting. And after a morning of avoiding the clutches of both George – whose research on 'European women' must have come from hours of watching *Carry On* movies – and Donna – who I was beginning to suspect must really fancy our PR agency like a teenager because she seemed to want to drop it into every conversation – I was ready to hide out.

I grabbed an early lunch from the buffet table and was sneaking it back up to my room when I met Jamie in the corridor.

'Well, well, if it isn't Cupid himself,' I said.

'Well, well, if it isn't Bella Notte's very own heartbreaker. Where are you going with that?'

'I needed a break from everyone; I was going to eat it in my room.'

'I know a slightly more interesting place to hide out, if you want.' He led me further down the corridor, past Laurie and my rooms, past those of the other guests, and around the corner to a door marked 'fire escape'. He opened it, and I stepped out onto a stone veranda that ran along the back edge of the building, shaded by trees and foliage. We sat down on the wall and he helped me plough through the slightly excessive amount of Pecorino I'd helped myself to.

'Jamie. Can I ask you a question?'

'Of course, if I can have a bit of that chilli jam.'

'Sure. What's the deal with you and *You Had Me at Merlot Holidays*? You don't seem to ... like them very much.'

He looked a bit bashful. 'Yeah, I'm a little bitter, you could say.'

'Like an unripe grape.'

'Just like that. I will tell you why, because you seem nice. Are you nice?'

'So nice I was voted Nicest Person in my school yearbook.'

'Really?'

'No. But I do give generously to a cat-shelter charity.'

'That's pretty nice. Okay, the problem is that Bella Notte, as a winery, is not doing too well. Don't get me wrong, our wine is the best in the whole of Italy, but there's a lot of competition, and whereas a lot of our income used to come from wine clubs around the world, and past visitors placing rolling orders, now supermarkets abroad offer big-brand wine at cheap, *cheap* prices and ours is getting pushed out. Like many winemakers, we are nearly at the last resort, which is to sell our brand to one of these supermarkets, let them repackage and put their name all over it, but then Bella Notte wines become faceless. It fades away.'

Sadness washed through his voice and he rubbed his hands across his face. I wanted to make it better, make him smile, but what could I do? So I lamely handed him another lump of Pecorino.

'This place has been in *mia mamma*'s family for hundreds of years. I don't want it to fade away.'

My heart bled for him. He wasn't scornful or grumpy, he was lost. He was scared. We all get that sometimes, and instinctively my hand reached out and rubbed the back of his neck.

'I don't want you to get the wrong impression of me,' he continued, 'and think I don't want you or the other guests here. My parents have been running *You Had Me at Merlot* for a year now, in a last attempt to bring in money and drum up new business. I should be less stubborn because actually you're keeping Bella Notte alive.'

'I understand, though. I imagine it would be like the threat of losing your family home and having to open it as a B&B. You're grateful to the guests, but can't help but feel a bit invaded.'

We sat in silence for a little longer, until he looked up and gave me a lopsided smile. 'You are just going to have to fall in love with George, because we can't afford to have any unhappy customers.'

'If I end up falling in love with George I'm leaving the most furious review on TripAdvisor.'

♡

Come afternoon, Laurie and I scuttled off to the far end of the vineyard for a sunbathe and a catch-up.

Laurie rolled on to her front. 'Ouch. I'm lying right on a massive, twiggy vine.'

'Do you want to move?'

'No, that would take even more effort than ignoring it. Now listen, I don't want you talking to Jamie any more because we're out here to find me a husband, not you.'

I lifted my sunglasses in surprise. 'Are you being serious?'

'Yes, stop being such a crap friend.'

My heart thudded. Laurie and I never fought, unless we got on to a discussion about cryogenic freezing, which we had completely opposing opinions about. I didn't know whether to feel hurt or angry. 'I'm sorry – nothing's even going on between Jamie and me really. I didn't realise you needed me to be—'

'Love, I'm joking. I'm not that much of a cow. Tell me all about him, and I want all the details, especially if you've had any saucy dreams about him.'

'There have been no dreams.' My laughter trailed off. Or have there? 'It's nothing. We're a little bit flirty, I guess, but it's just harmless fun. He's just messing with me anyway; he seems far more interested in getting me together with George than with himself.'

'So basically it's like when a boy at school tells you he hates your face and it means he wants to snog it.'

'No, it's nothing like that. I'm sure there will be no snogging.'

'Oh, there'll be snogging. You need a snog. Even if it comes from me after too much Merlot.'

'You need to save your lips for all your men.'

Laurie stretched out like a cat in the sunshine and smiled. 'I love men, I love Italy, I love love.'

'Seriously, though, what are your thoughts so far? Anyone that you think might make you happy?' I asked with delicacy. I didn't want her to wallow, or get teary. The Botox had only just started to settle.

'I don't know. I don't know if I'm being too cautious. Or maybe too desperate. I don't feel a click yet, but it'll come, I'm sure. It's only the third day. It'll come.' I wasn't sure who she was trying to convince, her or me, but either way I sensed the conversation was over and we went back into a peaceful lull.

A while later, as my eyelids were drooping and the page of my John Grisham was becoming blurred, Laurie let out a snort and sat bolt upright. 'Well, sunshine and wine are having a wild old time reminding me I'm getting old – I think I need to head in for another nap.'

We dragged ourselves up, stretched and gathered our belongings.

'See you downstairs tonight though – good luck!' said Laurie with a yawn.

'What's tonight?'

'It's the lucky-dip date. We all have to show up at eight and the first person you see, you have dinner with. They're setting up little tables for two outside on the terrace, I saw Sebastian and Sofia getting it ready earlier on.'

Urgh, who would I have to make small talk with? It was sure as hell not going to be George this time.

❤

Clearly I am also ancient, because when we got back to our rooms I went straight to sleep, feeling utterly crumpled and in need of a wash when I woke up at seven. Stepping out of the shower, my stomach growled. I didn't care who I had to sit next to at dinner, I just wanted to eat. Unless it was George, but then I'd probably be put off my food anyway.

As I was debating whether it would be considered rude to not bother dressing up for my lucky-dip dinner date, and instead wear pyjamas and no bra, I noticed a note had been slipped under the door.

Dear All,

The chef is running a little late, please come down at 8.30 instead.

Grazie,

You Had Me at Merlot xx

The beast in my belly roared with anger and I scoffed half a pack of Smints that were in my handbag.

Eventually, at eight twenty, I couldn't wait any more and decided it was close enough. I put on my bra (sigh) with a T-shirt and jeans (compromise) and scooted downstairs, out the door and round to the terrace.

Even an unromantic cynic like me could see this was perfect for an evening of romance. The terrace had been transformed with a dozen bistro tables, beneath hanging stained-glass lanterns. On the tables were red and white checked cloths and tall glasses filled with breadsticks, while low accordion music played out of who-knows-where, giving the ambience of a real little Italian nook restaurant.

The only thing that ruined it for me, and it was a tiny thing, was that everybody else was already paired up and seemed to be tucking into platters of antipasti.

'There you are,' cried Sofia, running up to me and

weaving me by the arm through the tables. 'Elle, I'm sorry about this, but only one other person turned up late as well, so here is your date.' She stood aside and pulled out a chair, and of course – *of course* – there was George's face grinning up at me like the cat who'd got the cream.

'Baby, baby, this is just meant to be! And I like that you didn't dress up, playing hard to get, making me work to see your body.'

'I don't understand,' I said to Sofia. 'I'm not late. The note said to come down at eight thirty.'

'The note?'

I turned to George. 'Did you get a note? Saying the chef was running behind and we should come down later?'

'Sure did.'

Sofia wrung her hands. 'But Sebastian is your chef tonight, and he is always here. I'm sorry, I don't—'

'Did you *write* the note?' I butted in and glared at George.

'Guilty of a lotta things, but not this, baby. Though I'd like to shake the hand of the man who did.'

And the penny dropped. I'd like to shake the neck of the man who did.

♥

'I don't even use Viagra, I don't need to. Now, I think we both know that's a lie, but if role-playing is what you're into I can play the virile younger man. You wait and see, baby.'

And people wondered why I didn't want a boyfriend. 'I just reeeeeeeally don't want to sleep with you.'

'You say that now, but we'll see.'

'No we won't.'

'How's your pasta?'

'Delicious. Yours?'

'It would be better if I were eating it off your body.'

'George, I am *this close* to getting up and leaving you sitting here all on your own.' Except I wasn't, because the pasta was amazing and no one else was going to get their hands on it.

'How are the love birds?' cooed Jamie the puppet-master, appearing out of the darkness with his guitar and a tea light in a heart-shaped stand, which he placed in the middle of the table.

'Close to flying away.' I glared at him through slitted eyes.

'Flying away together to the Bahamas on our honeymoon!' George roared with laughter. 'Can you picture this one in a bikini, holy hell . . . '

'Save me,' I begged Jamie.

'Elle, you just need to feel a bit more romantic. Give George a chance. He's a remarkable, macho man—'

'With a huuuuge—'

'George, leave it to me. Close your eyes, Bella Ella, and let the mood take you.'

I closed my eyes, but not to let the romance in. It was purely to shut George's face out. Jamie strummed and started softly singing *Bella Notte* from *Lady and the Tramp*. His voice, though not perfect, was gentle and husky, and it lulled me like a soft wine into a blissful state. I almost forgot who I was sitting opposite as I revelled in the pure, unadulterated cheesiness that being serenaded under the moonlight brought. If the ladies back home could see me now ...

'Well now that's a nice smile,' said Jamie when he finished and I opened my eyes to see him crouched next to my chair, peering at me. A big dopey grin had indeed crept over my face, and for a moment my eyes just twinkled with his and I wasn't sure what to say.

And then George broke the mood. 'Hot diggidy damn, Jamie, you've done it. I think she's just fallen in love with me.'

♡

The boiling sun was in the very centre of the sky and tendrils of my hair were sticking to my face and neck, but I couldn't move them.

I was knee-deep in an enormous vat of grapes, the hem of my dress soaking, my hands stained mauve. I moved a few inches to the left and my feet squashed and squelched another dozen bunches. It was messy, but the most satisfying experience you can have outside rolling down a hill in a bubble-wrap dress.

Laurie, Marco, Pierre and Vicky were also in the vat, with George and everyone else on the sidelines. We'd been divided into small groups to try the grape-crushing, and just this once I'd refused to let go of Laurie when she was called up.

'Now everybody hold hands and run on the spot as fast as you can,' called Sofia, to the whoops of the other guests. The last thing I felt like in this heat was a burst of cardio, but I wasn't going to be Donna, sitting at the side away from the others, not joining in, so I grabbed the hands of Pierre and Vicky and ran like mad.

With a sudden *whoosh* Laurie's foot slipped and she tumbled backwards into the mushy grapes, causing bursts of laughter from everyone, including her. Pierre and Marco fell over each other trying to help her, splatting face down into the grapes themselves. In the end Jamie reached in and hauled her upright, catching my eye and chuckling. It was nice to see him having fun.

I waded over to Laurie, who threw sticky arms around my shoulders and we both slipped and fell back down with screams.

'That's what I'm talking about!' yelped George. 'This is better than jello wrestling!'

I gripped the sides of the vat and yanked myself up, darting a look at Donna. That was not the kind of thing you want your potential future boss to remember you for. I expected a raised eyebrow, a contemptuous look, but she was staring off into the distance, quite oblivious to the whole farce. And I found myself wondering, for the eightieth time so far this holiday, why she was here.

Jamie took our hands and helped us out. Once my feet were back on the solid, if rough, terrain I flicked chunks of grape from my dress. 'How do I look?'

'Like my favourite wine,' he said.

'Like your favourite wine, or your favourite wino?'

'Wino?'

'Drunkard.'

'Ah, both: my favourite everything.' He removed a crushed grape from my hair, sending a cold shiver down over the sweat on my skin. 'George,' he called. 'Have you ever seen such a beautiful creature?'

'Hey, Bella, how are ya?' said Sebastian, squinting into the evening sunshine as I walked back to my room to clean off.

'Good, thanks, though I look like an extra from *Carrie*.' I motioned to the blood-like splatters of juice that covered my feet, legs, hands and forearms.

'Fun, though, isn't it?'

'It was so much fun. It's satisfying just to squash the hell out of something – not to sound like a psychopath – and watch it splatter all over the place, knowing you don't need to clean it up.'

'Did Jamie work you hard in there?'

'No harder than anyone else,' I countered.

Sebastian hauled a large wooden bucket onto his shoulder and we walked up towards the house. 'So he hasn't asked you to be my daughter-in-law yet? What's wrong with him?'

'I think you should give up.'

'Never.'

'He clearly isn't interested.'

'Now why would you say that?'

'Because never has a guy devoted this much attention to setting me up with another man.'

'But you're interested, right? I can see you like him. You look at him the way most women look at me.'

I laughed. 'But it's kind of beside the point if the guy

would rather marry me off to some old American dude rather than be alone with me.'

'He's just testing you, Bella. He wouldn't admit it, but he's a little broken, and he's seen many women – and men – come and go on these holidays. They get seduced by the wine, and the food, and the sun, and more wine, and their attention can swing back and forth like a bloody great pendulum.'

'Are you saying he's trying to push me away to see if I'll stay?'

'Well, I wouldn't have put it in such a self-help book way, but yeah, that's the gist of it.'

♥

I watched Jamie as he skirted around the edge of the lounge that evening, pausing to examine nicks in wood-work or to brush dust off wine bottles.

'I'm gagging for a coffee, do you want one?' Donna asked. She hadn't left my side since dinner.

'Sounds perfect.' Off she went and I continued to watch Jamie with interest. Eventually he reached me.

'*Ciao* again.'

'*Ciao*.'

'You told my dad on me.'

I laughed. 'I what?'

'Yeah. He just told me off, said I had to stop being mean to you.'

'Did he now?'

'I said I wasn't being mean, I just really believed in you and George. But he was all, *you'll regret it if you don't treat her well*, blah blah blah. So I have a question for you.'

Little teenage butterflies awoke inside me. 'Yes?'

'Would you like to escape for the day tomorrow? Go to Florence with me?'

'Just me and you?'

He kicked at the ground. 'If you want.'

'To Florence? We can do that in a day? Or did you mean ... um ... an overnight stay?'

'No, it's, like, an hour away; we don't have to spend the night together. There. Spend the night together there.'

'Good. I mean, cool. I mean, that sounds brilliant. How will we get there?' As if details like that really matter when Jamie has just asked me on a full-day date and I have to be entertaining and fabulous for hours on end. Holy crap, I just agreed to a date. Maybe I should just have said no.

'We could go on my Vespa. If you'd be happy with that?'

'Yeah, that sounds ... really not like a hardship.

Thank you, I've always wanted to go to Florence. I can't believe I'm going tomorrow!'

'I like seeing you smile like that.'

'We're going to Florence tomorrow? How lovely!' Donna reappeared and handed me a coffee, which for a moment I wanted to throw in her face.

'Florence?' said Jane. 'That's where they filmed *Jersey Shore* season four.'

'That was the best season,' chimed in Vicky. 'Do you reckon they do a *Jersey Shore* locations tour?'

'I'll go to Florence! Pierre, Jon, Marco – you'll come, won't you?' said Laurie, appearing with her band of suitors.

'We're going to Florence?' asked George, coming over and standing – as usual – right next to me. 'There's a lotta statues there in just their birthday suits, Elle, it's gonna be harder than ever to keep your eyes on me.'

Jamie held his hands up. 'Actually, I was just asking—'

'Did I hear we're going to Florence tomorrow?' interjected Bridget, her eyes wide. 'I haven't been there since my honeymoon. I'd love to go again, it's a beautiful place.'

I met Jamie's eyes and he nodded, lowering his hands and brushing one down my arm as he did so. 'Fine. I will have a minibus or two ready to leave at eight tomorrow morning for anyone that would like a day trip. But it will be a free day, a self-guided trip around the major sites at your own leisure and pace.'

The group broke up into excited chatter and Jamie bent down to my ear. 'I will have a little alone time with you,' he promised with a grin that made me melt that little bit more under the Tuscan sun.

♥

I woke up early as usual, my shutters wide open and the dawn light streaming in. If my bedroom view in London wasn't of the windows of the townhouse directly across the street, I would do this more often; it was a thousand times nicer than waking up by alarm clock.

Florence was a popular decision – nearly everyone had said they would come on the day trip – but although I wouldn't be flying down dirt roads with my face pressed against Jamie's warm back on the back of his Vespa, I was still breaking out into sporadic happy dances at what the day might bring.

It was as I was whipping my scruffy, slept-in ponytail back and forth with joy that I spotted a note slipped under the door.

Breakfast is served! These are absolutely delicious to eat — you have to try them (before Enzo gets to them all). See you at 8. J x

And I thought I was up early. I opened the door a tiny crack and there, in a little wooden bowl, was a bunch of perfectly round, tightly packed violet grapes. I tried one and it burst in my mouth, as sweet and soft as a blueberry, so I scuttled inside with the rest – there was no way I was going to share these.

I decided to be a Decadent Daphne and took the whole bunch into the bath with me for my morning soak with vineyard-view porn, and as I laid them against my bare chest and munched away I felt very like I was in a Renaissance painting. How lovely of Jamie to think of me and bring these to my room. I've quite literally never been brought room service before, and could definitely get used to this.

♥

We all gathered in the morning sunshine, some still chewing on breakfast, some already getting their tan on, some hiding hungover eyes behind sunglasses. Laurie was chattering to me about how her own dinner date went the night before.

'I just get concerned whenever I talk to Marco that anything I say will go straight into his magazine article. But the problem is that after a glass of wine I say a lot of things. And here, there's a lot of wine.'

'But he did say he wouldn't write about any of us, and he seems genuine. Don't let yourself worry like this.'

'You can tell I'm worried? Even through this Botox? What a rip – I want my money back when we get home.'

We began piling into the minibus, then Sofia waved us off, clutching a large mug of coffee in her other hand. 'Remember, everyone, that Firenze is a very romantic city. Take this opportunity to spend some quality time with your potential love.'

Without thinking I turned to beam at Jamie, only realising what I was doing at the last minute and trying to turn it into a communal grin, which meant I was smiling like a lovesick fool at Bridget.

I sat by the window with Laurie, but as Jamie boarded she leapt up and ran to the back of the bus, leaving the seat free for him. He relaxed down next to me, only us knowing we were on a sort-of date. And with that the bus set off for Florence, full of singletons ready to up their game in a medieval city famed for its sensual sculptures and fleshy paintings.

There was a school-trip feel to the journey as we sped down the hill and through the countryside towards

Florence. Even Donna seemed to be lightening up a bit. 'Jamie, do you have any horror stories about past guests? Any as bad as George?'

'As bad, or as sinfully good?' George wisecracked.

Jamie shook his head. 'No, no, I will not speak badly of past guests.' A shadow passed over his face, then left as quickly as it had come. 'They've all been *magnifico*.' There was a groan and he laughed, turning back to me and ducking down in his seat. 'I will tell you one story, though, because you're my favourite.'

A warm wave flooded my insides. I couldn't help but feel elated when he confided in me – it felt like I was the only one in his world. I snuggled further down in my seat, our heads so close I could feel his grape-scented breath tickle my eyelids as he talked.

'Last year there was this woman, and she was head over heels for this very shy guy. She was a – do you know what I mean if I say a "Stifler's Mom" type?'

I guffawed. 'Yes, and I love that you do.'

'She tried every trick in the book to get this poor guy to fall in love with her, and on one of the last nights she went out to the vineyard in the middle of the night, took off all her clothes and lay among the vines, her body decorated with carefully placed bunches of grapes. I think she was trying to recreate a Renaissance painting or something.'

'Well that's just totally insane.' I turned a little pink thinking of my bath that morning.

'I know. She'd asked him to come and meet her out there, but he was so drunk he'd passed out in the kitchen long before she'd even removed her bra. And she was pretty sloshy too. After waiting a while she fell into a deep snooze. It was Enzo who found her, because he always goes to investigate a noise and she was snoring pretty loudly. By the time I arrived he'd eaten half of the grapes right off her.'

'Maybe she thought it was her man, and he'd come after all.'

'Maybe.'

It felt strangely intimate, curled up together on this seat, talking about midnight nudes and eating grapes off bodies. My mouth was a little dry. 'What did you do?'

'I gave her a blanket and walked her back to her room, and that's where I left her. But – I'm not sure how – the following morning both her and her man were in there together.'

'A happy ending, then.'

'Indeed. It was a waste of grapes, but Enzo had never been happier.'

We chattered for the rest of the journey, and it was as easy as talking with someone I'd known for years, if you ignored the butterflies that fluttered up every single time we made eye contact. By the time the bus rolled into Florence I was ready for a little fresh air.

'Here we are,' Jamie said to everyone. 'Florence is beautiful, and there's a lot to see and do, so make sure you pack in as much as you can. I suggest you start just there at the tourist information office.' He held his hand out to me and helped me off the bus.

'Where are you two going first?' asked Donna.

'We're going to see the Duomo di Firenze, the cathedral of Florence,' said Jamie, though I knew he was wishing he didn't have to tell them.

'Is that the bloody great one with the whopping orange roof?' asked Laurie.

'That's the one.'

'Maybe we should all start there, then I can keep an eye on you with my girl,' George joked without joking.

So off we trundled, all of us, until we reached the Piazza del Duomo, a wide and bustling space in which the cathedral stood prominently in the centre, towering above everything, its pale stone walls high and the vast, bright dome dominating.

'Here we are,' exclaimed Jamie. 'You guys have an amazing day, okay? Get lots of stories to tell us all on the way home.'

'Jamie, can we go in there?' purred Annette.

'Yes, go in, look around, go up the dome if you dare.'

Jane stepped forward. 'Is there a lift?'

'There's not going to be a bloody lift, you bloody idiot!' shrieked Vicky.

'*Shut your bloody face. Who bloody asked you?*'

'Jane, shut up, have you seen that guy over there with the greasy hair? Urgh, he's totally looking at your arse.'

'Urgh, bloody pervert.'

'Urgh, look at all them muscles.'

'Urgh, shall I go and talk to him?'

And with that the Bristolians left us. Jamie subtly placed a hand on my back and, on the pretext of showing me the carvings on the wall of the basilica, tried to lose us from the group.

'Hello.'

We turned around and Pierre was behind us. '*Ciao*, Pierre, what can I do for you?'

'I am wondering if going up the dome is suitable for a lady. I would like to take Laurie, but she is a delicate flower.'

'No she's not,' I said. 'She'll be fine.' Behind Pierre's shoulder Laurie was being anything but a delicate flower, ordering a round of limoncello shots from a street-side café.

'I think you should go for it, Pierre, just go in the front entrance and they'll tell you all about it.'

With a nod, Pierre strolled away, finally leaving Jamie and me alone. We circled the entire building as he told me little facts about Florence's history, some of them blatantly made up.

'I find it very hard to believe that Sofia Loren was born here in the Santa Maria del Fiore.'

'Why?'

'Because about five minutes ago you said the same about Frank Sinatra.'

'Ah, busted.'

'There you are,' said Annette, appearing in front of us, hands on hips, trying to give Jamie sexy-eyes but refusing to look at me. 'I seem to be man-less right now; one of the other girls, whose name I can't even recall, is all over mine.' She threw me a deliberate glance and I ruffled my feathers on behalf of Laurie.

'I guess some people just aren't that interested in being around certain other people.'

Annette rolled her eyes and put a hand on Jamie's arm. 'If you want to spend some time with me, I'm right here.'

How dare she? He was my date, and even if she didn't realise that's what this was, it was pretty obvious we were into each other. Yes, I was admitting it. Yes, I was having my first jealous patch in years, and it was kind of interesting.

Jamie extracted himself and put his arm around me. 'Thank you, Annette. Although I think I saw Marco going into the Duomo alone just a few minutes ago.'

'You did?'

'*Sì.*'

She cracked a coy smile as a goodbye, and raced off.

'You did?' I asked.

'No. He's over at that café with Laurie, Jon and Bridget.'

I laughed. 'Well, this is beautiful. Good first stop, even if the others have dragged themselves along too.'

'Florence is small, but with all the little streets and secret walkways, I think we can lose them.'

I liked the sound of that. We explored the cathedral inside and out, often veering off to one side, into an alcove or to carefully study a mural when another member of the group neared us. And besides, from the hand-holding and eye contact I saw going on, it definitely seemed this lot wouldn't have welcomed us chaperones.

♥

The next stop was the Ponte Vecchio, which looked rather a lot like the Pulteney Bridge in Bath, lined on both sides with boutiques that were crammed together and spilling over the sides, like stubborn old ladies using each other's bodies to stop themselves falling down.

We strolled down the centre peering into the jewellery stores, over the wonky paving slabs of the arched walkway to the middle of the bridge where the shops gave way to views out across the river. We stood for a while, tourist-watching.

'Is that Laurie?'

Jamie shaded his eyes from the sun and looked in the direction I was pointing, where a woman was loosely draping herself over a man in an embrace that rivalled any Jack Vettriano painting. They were kissing, tenderly, and when they broke for air she rested her head on his chest and looked out over the river.

'And Jon! Lucky man. I thought he was going to be ousted by Marco for sure,' said Jamie.

'Me too, but look how content she looks. I don't mean this to sound like my friend's a man-eater, but usually when she kisses she's all hair-pulling, legs wrapped around, suck the life out of them like she was the last vampiress on Earth.'

'*You Had Me at Merlot* – one, us cynics – nil.'

'I'm beginning to feel a little less cynical, to be honest.' I wondered if he knew that was my embarrassingly lame attempt to tell him I desperately wanted him to kiss the hell out of me on this bridge.

'Me too. They seem to be having a nice time.'

'Happy.'

'Happy,' he agreed.

'There must be something about this bridge – look at all these couples.' God, I was disgusting, practically begging for a snog.

'Hard to think about anything other than love.'

'And kissing.' URGH, where was my filter? I had to remember to punch myself in the face when I got back.

Jamie turned to face me straight on; I mirrored him. His eyes searched mine, and he raised his eyebrows playfully. I mirrored him again, because apparently I'd forgotten how to speak English now. He stepped closer, inviting me to do the same, until we were inches apart, and there was no question that this was going to happen. Our heads drew closer.

'*Jamiiiieeee*,' shrilled a high-pitched West Country accent. We pulled apart just as Vicky and Jane screeched to halt by our sides and grabbed Jamie's arms, swinging him around.

'Jamie, we need you to translate for us,' giggled Jane, pointing out two pumped-up Italian men with slicked hair who couldn't have been older that eighteen.

I wanted to throw every one of them off the bridge.

'So this is, um, Franco or something, and I need you to tell him I'm just here for the day but I totally want to go drinking with him.'

'And this is my one,' said Vicky, pulling forward her nameless teenager. 'And I need you to tell him I'm a model back in England.'

'And tell mine that I'm a model too.'

'And tell mine that English girls are the best kissers.'

'That is true,' I said through gritted teeth, catching Jamie's amused eye.

Jamie, ever the gracious host, dutifully translated a stream of embellishments about the girls for the poor boys, and by the time they left there was much neck-kissing and bottom-slapping.

I was hoping we could start again right where we'd left off, but as the mood had been ruined somewhat Jamie took my hand in his big, rough one and announced that we were off to look at another man's penis.

♥

Jamie must have some kind of tour-group deal with the Galleria dell'Accademia, because we managed to skirt the long queue and head straight inside.

'We only have one day in Florence, so I'm just going to show you the must-see.'

We wove through halls and galleries festooned with Renaissance artwork until, standing seventeen feet high, was Michelangelo's David.

'He's ginormous!' I cried, not especially talking about his not-so-private parts that were dangling about for all of Italy to see. The sculpture was perfectly carved, from his lifelike toes to his straight Roman nose. There was something humbling about standing in front of an iconic work of art, whose image is seen the world over. I'd never before been taken on a date where I'd been shown something so paramount and prominent that I felt my life had changed, just a little bit, for the better.

There were signs everywhere saying no photos, but how could I not capture this? What would happen if I was old, and Alzheimer's had set in, and someone was trying to tell me about the day an amazing Italian man showed me this masterpiece and I just couldn't picture it, couldn't remember him?

'Jamie, shall I try and take a photo?'

'That's a million times illegal, you criminal.'

'But I really want one, and you have to be in it. I need to remember this.'

'Okay, but if you go to prison it's nothing to do with me.'

'I'll take it really subtly. You just stand next to him and pose in the same way.'

'In the same way as David?'

'Yes. Left hand up, jutting hip, look to the distance like you're thinking, *I wonder if anyone's noticed I've got my man-bits out.*'

'Okay. Should I take my pants off?'

'Yes.'

'Okay.'

Jamie strolled over to the statue, uber-casual, taking his time to look up at the penis, circle to the back and study the butt cheeks. All the while I pretended to text on my phone, keeping an eye on him. Suddenly, he appeared to the side of David and fell into his pose, and I tilted the phone up and – *CLICK*.

Shit, how could I have forgotten to turn the volume off? The security guard's head snapped to attention and she began marching directly for me. I panicked and stuffed my phone in my bag, and Jamie reached me in record time, slinging his arm around my shoulders and whirling me to face the door, where we speed-walked to the exit.

'Mi scusi. Signora. MI SCUSI.' The security guard was right behind us but we ignored her, only steps away from the exit. Jamie pushed open the door, shoving me in front of him, and we both fell out into the sunshine.

And straight into two Polizia who were leaning against their motorbikes.

'*Signora*,' said the security guard in a stern voice, catching the attention of police officers. Jamie turned to the three of them and they all started speaking at once in rapid Italian. The security guard seemed very angry, and the Polizia looked annoyed at having their break interrupted. Jamie was charming and apologetic, and though my heart was racing there was also something adrenalin-pumpingly delicious about watching this man defend me in a beautiful foreign tongue.

Just look at him go ...

I caught the Italian words for 'wife' and 'doesn't speak Italian'. The two male police officers nodded but the security guard shook her head and turned on her heel, going back inside the gallery.

Jamie strode back over with a grin and put his arm around me, and then just to make my knees turn completely to jelly after his Italian-language lesson, he did something deliberately intended to make me melt like gelato. He made a show of giving me a husbandly kiss on the lips, taking me by surprise though I knew I had to act like it didn't. So I kissed him back, Florence spinning around me, my mind muddled with thoughts of how long it had been since someone had their lips on mine and how I could feel his soft stubble and hot forehead.

As quickly as it started he broke away, slung an arm around me and strode us off across the piazza.

Once we were a safe distance, and I was quite sure I wasn't going to spontaneously combust, I pulled a grinning Jamie to a stop.

'Sorry about that, but I had to tell them you were my wife, and I had to make it convincing.'

'Were they going to deport me for taking a photo?'

'No, but I just felt like it. Sometimes the little embellishments can make a story more fun.'

'And what story did you tell them, exactly?'

'That you were my new wife from a foreign land, and you didn't understand Italian very well but are absolutely entranced by our culture anyway. And that you are very vain and like to take a lot of photos of yourself wherever you go.'

'You told them I was taking a selfie?'

'Yes. I was like, look how beautiful she is, why wouldn't she take a lot of photos of herself?'

'Thank you, for the compliment, and for saving me from ending up in an Italian prison. Can I buy you a gelato?'

'Um, YES.' Jamie led me straight into the nearest gelateria, of which there was one on practically every corner, and we were faced with the agonising decision of which flavour to choose from the rows of tubs, overflowing with soft, pillowy ice cream, all swirled with sauces and decorated with carved fruit.

'What's *fior di latte*?' I asked Jamie.

'It's "flower of milk" – it means the best bits of milk. It's a little bit sweet, like thick cream.'

'Sold, I like trying new flavours. What'll you have?'

'The best flavour, *stracciatella*. It's the same as yours, but with chocolate flakes in it.'

I ordered and paid, all in broken Italian which had Jamie sniggering beside me, and we stepped back outside onto the cobbled street.

'I just have something I need to do, really quickly, and then I'm going to take you to secret Florence. Will you be okay just hanging out here for a few minutes?'

'Of course,' I said through a mouthful of gelato, which I couldn't bring myself to stop eating, even to talk.

Off he went, and I took a slow stroll down the street, peering through the glass in the many arched windows of the shops. I stopped outside an Intimissimi, and gazed at the slim, slowly rotating mannequins with pert bottoms in chic, frilly undergarments.

I took a spoonful of ice cream. I was not the owner of any chic undergarments. Don't get me wrong, just because I'm single doesn't mean I only wear multi-pack briefs from Tesco (or at least only on gym days). I possess a fabulous array of brightly coloured thongs and sequin-bedazzled bras, but it's been an awfully long time since

I've bothered to match them. Or buy anything sexy. The sexiest thing I own is a way-too-small corset I forked out for at an Ann Summers party at university, which I keep for that special occasion that has never happened and if I dragged it out now I'd feel like a right lemon.

But this lingerie was pretty, feminine, stylish. It was all dusky pinks and creams and carbon greys. I wondered if I should get some.

I took another spoonful of ice cream. Would Jamie like this kind of underwear?

'Going shopping, or just admiring the view?' he asked, standing next to me and making me snort ice cream and blush all at once.

'Well, those mannequins do have fantastic bums,' I coughed. 'Shall we go?'

'I got you a present.' He handed me a brown paper bag and I tried to shake from my mind the present I'd just been contemplating giving him. I pulled out an electric blue T-shirt and unfolded it to see emblazoned on the front, in the Coca-Cola font, the words 'Ciao Bella'.

'For me?'

'For you. To remember Italy by. I thought it was perfect.'

'As if I could forget Italy.' I was touched and looked up at him, holding the T-shirt close to my chest. 'Thanks, Jamie, this is sweet of you.'

'It's nothing really, just ... you suit the name Bella. It suits you.'

I ran my fingers over the words. 'I'm having the best time so far. I really didn't think I would. And you're helping.'

'You didn't think you'd have fun?'

'Not this much fun. You know, with the whole not-looking-for-love thing.'

'I'm having fun too. Now, how are your feet? Can you handle a walk or do you want to take the bus to our final stop?'

'I'm walking; I don't want to miss a thing.'

We set off, following broad, leafy roads to the out-skirts of the city, crossing over the Arno River and on to the south bank, where we started to climb a hill, chatting all the way. Jamie was keen to know what my favourite parts of the day had been, and I was torn between the cathedral and the gelato.

'It's just that I've never tasted anything like *fior di latte* – it was just like frozen double cream, which is a big plus. But on the other hand, the basilica was kind of impressive too ...'

'The gelato has won, hasn't it?'

'I believe it has. Am I horrible tourist?'

'My whole business is based on taste, and people enjoying a taste so much that they want to stay in that place. The fact you've chosen a flavour as your favourite thing about our day trip just makes me think more highly of you. We're nearly there.'

We reached the top and turned, and only then did I look up to see what we'd been aiming for. We stood looking down across the whole of Florence, a sea of sparkling red roofs with the majestic Duomo di Firenze rising above them all, shimmering in the late afternoon sun. 'Wow. Look at that. Where are we?'

'Piazzale Michelangelo,' Jamie said, taking my hand and leading me to the walled edge, where we perched and admired the view. 'This is Florence. This is Tuscany. Do you like my home, Elle?'

'I like it so much I don't want to go back to *my* home,' I sighed. We were still holding hands, and though I was gazing ahead I was aware of Jamie looking at me. 'Are you looking at me?'

'A little bit.'

'Why?'

'I don't know. Nice views all around, I guess.'

I leant my head on his shoulder and we sat for a long time watching the sun sinking, looking like a happy couple, feeling like a first date.

The minibus rolled back into the vineyard some time after eight. Laurie and her three men had boarded with stacks of pizza boxes for everyone, so there was no need to scavenge for food when we returned. Jamie helped me off the bus.

'Can I show you something? If you can bear to be around me for a bit longer?'

'Sure.' *Of course.* He took my hand like it was the most natural thing in the world now and began leading me towards one of the outhouses. I looked back at Laurie who was stood giving me a dramatic lunge and two thumbs up, and I widened my eyes back at her. Where was he taking me? Were we going to make out again? I licked my lips in anticipation, hoping they wouldn't taste of pizza.

Inside the cool building, which was all stone walls and wooden beams, there was a thick aroma from the oak barrels that were stacked high.

'Are these all full?'

'Every one of them – this is the 2008 Merlot, which was a great year for us.'

'That's a lot of wine. Don't let Laurie in here alone.'

'Come on, this way.' As he walked me to the far end of the room I ran my hand over barrel after barrel. At the end a wooden staircase led downwards, and when Jamie flicked a switch a line of dangling light bulbs lit the way to the cellar below. 'After you. I promise I'm not going to murder you.'

'If you're a murderer, I can't exactly trust that you aren't a liar as well.'

'This is true. What if I tell you there's some open wine down there.'

I shrugged.

'And some chocolate.'

'You better not be messing with me or so help me God . . .'

'I would never joke about chocolate with you, trust me.'

Down I went, and the stairs opened out to a perfectly curved cellar, lined with more barrels, but these ones upright. There were also some cooking utensils at the end that appeared to have been stolen from the Bella Notte kitchen.

'Take a seat.' He gestured to one of the barrels and I hopped up. He handed me a glass and poured from a black bottle an inch of thick, blood-red liquid. 'Try this and tell me what you think.'

'Is it blood? Are you a vampire?'

'Yes.'

'Well it smells like wine, that's good enough for me.' I took a sip, and it was like a hundred raspberries bursting in my mouth – both sweet and tangy – and something more. Jamie was watching me carefully and shuffling on the spot, eager for my reaction. 'Oh!'

'What? What can you taste?'

'Oh! It's ... oh, it's spicy!'

'Too spicy?'

I took another, bigger sip. 'No, it's absolutely amazing. It's delicious and moreish, and has more than a little fire.' I looked directly at him, afraid I was sounding a little too soap-opera innuendo right now. He was looking down at me, watching me intently with those dark eyes. 'And my, it's potent,' I said polishing the glass off and dragging my gaze away. He topped me up another inch and poured himself a glass too, breaking into a happy grin.

'You really like it?'

'Mmm,' I said through my gulp. 'Did you make it?'

'It's just something I've been working on. The wine is fortified, and then I've been infusing chilli in it.'

'Chilli, huh? May I have some more?' He refilled my glass, this time with a slightly more decent measure. 'You are a very talented chap.'

'I've been working on it for a while but you're the first to try what I think might be the finished product. My first attempt was so hot I cried for days!'

'Well I am honoured. It really is delicious.' Jamie's smile could have lit up the room if the light bulbs weren't already doing so. It was nice to see him so happy, and so passionate about something. Was I ever *this* passionate about work? I know I loved my job and all, but did I ever beam like a ball of sunshine if someone complimented a report I'd done? I guess it's different if it's something you made from scratch, something that's all for you and your own company.

'It's strong alcohol content though; be careful,' he chuckled.

'Yeah, yeah, I think you mentioned something about some chocolate.'

'Right!' He pulled out a cling-film wrapped brick of chocolate so dark it was nearly black. 'I made this too,' he said shyly, getting out a small hammer.

A man who makes chilli wine and his own chocolate? I don't care how much the ladies would be all '*We told you so*', I had to walk down the aisle and marry him immediately.

'Close your eyes,' he instructed.

Please kiss me. Something cold nudged my bottom lip and I breathed in sharply.

'Drink,' he murmured, and I took a long sip from the glass, perhaps more than I should have but a blissful tingling of nerves was setting in. 'Now open your mouth.' I opened it a touch, in an alluring way. Or in a slack-jawed, slightly drunk way. 'A little more.' I obeyed, because that definitely sounded like an invitation to snog with tongues.

And then he placed a small chunk of smooth chocolate on my tongue and the flavours melted all over the fiery chilli. 'You didn't really make the chocolate too, did you? Because if you did I'm never leaving.'

'I made the chocolate too.'

I sighed with happiness and reached for my glass again, my body relaxing and swaying a little, my eyes still closed. 'How do you have so much patience to make all these things yourself? What about supermarkets?'

'Supermarkets can't give me the exact combinations that I need, which is such a dark, bitter chocolate that it becomes mellow and balances the chilli. It's like a science. But . . . tastier.'

'Amen.' I drank more, and then a little more. This wine was perfection, and it was making me heady quickly. 'You could sell this anywhere. Seriously. Like, even at a baby shop. You could package it right up and sell it as a special offer when someone buys a pack of dummies.'

'Dummies?'

'You're a dummy.' I hiccupped, and stood up. 'Woo-wee, this really is strong.' *Gulp.* 'You're coming home with me.'

'Am I?'

'Yes, to make me wine and chocolate for ever more.'

'Okay. Are you feeling okay?'

'I feel . . . unsteady.' I laughed.

'Maybe I should take you back to your room now.'

'Really? Will you kiss me again?' Hello, where did that come from?

He chuckled. 'Maybe. We'll see. Come on.' He led me up and out of the cellar, but not before I leant back and grabbed the rest of the bottle of chilli wine to take with me. I was drinking more than I ought to, knowing it was making me behave in a way I would never normally behave, and bringing me closer to Jamie than I'd dare.

'Look at all these barrels,' I said as we staggered through the top level. '2008 was a good year for us.'

'Yes it was.' He opened the door and I stepped outside, where it was now twilight and no one else was around.

'No one else is around,' I stage-whispered. 'Maybe you should kiss me.'

Jamie reached for the bottle and took a swig himself. 'Chilli wine, what have you done to my sweet Bella Ella?' We stumbled away from the outhouse, crunching through the pitch black, over the dirt path and in the direction of the main building, whose lights were glowing warmly from inside. Inside, where all the others probably were. George. *Donna*.

I stopped. 'Can I tell you a secret? Sometimes I get so bored at my work and I think, I hate you all, and I think that when I'm CEO I'm just going to fire them all for being boring and for making me talk about work aaaaalll the tiiiiiime.'

'I don't think you mean that.'

I slumped against the wall. 'You're right. They're all fine. Maybe I talk about work too much? Do I talk about work too much?'

'Not to me.'

'Well you're special. Where's my kiss?'

Jamie moved in close and pulled my body weight against him, and kissed me softly on the forehead. I sighed and wrapped my arms around his chest, feeling like our bodies were magnetically drawn to each other.

'Fine,' I said. 'But I really don't want to go back in there. I don't want to see everyone or have people asking all these questions like, "*What's going on with you and Jamie?*" and "*How yummy is Jamie's chest?*"'

'What do you suggest, Bella?' he murmured in my ear.

'Where's your room?'

He was quiet for a moment, and I just stood there, leaning against him and breathing in his neck, my mind swirling with wine-fuelled giddiness and small drips of crystal clarity about the implications of what I was saying.

'You can stay in my room with me, if that's what you're sure you want.'

'Yes please,' I yawned. I didn't want to move my head from his chest, I could suddenly have fallen asleep right there, but even with this cloudy mind my heart was thump-thumping.

He took my hand and we turned, walking back through the vineyard.

'Are you drunk?' I side-eyed him.

'No. Maybe a little, I'm a bit more used to it than you. Are you?'

'Drunk in love,' I sniggered, then let out another enormous and very attractive yawn.

'Are you tired?'

'Maybe a little. It's been just the best day, but very long, and you have a lot of sunshine in Italy. And a lot of wine.'

We stopped at what seemed like a garage, but on entering turned out to be a lovely converted studio. The stone walls had been painted white and small touches made it homely and warm inside. Jamie switched on a lamp and turned to face me, his face nervous and apologetic.

'It's not much, and it's not as fancy as your guest

room, but it's mine and it's away from everything else.'

I ran my hand over a collection of photos of Enzo in little wooden frames, from (still fairly massive) puppy to the huge dog he was now. 'I think it's perfect.'

'Should I . . . leave you to . . .'

'Can we lie down for just a minute? Do you mind?' He shook his head, and I wondered if I was crossing the line, or being too forward. But I genuinely just wanted to rest, just for a moment.

He climbed on to his bed and stretched his arm out for me to lie on. I went to him, and as we lay there I wondered why I'd left it so long to lie with someone. It felt nice to be this close to another person. Safe, warm, intimate. But also scary, and I didn't know what to say any more because all I could think about was his breathing, and my breathing, and how much had changed in the space of a day.

He sighed, exhaling through his nose, which blew a tuft of my hair up and over my face. Jamie reached over to push it back and I instinctively nuzzled into his hand, kissing his palm lightly.

'Elle . . .' he said, and I shifted my body up so my face was level with him. I wanted that kiss. Did he want it too?

Suddenly he brought his head up and crushed his

lips against mine. I hadn't kissed anyone for a long time, bar earlier today, and my body wanted to make up for it. I had the feeling he was the same, from his urgency.

We kissed, our tongues tingling from the chilli, and pressed our bodies together on his bed, and the roaring fire slowed to softly crackling embers as we melted into it. I hadn't thought there was a more delicious combination than chilli, wine and chocolate, but add the fourth ingredient of Jamie's lips and finally my mouth was in heaven.

♥

My mouth felt like I'd been chewing on cotton. And when I opened my eyes, sticky with yesterday's mascara and found myself staring into the T-shirt of Jamie, half of it balled in my mouth, sucked in through a sleep vacuum, I realised this was exactly what had happened. I lifted my head very slowly from his chest, leaving a trail of dribble on the bunched-up T-shirt. I glanced up, but he was snoozing like a very attractive baby.

What the hell happened here last night? How did I fall asleep right on him? Was he even still alive, or had I crushed him to death?

I moved a hand as carefully as I could and held a

finger under his nose. Yes, he was breathing. Now the real question . . . was I wearing underwear?

Yes. Although my dress had ridden up to my stomach, my knickers were very much in place, even if they were rubbing up against the crotch of his jeans. Okay. So we can't have done 'it'. Probably. But we were very close together, so much so that, to be honest, I felt a bit clammy. I used my spare hand, i.e. the one not screaming with pins and needles as it was currently wedged under Jamie's tricep, to rub my fuzzy teeth until they squeaked with a whimper of cleanness.

I lifted my head again and – ooo – that was a hangover waiting to happen.

Jamie opened his eyes and met mine. We stared at each other for a moment, my body tense, very aware of it pressing down on his, and suddenly very aware of my full bladder.

'Hello.' I tested the waters.

'*Ciao*, Bella.' He cracked a smile. He wasn't revolted by me; this was a good start.

'How are you?' Formality is always a good start when lying atop someone, in their bed, with a big old mind-blank and a rucked-up dress.

'Very well, and yourself?'

'Not too bad. Thank you.' I peered around his room, searching for conversation or at least a way to say *Please*

155

could you tell me if your bits were introduced to mine last night. I saw the empty black bottle that had housed the chilli wine that was now thumping about inside my bladder like an angry inmate. 'That chilli wine . . . that's some good stuff you've got going on there. Strong.'

Jamie nodded. 'But without it, this magical night may never have happened.'

Oh God.

'Magical . . . did you have a, um, favourite part?'

'Every inch of your body.' Jamie inhaled, a lazy smile spreading across his face before he stroked my hair and I struggled not to pee myself in panic. 'What about you? What was your favourite part?'

'Hahaha, your body is pretty good too, mister!' *Shit, shit, shit, REMEMBER.*

'But as wonderful, as unforgettable as our lovemaking was, it was nothing compared to the honour you did for me afterwards.'

I had no idea what I did. Did I give him a—

'Thank you, *mia Bella*, you have made my heart sing.'

'No problem . . . ' I sat up and he sat up too, wrapping his arms around me.

'Oh Bella, when you said you'd be my wife you made me the happiest man in Italy.'

Whoa. 'Your wife?'

'As soon as possible, just like you insisted last night.'

He leapt out of bed and stood in the middle of the room while I frantically adjusted my dress and my life flashed before my eyes. 'Today I will take you to meet my grandmother!'

'Brilliant.'

'And she will love you.'

'*Yes.*'

'And we will be married!'

He spread his arms wide, my headache kicked in, my bladder nearly gave up and bile rose in my throat, and all I could say was, 'GETTING MARRIED IS JUST WHAT I WANTED.'

Part Three

'Marrying you is going to make me the happiest man in the world,' declared Jamie, bouncing onto the bed next to me and making my stomach heave. How did this happen? *How?*

'I'm sooooooo excited,' I forced.

'You are?'

'Just so *fall-on-my-face* excited.'

'You really are?'

'I LOVE MARRIAGE.'

'So do I!'

'Well we are just meant to be together then.'

'This is fantastic. It's fantastic! You know, from the way you've spoken about love since you got here, I didn't think you'd even be thinking about something like this, so when you asked me if I'd marry you I was—'

'*I asked you?*' I interrupted in disbelief.

'You don't remember? It was beautiful.'

'I mean, obviously I asked you, I remember it like it was yesterday. I just think, really, you were asking me first, with your . . . eyes.' I am never drinking chilli wine again. I am never drinking anything again. Damn you, alcohol, for this treachery.

'I would have if you hadn't – I wouldn't have let you slip away. Happy days!'

'I don't think I've ever been this happy,' I said miserably, weighing up whether it would be better to break his heart now, grab a Vespa and make a dash for the airport, or just go through with it and save an awkward conversation.

'Neither have I. How many babies do you want?'

I shrugged. 'One?'

He shook his head.

'Two?'

'No, let's have a whole brood of them.'

'Three? Four? *Five?*'

'Let's say no more than half a dozen.'

My poor vagina.

'Bella Ella, my blushing bride.' He gazed out of the window, a far-off happy look on his face. In my blurry, hungover state I didn't have the strength to be the cause of someone else's heartbreak. I'm sure I could get out of this later, when I could think of a way we could laugh about it. Knock-knock. Who's there? Not your wife. HAHAHA, now can I get you a cappuccino?

'When shall we do this?' he asked, his eyes positively glistening.

I pasted on a manic grin. 'As soon as possible, please!'

'Are you serious?' he asked, his smile dropping a millimetre.

'Mmm-hmm,' I said, amping the brightness up another notch.

'You really do want to get married?'

'Of course. I'm planning it in my head already.'

'You are? Already? That's some forward planning.'

'I think there should be ... swans.'

'Perfect ... '

'Um, what time are we going to meet your grandmother?' How long did I have to formulate a plan?

Jamie sat down next to me, all trace of humour gone. 'Elle?'

'Just call me Mrs—' Jesus Christ, what the hell was his last name?

'Oh Elle, I have something to tell you.'

'Yes, *hubby*?'

He gulped. 'I don't want you to hate me, and I really didn't mean to play about with your heart.'

'Quit Playing Games (With My Heart)' started up in my head. *Focus, Elle*. 'What?'

'I feel awful ...' Jamie faced me, then looked away, then turned back to me again. 'Don't hit me, okay?'

'Okay.'

'Oh, you're going to hit me so hard.'

'Get on with it.'

'You didn't ... *exactly* ... ask me to marry you.'

'I didn't?'

'In actual fact, we didn't get engaged last night at all.'

'We didn't?'

'And while we're being open with each other, we didn't even ... do it.'

I instinctively lifted the duvet and peeked at my knickers. Yes, they were definitely still there. 'Not even a little bit?'

'Not even a fondle. Elle, I'm so sorry. It was a joke; I had no idea this would actually be something you wanted, and now you're heartbroken and ... You know what, would you like to kick me in the balls? It might make you feel better. Go on, I deserve it.'

In fact, far from gathering up its pieces, my heart was heaving a bloody great sigh of relief. I fell back onto the bed. 'Oh, thank God.'

'I don't understand. Are you sad? Are you passing out with anger?'

'No, Jamie, I'm relieved.'

'Relieved that you can kick me in the balls?'

'Relieved that we're not engaged.'

'You *didn't* want to get married?'

'No way! No offence.'

'Offence taken: "no way" is a little harsh.' He answered my cheerful grin with a confused smile. 'Why did you say how happy you were about it all then? I expected you to freak out immediately.'

'It's just that you looked over the moon. I didn't want to make you sad, or make it awkward between us.'

'That is the most British thing I've ever heard – agreeing to marry someone just to avoid being rude. So you aren't angry? Even though we're not getting married?'

'No, definitely not.'

'How about because I'm an asshole for telling you we were – are you angry with me about that?'

'Still no. Lucky for you, I have a fabulous sense of humour. Perhaps you could take me to breakfast though; I'm in need of a big scoop of Nutella on lashings of toast, stat.'

He helped me up and I straightened myself out in his mirror, licking my thumb to wipe away the smudges of mascara that had pooled under my eyes. 'You're saying we absolutely didn't, you know, actually *do it*?'

'Nope, all clothes remained on all bodies.'

'Did I do anything else embarrassing?' Why do we all feel the need to ask that question after a boozy night?

'Not at all,' he said, coming over and wrapping his arms around me. 'We kissed a little, which was lovely – you tasted like some *delizioso* wine and chocolate – and then you fell asleep on my chest. You dribble a lot in the night, you know.'

'Good, you deserved it. The kissing was nice?'

'I can show you again if you like.'

'If you think it might jog my memory . . . '

Jamie bent his head, and the last thing I saw before our lips touched was a lazy smile cross his face, a row of neat teeth and his eyes fluttering closed.

It was over within a few seconds; no one needs to use tongues when hungover and with a mouth drier than a tumble dryer. But it was delicious.

And with that he took my hand and we stepped out into the bright morning sunshine, straight into the vineyard. And it felt so *easy*. There was no awkwardness, no 'where do we go from here', just two happy little lovebirds with a blossoming romance.

Who *was* I?

♡

I stuffed my face with all the things we're trained not to desire for breakfast in England, as we chew our soggy Special K: cookies, sweet buns, doughnuts, pastries and cream-filled *cornettos* – Italian croissants rather than the ice creams, though I would have happily scoffed one of them too. With a handful of extra cookies, I went to my room for a much-needed wash and change of clothes.

I lay back in the bath and thought about the night before, and about me (before the snogging began and it all got a bit hazy). I smiled to myself. That wine ... that wine made me carefree for a while there. Fun, silly and open. I'd been happy to live, happy to laugh and happy to love with wide-open arms. I'd been begging for a kiss, but I wasn't embarrassed. It made me be who I wanted to be in real life.

I'd been engaged this morning, for a short while. Ha! Me, engaged!

Me, engaged ...

These were very silly thoughts so I dunked under the water, shaking my head to fan out my hair, and let them float off into the bubbles.

♥

Clean and shiny, I went to Laurie's room so we could debrief one another on the past twenty-four hours. I tapped on her door and waited. Nothing. I knocked a little harder, though I knew she probably wouldn't appreciate if she was trying to sleep off another hangover on the windowsill. But still nothing. Perhaps she was already up and at breakfast, or had taken herself off for a walk. Or perhaps she had someone in there ... I squashed my ear against the door, held my breath and listened for sounds of movement, talking or – what I was really hoping for– the sounds of a little morning delight.

I heard nothing, which was disappointing. She must have been up, or selfishly in someone else's room.

With Jamie back to work, Laurie MIA and me with no idea if there were any activities planned for the day thanks to spending all evening and night on the other side of the vineyard, I was on my own.

I grabbed my book, then put it back again – sometimes it's better not to have other means of entertaining your mind and just to let it think on its own – and with a large, floppy sunhat on my head I went to the kitchen to make myself another cappuccino, extra foam.

Downstairs was deserted; either everyone was sleeping in or they were all off doing some flirt-tastic activity with Sofia, who'd be clapping her hands with glee every time two people made physical contact. I took my time crushing a portion of smoky-smelling coffee beans and fiddling about with the milk frother, and eventually stepped outside clutching an oversized mug.

It was very peaceful, and I looked across the vineyard

to Jamie's tiny house in the distance. I strolled so slowly that my feet barely made a crunch in the dust as I rounded the building to the terrace, where I stopped short.

There was Donna at one of the far tables, gazing out at a view, her arms folded and large sunglasses on her face. Well it was no surprise she wasn't out enjoying the activities, but more than ever I didn't want to ruin my good mood with talk of work, or having to think about the consequences of everything I said.

I was about to back away, ninja-style, and find somewhere else to sit with my coffee when I saw her wrench off the sunglasses and drag a hand across her eyes. Her shoulders sank further. *Oh, Donna*. My heart panged. There's nothing that grabs hold of my empathy more than when I see a person cry; it has the potential to set me off in mere seconds (seriously, even if it happens to a character in *Hollyoaks*). It's just horrible for someone to feel that sad and helpless.

I wouldn't leave her like this, not without making sure there was nothing I could do, but I did manage to resist running over and throwing my arms around her, pulling her head to my bosom and stroking her hair.

Sitting down next to her, I looked out at the view. Her head tilted in my direction, briefly, and she let out a big sigh.

'It is a bit of a rubbish view, isn't it?' I quipped gently.

She nodded. 'It's crap.'

'Is there somewhere you'd rather be?'

'Anywhere . . . nowhere . . . I don't know.'

'Would you like to go home?'

'No.'

We sat for a while, staring out. I waited for her to tell me what was wrong, but I wasn't really sure if that was ever going to happen. The little I knew of Donna, she didn't seem much of a sharer.

Eventually I said, 'It's a bit quiet around here today. Do you know where the rest of the singletons are?'

'They're all in one of the cellars. Something about spin-the-bottle wine-decanting. Not my cup of tea.'

'No . . . How have you found the holiday so far?' As if I didn't know she'd hated every moment.

'It's a beautiful place. It's just best when there's no one else around. Present company excepted.' She gave me a small smile.

'You haven't found anyone you . . . you know . . . like?'

'I really don't want a *boyfriend*,' she spat, resentment firing out, but I sensed it wasn't directed at me. She was shaking slightly, her jaw hardened.

'Would you like a coffee? I just worked out how to make the best cappuccinos and now I can't stop drinking them.'

She nodded, like a child who needs a bit of looking after but doesn't know what would make her feel better. I returned to the kitchen to make two fresh foamy coffees, giving her time to calm down. Armed with the drinks and a little plate of biscotti I went back outside, where Donna had placed the sunglasses on the table and twisted her hair back into a messy bun. It suited her, the off-duty look.

'Thank you, Elle,' she said, reaching for the cappuccino and bringing it to her lips with a satisfying slurp.

'No problem. If you're not going to take a boyfriend away from all this, you might as well make your money back in coffee and biscotti, right?'

I hoped I hadn't crossed a line, but Donna chuckled. 'That's the type of problem-solving brain I like. So, have you found anyone *you* like?'

'Er . . . No, I'm here for the wine and biscotti, not for the silly boys. I'm being moral support for Laurie – the gooseberry friend, if you will.'

'That's nice of you.'

I munched my eighty-fifth piece of biscotti. 'It's not the worst deal in the world, and I'm making the most of it so far. Can I ask you a question?'

'Okay,' said Donna, a little guarded.

'If you're not here to meet someone, and you're not playing gooseberry, can I ask why you chose this holiday? You don't have to tell me – I don't mean to pry, it's just, if you want to talk about it . . . ' I stuck my face so far into my mug my nose got covered in foam.

'It's not that I don't want to tell you, but I don't think I should burden you.'

'It wouldn't be a burden. I have literally nothing else to do.'

Donna lapsed into silence for a time; the only noise between us was the crunching of biscotti. Finally, she spoke.

'I don't want a boyfriend because I was genuinely happy with my life. I divorced years ago, and I don't want a new husband or someone to move into my house with me. I've been there and done all that. I have just the best, most patient and selfless daughter in the world, and I really don't think having a partner is the only way to make me happy – because I already was happy. Not just happy for now, but for life. Does that make sense?'

'Perfect sense.'

'I don't believe for a second that you can only be validated as a woman if you have someone sleeping on the other side of your bed.'

'Absolutely.'

'And don't get me wrong, I'm not anti-marriage: like I said, I was married. It didn't work out, but that hasn't made me hate love or anything. If people are dating, or married, or having families and they're happy then brilliant, I'm happy for them. And I think they should be happy for me if I'm single and independent and perfectly content.'

'Is someone not happy for you?'

'It's actually a slightly bigger picture than that.'

I waited for her to continue.

'To be honest, I'm a little embarrassed to tell you.'

'Well I'm a little embarrassed that you saw me having a wet T-shirt contest in a pool of grape juice the other day, so perhaps we could be even. What happens in Tuscany stays in Tuscany?'

'Maybe we could stay in Tuscany, start our own company.'

'Hear, hear.'

'You're not happy at work?'

Oops. 'No, no, that's not what I meant, I love work. I love my job and the people are great, and it's really interesting and varied, it's just nice to have a holiday occasionally. Sometimes I think my main problem is that I'm *too* dedicated.' I side-eyed her, wondering if she'd noticed I'd just played the ultimate brown-nosing interview question card.

'You do work very hard: I've noticed.' My heart gave a happy jump, but I kept a straight face – this wasn't the time to fish for performance compliments. 'They don't appreciate you like they should.'

I wondered who 'they' were. My co-workers? My bosses? *Her* bosses?

'They ask so much of your life be dedicated to them and they take it totally for granted. They wouldn't even have a company if it wasn't for you, putting in all that hard work.'

I wasn't sure that was totally accurate, but I also wasn't quite sure if we were still talking about me. 'I do really like what I do, though. I could leave earlier if I wanted, I just like being on top of things and seeing clients happy and helping our profile grow.'

'But those things are all for *them*, not for you directly. If you left, you'd be replaced and it would carry on. You give, give, give, but where's the direct benefit for *you*?'

This was a downer. And I was yet to understand how boyfriends, work and being on an unwanted singles' holiday all linked together. 'I guess the benefit for me would be moving up the company and building my career. Promotions and such larks.'

'And there it is,' sighed Donna. Did I say something wrong? 'Do you know how long I've worked there?'

'I'm not sure—'

'Over twenty-five years. And do you know how long I've been in my current role?'

'No.'

'Ten years.'

'You're very good at it,' I offered; probably the most patronising thing I could say.

'Yes, I am, but ten years? I deserved a promotion.'

I thought back over my seven years with the company. I'd worked my way up from marketing assistant to marketing executive to marketing manager, and had always been pleased with how encouraging everyone was there about furthering my career and reaching higher. But was there a point the promotions stopped?

Donna continued: 'I'm pressing so hard up against that glass ceiling the board – and Andreas – thought it might crack. Perish the thought.' Andreas was our CEO, a slight man who looked like Mr Burns crossed with Beavis and/or Butthead. At my level we rarely saw him, unless he was showing an obviously bored member of the board around the office.

'Do you really think there's a glass ceiling there?' I didn't think Donna was flaky or paranoid enough to imagine such a thing, but the thought made me queasy.

'Trust me. I didn't want to believe it for a long time. Like you, I've dedicated a lot of time to this company; it's been a huge portion of my life. I hated to think there was this seedy side of them. But I couldn't ignore the facts.' She gnawed on a biscotti for a while. This must be killing her to have to admit all of this. 'I am good enough. I am worthy of being on the top rung. I've achieved a lot in this position, I'm more than qualified, but I'm not taken seriously because I'm a woman. I'm constantly pushed aside and, lo and behold, another high-ranking job is filled by a man who's been recruited from another company or brought in from the board.'

My breathing shallowed as she spoke. This could be my future.

'Just so you know, I'm not anti-men—'

'No I know, and I hate that when women demand equality it's often met with "Ooo, she's a man-hater." It's nothing to do with that,' I said, exasperated.

'Exactly.'

'Do you think it's a conscious thing, like Andreas is sat there with the board saying, "Obviously we won't hire her because she's a woman," or do you think it's unconscious and they just don't even consider women as serious candidates?'

'Does it make any difference? Both are as bad as each other, in a way.'

'I guess you're right.'

'But right now, if I had to guess, I'd say the first one. There's been a shift in the past few months. There are rumblings of significant changes to management, restructuring and such things. I was excited to begin with, but have noticed that a cold shoulder's been turned my way more and more frequently of late.'

The way Donna spoke was admirable. She described her situation with controlled dignity, whereas I could feel my blood heating as she went on.

'Then the comments started. About how I'm getting older, about how surely I wanted a man in my life for those times I'm not at work.'

'That's awful; surely it's illegal for them to say that kind of thing to you?'

Donna rubbed her eyes, which were by now bare of make-up. 'It was Andreas that advocated and paid for me to go on this holiday.'

'Well that's . . . really wrong.'

'Yes it is, it's horrible, and I was so taken aback, and angry and confused, that I agreed. And I'm so ashamed. Not that this place, this type of holiday, is anything to be ashamed of, but I feel like I gave up and let the bully-boy win. It was the weakest moment of my life.'

She broke down and, feeling her pain, my heart broke with hers. All her life and her dedication thrown aside. Donna wasn't weak, she didn't deserve to feel ashamed, she deserved the whole company handed to her on a stick. Those utter bastards.

'Those utter bastards,' I mumbled through my own snotty tears.

'It's obvious they're going to make me redundant. They couldn't have made it any clearer that I was just in the way now, a bag of old rubbish.' A loud sob choked its way out of her.

'You're not rubbish, you're my idol. You're strong and powerful and to hell with them and their stupid man-bollocks. What they're doing is completely wrong. Maybe you could sue them or something.'

'Don't get me wrong, I won't go quietly. I'll fight it, but what a bitter taste that'll leave, what a way to end my career. Besides, stupid old me accepted the holiday, feeling for a fleeting second like I deserved a free trip and a break from their bullshit; they'll argue that I can't be that upset. I should never, *ever* have come.'

'But you did come, and I was here as well – I know that was a shock for us both but I'm really glad now that you weren't on your own. Stop beating yourself up about something you can't change. You made one mistake in the last ten years. It's not like doing the correct thing up until now ended up having a different effect.'

To be honest, I don't know how I was delivering this calm advice because inside I was fuming, wanting to get on the next plane, march into the fancy meeting room at work and rip every one of their penises off and lob them out the window.

Sorry, but it's true.

At that moment the group appeared from one of the far-off outhouses, their chatter and laughter carrying across the vineyard. Donna threw on her sunglasses and stood up.

'Elle, thank you for listening, I'm sorry for lumping this on you and I hope it doesn't affect your holiday. I'm a horrible person for even making you talk about work while we're here. I'm going to go to my room for a bit; I don't want to see anyone else right now.'

With that she left, quick as a flash. I stood up slowly, unable to think straight since an earthquake had just knocked a huge part of my world sideways. I wasn't ready to smile or listen to stories of who fancied who, or field innuendo from George. Right now, they could all go to hell and leave me alone.

♡

I stood in the middle of my room, the aim being to calm my fast-pumping heart, but the longer I stood there, thoughts brewing, the more I felt like I was preparing for battle.

How dare they? How fucking dare they?

Misogyny. Sexism. Segregation. How dare they decide that's going to be part of my life? How dare they push that on me?

I'm tired of women being the victims of things like this. Of anyone being the victim of this kind of bullshit. Is the idea of equality that damn hard for these tiny, worthless brains to understand? I don't think I'd ever felt so angry.

And I felt like a fool, being so passionate about a job, dedicating so much time and energy to it, when now it seemed ... false. Pointless. They didn't really care at all.

I stormed down the corridor and banged on the door of Donna's room, perhaps a little louder than I should have. She opened the door, an arm full of toiletries and a towel.

'They don't care about us,' I cried. 'At all. They don't give a shit.'

'I know.'

'Well they *should*.'

'Yes, I know.'

'They should give a shit. We're good employees, we all are. But they really don't care. And it makes me want to—'

'Trust me, I know – I feel the same. I've been through every emotion you're feeling now, and more.'

My nostrils flared and I nodded, then turned on my heel and marched back to my room where I paced back and forth a little more. If this was how they treated women when they got close to the top, I sure as hell didn't want to keep working there. They'd had seven years of my life; they weren't going to get twenty-five. They worked me to the bone, they made me believe my spare time was more precious if I gave it to them, they promised me a future, but they wouldn't hold me down or trap me under that glass ceiling until they were done with me. They would never have me.

I stormed back to Donna's room and banged on the door again to impart this further wisdom, but there was no answer. I pressed my ear against the door and heard the shower running.

Fine. Then I was off to see someone else.

♡

'Jamie? *Jamie?*' I leant against the wall outside his house, arms folded, cross at the world. Out he came, wiping his hands, a big grin on his face at seeing me.

'Hi, beautiful— whoa, what did I do?'

'Nothing; it's not you. Can I come in?'

'Of course.' He put his hand on my back and led me in, his touch sending tingles down my hot spine. 'What's wrong? Is it George?'

'No, actually George is a positive angel compared

to some people. Why are some people such *shits*?' I winced. I wished I could spit this out without it being laced with bitterness. Donna was a better woman than I.

'Hey, Bella, calm down,' he said with concern, facing me and running his hands down my shaking arms. 'Talk to me. Has someone hurt you?'

I tried to form the words, but the lump in my throat blocked them and I wobbled. Jamie pulled me in close and I stood for a while, my face pressed into his chest, mascara going all over his shirt, silently weeping while wishing I wasn't weeping.

'Shhh. Breathe,' he cooed, tenderly stroking the back of my head.

'This is stupid, I don't know why I'm ...' I tried to pull back but he held me firm, taking deep breaths and not releasing me until I matched them.

'Now, what's happened?'

'I was talking to Donna.'

'Oh no, Donna again?'

'No, it's not because of her, it's because of my job. Our job. She told me why she's on this holiday, and it's because the company we work for are horrible, sexist knobs who apparently fire women once they get to a certain age or get that bit too ambitious.'

He blinked. 'Why don't you start from the beginning, let it all out?'

I told him everything, and I think he kept up pretty well despite the fact I was speaking into his shoulder. My words were laced with anger, confusion, sadness and always back to anger, and by the time I had finished I felt drained.

Jamie kissed my deeply frowning forehead. '*Bastardi*. And these men are your bosses too?'

'Yep, so I guess that's my future out the window.'

He wrapped me in a tighter hug and I breathed him in, his clean-ish shirt, his warm chest. 'I wish I could go and knock their heads together. What century are they living in?' he mumbled into my hair.

'You know what pisses me off? I feel stupid. I was just in love with that company, always telling people it was this great place to work, that they valued everyone, that it was worth me spending all my extra hours there because I was going to be someone one day.'

'You don't need them to be someone. You're a pretty fantastic someone already.'

'But I'm talking about the principle of it. What have I missed out on by giving so much of myself to them?' I ran my fingers up the back of his neck, looking up at his face. I hadn't been with a man in years. *Years*.

'It's not too late. Maybe it's time to move on.'

Maybe it was time to take some things back for myself. I was hot and angry, blood sprinting through my veins, and what I wanted, and what I didn't, presenting itself in black and white.

I tugged Jamie by the collar and pulled his face towards me, pressing my lips hard against his, my body not allowing a millimetre to separate me from him. His eyes showed surprise for a moment before glazing over and fluttering closed as he gave in to the intensity of the kiss. I bit his bottom lip and dragged my nails through his hair. The nice girl, the dream employee, was sent outside while the Elle who'd been given sleeping pills for way too long woke up.

Jamie picked me up and I wrapped my legs around his waist. We stumbled back against his wall, the cold concrete sending a shock down the skin of my back as he pressed me between it and his strong body. His hand was high up my thigh as he held me up, the fabric of my dress falling over the top of it. I wanted him to touch me; I wanted to feel his skin against mine. I wanted him to change me.

He pulled his mouth away from mine. 'I want you so much,' he whispered.

'Show me.'

His hand moved under my dress, his fingers sliding a centimetre higher and then stopping. 'We shouldn't do this now, not with these things on your mind.'

'To hell with that – I want this.' He couldn't stop now.

'I'm afraid you might rip my head off like a praying mantis.'

I let out a laugh, which felt good. 'That might happen. Can't we risk it?'

'I really want to, but ...'

I rested my forehead against his, our brows both beaded with sweat. Our breathing slowed and we looked into one another's eyes. I sighed, and gave him a lopsided smile. He returned it with a relieved one of his own, and with a delicious, gentle kiss he lowered me to the ground, his hands leaving my thighs.

'All right, I guess I'll go and get my rocks off with Gorgeous George then, if you won't have me.'

'Okay. I hear he has quite the stash of Viagra. Have a great afternoon.'

'Thank you for listening. That was quite, um, therapeutic.'

'*Any time.* You okay?'

'I'm sure I will be. I have a lot to think about, but I might go and catch up with Laurie. I could do with an easy-going gossip session right now.'

'Will you talk about me?'

'My fiancé who won't even sleep with me? I don't know ... where's the story there?' I winked and left him to it. For now.

When I got back to the main house I found Laurie sitting cross-legged against my bedroom door.

'There you are!' she cried, pulling herself up. 'Have you been doing it with Jamie since yesterday evening?'

'No,' I laughed, pulling her inside my room, where she clocked my un-slept-in bed and raised her eyebrows. 'I made it this morning.'

'Liar – that's the chocolate they put on the pillows at night.' She popped my chocolate in her mouth and kicked off her flip-flops. 'Tell me everything. *Wait* – is it too early for wine?'

'Urgh, you go ahead. Think I'm going to stick to *acqua frizzante*.'

'Feeling a little rough?'

'In more ways than one. But what I could really do with is just to hear something other than my own thoughts for a bit. Can you tell me your gossip and I promise to tell you mine after?'

'I don't have any gossip. What do you take me for?'

'Really? Because I spied with my little eye something beginning with "s" on Ponte Vecchio yesterday.'

'Slut?'

'No! Snogging!'

'Oh, I did do some snogging. Some very lovely snogging.' Laurie grinned. 'With Jon, who, by the way, has a tongue piercing.'

'Really? But he's so timid.'

'I know. He's like this lovable geek with a sexy-as-hell mouth.'

'Was there anything more than snogging?'

'Do you mean did we *dooooo it*?'

'Yes. Did you?'

'Just a little bit.'

'A little bit? What does that mean?'

'It means . . .'

'On a scale of Enid Blyton to *Fifty Shades*?'

'Let's say around the *Bridget Jones* area. Not too explicit, but kind of fun. There was a lot of laughing.'

'Did you see his willy?' I whispered.

'I did – that wasn't the cause of the laughing though, just to clarify. And no, it wasn't pierced, if that was going to be your next question.'

'It wasn't!'

'Oh – it was mine.'

'I'm glad you had a fun night, and he seems really cool.' I smiled at my friend as she blushed a light pink and nodded. 'What happened to Marco?'

'Marco is very cool, and I thought that us having similar-ish careers would mean we'd be completely suited to each other. But when we talk, it's like ... like a really good networking event.'

'No spark?'

'A tiny one. Like how you'd flirt with a co-worker just to brighten up a dull day at the office, but that's about it. Now you tell me: did you lose your virginity last night?'

'Laurie! It's not been that long.'

'There've been like, fourteen new Sugababes since you last did it.'

Actually, that could be very true. 'We didn't do the honkytonk.'

'The what?'

'Gettin' jiggy with it. Driving the o-train. We did not get down with the trumpets.'

'Honey, sometimes I swear you are not single through choice, whatever you might say. So you didn't have sex with Jamie?'

'No.'

'I'm going to need something juicier than that, so tell me what you did do.'

I relived Florence for Laurie, blushing at some memories and sliding into daydreams when I got to other bits, then gave her the scaled-down version of the evening and the morning, which she was having none of, so I was made to retrace my steps and tell her everything.

188

Then I went on to what happened with Donna, and I could feel the unpleasantness rising again.

'Those shit-for-brains!' she exclaimed, indignant on my behalf. 'And there's no likelihood that Donna would have read the situation wrong?'

'No, I don't think so. The more I think about it the more it seems blindingly obvious.'

'Well, Arsing McArseburgers.'

'Indeed.'

'I'll try and get photos of them being corporatey twats at a strip club or something and we'll get some revenge. Have you told Jamie?'

'Yes.' I went a bit red again. Sometimes I think my body enjoys dropping me in it.

'What happened? Did you show him your boobies in anger?'

'Not quite.'

'Not quite?'

'Laurie, I nearly had angry sex,' I whispered. 'But we stopped before anything really happened.'

'Blow down my giddy aunt and wait right there – I'm going to need some wine and a step-by-step account.'

I didn't see Donna for the rest of the day, but I left some snacks and a coffee by her door; I knew she was in there. The afternoon was free, but the last thing I now wanted was to relax somewhere with just my thoughts for comfort, and Laurie was adamant she wasn't leaving my side in case I did something rash in my state of depression. The only rash thing I'd done so far was nearly have sweaty, primal sex with one of the owners, and it really wouldn't have been the end of the world if my mood led me to there again.

'Yes! Via Roma, that has to be good, right? I'll take it.'

'What do I know? I've spent almost the whole game in *prigione*.' We were sitting outside under the cool branches of a tree, playing the Italian version of Monopoly. Laurie was royally whupping my arse.

'Well, that's what you get when you stay up all night with a hunky man.'

'Jail?'

'Yep. Times have changed, my girl. Frankly, I expect everyone thinks you're a harlot now. Speak of the devil: hello, Jamie.'

'Hi, Laurie, how are you?' he said, coming by the table. I looked up at his sunny face, and at those lips I had been sucking on earlier.

'Hey you,' I said.

'*Ciao* yourself.'

'Off work early today?' As if he really had to stick to anyone's timetable – he was a free man, working for himself. Lucky.

'I just got a call from my parents; they said they need to speak to me about something. How are you feeling?'

I excused myself from Laurie, knowing full well she'd be stuffing her pockets with money from the Monopoly bank while I wasn't looking, and walked a short distance away with Jamie. 'I'll be fine. It's still rubbish, when I stop to think about it, so I'm trying not to – I'd rather worry when I get home. Sorry about earlier; I let the crazy lady out for a while there.'

'No, don't apologise: that's what you were feeling, I'm glad you shared it with me. It's good to be angry when you're angry, or sad when you're sad, or drunk and happy when you're drunk and happy. Besides, I'm Italian; we don't like to keep our emotions in bottles.' I think he meant bottled up. 'You think I want a girl-friend who is a robot?'

'A girlfriend?'

'This morning you agreed to be my wife, now you don't even want to be a girlfriend?'

'It's just ... I don't know ... *girlfriend*?' But I told everyone at home that I wasn't looking for a boyfriend. And besides, wouldn't it be silly to have a boyfriend who doesn't even live in my country? 'That would be a pretty long-distance relationship.'

'Do you see just one nationality here on the *You Had Me at Merlot* holiday? It can work. It is literally my business to know it *can* work.'

'I thought your business was wine, and your parents' was matchmaking?'

'Wow, my girlfriend is such a smarty-pants.' He put an arm around my back and leant over, giving me a quick kiss on the forehead. 'I'll see you in a while, okay? Carry on with your game before Laurie pulls off Italia's biggest bank heist.'

I walked back to the table where Laurie was fanning herself with the pretend bank notes. 'I'm not going to lie: I took money from the bank and I took money from you, because that's the kind of friend I am. Now, feed my fantasies with the latest on you and the hunk and I might give some of it back.'

'What am I going to do with that money? I'm a jail-bird, I trade in cigarettes.'

'What if I give you my Get out of Jail Free card?'

'Okay. But you have to promise you won't laugh, or go and blabber this to the ladies at home.'

'No.'

'Hmph. I'll tell you anyway. He was sort of . . . I don't know how to describe it . . . telling me I should be his girlfriend.' I cringed as I said it, feeling like a total schoolgirl.

'He asked you to be his girlfriend?'

'Not in so many words, but kind of.'

'Hold your horses, ring the alarm, call the Prime Minister: would that mean Ever-Single-Elle has a *boyfriend*?'

'No, and if you breathe a word to any of the other ladies I will chop your hair off in the night.'

'You don't like him?'

'I do like him, he's yummy, but it's too soon.'

'You did practically dry hump against the wall.'

'Thanks for that, it was a beautiful moment. But since when did nearly doing it – or even actually doing it – immediately equal being boyfriend and girlfriend, Grandma?'

Laurie boomed with laughter. 'I like you in the sunshine, blood alcohol levels just always that bit too high, sudden disregard for your job. You have a bit more spice to you.'

'Thank you, I think. It's good to live my life a bit more, I suppose. Slowly does it. And we'll see what happens later in the holiday, but no one's calling me their girlfriend yet. On that note, I'm off for a pee.'

'Do you want me to come?'

'I'll be okay. I promise not to put my fist through a

mirror.' She looked a little startled that I'd even thought of that, but still let me go off on my own.

There was no one in the lounge; all of the other guests seemed to be out exploring, having taken themselves off in pairs or small groups, or had gone to their rooms for afternoon naps and to get out of the hot sun. I couldn't be bothered to trek up to my bedroom, and instead went to the disabled toilet by the staircase.

I was tinkling away when I heard raised voices through the crack of the open window – unmistakably Jamie, Sebastian and Sofia, arguing in a fluid rush of Italian and English. Crikey, I hoped they couldn't hear me peeing. I clenched, trying to be as silent as possible.

After I'd finished I couldn't stop listening, which was really rude of me, but I couldn't quite believe I was hearing it right.

'It's a success: people love *You Had Me at Merlot*,' Jamie was insisting. Sofia answered in pleading Italian, but Jamie seemed to be having none of it.

'It's not giving up—' Sebastian cut in.

'*Sì*, it is,' said Jamie.

There was a huge sigh, then silence for a moment, before Sofia replied and I definitely caught the Italian word for 'supermarket'. I caught my breath. Was Bella Notte in trouble? Then all three of them began to talk over one another and I strained to make out the snippets of English.

'A couple of months, it's nothing. Just wait,' Jamie was saying.

'*Perché?*' asked Sebastian. 'What's going to change?'

'*Non lo so,*' answered Jamie, who sounded exasperated. 'Don't do this.'

'I think we have to.'

The argument went on for a further five minutes, while I sat helplessly on the toilet, now too self-conscious to get up and flush as they'd know I was there, and that I would have heard them. I waited, pacing the floor of the bathroom, examining my face in close-up in the mirror, wondering if the cubicle was big enough to do doughnuts if you had a wheelchair, and generally trying not to eavesdrop (though I was totally trying to eavesdrop).

Eventually they stopped, and the sound of three sets of feet passed the toilet and went out the main door. I gave it another thirty seconds, to be safe, then flushed.

'Do you have constipation, or were you crying your eyes out?' Laurie asked me, quite seriously, when I finally rejoined her outside.

'Neither, I got stuck in the toilet.'

'Like, in the actual bowl? Urgh, go and shower.'

'No, in the toilet cubicle. I heard Jamie and his

parents arguing and didn't want to flush until they left, otherwise they would know I'd heard them, and then they went on and on.'

'What were they arguing about? You? Are you not good enough for their son now you're an ex-con?' She motioned at my sad Monopoly piece, still incarcerated.

'I don't really know what it was about. But I'll find out.'

♥

I wondered if Jamie would come and find me to have a vent, like I had him, but when after dinner he still hadn't shown up back at the main house I rambled down the dusk-covered vineyard to his house.

When I went in he looked up from a desk full of paperwork, rubbed his eyes and gave me a big, friendly beam, looking genuinely pleased to see my face. '*Buonasera*, Bella, come here.' He opened his arms and I perched on his lap, feeling like a bit of a twat and having sudden anxiety about having a too-bony bottom. Or too squishy. What hell was this? I wished I'd never sat down.

'What's all this?'

'Accounts. It's unbelievably boring.'

'It looks it. Everything okay?'

'Not really,' he sighed. 'We had some bad news today.'

I turned to face him, running my fingers over the soft frown on his forehead. 'What happened?'

'It's *You Had Me at Merlot*. It's just not doing well enough, not pulling in enough revenue.'

'What does that mean for Bella Notte?'

'It means our last chance has gone. My parents have been in contact with a supermarket abroad.'

'No!' My heart thudded. This was his worst nightmare. His eyes looked sadly into mine, searching for answers. 'Could you do more advertising or promotion, or increase your marketing budget?'

'I'm looking at our costings, seeing if there's anything we can do. Maybe I could hold it off for a month, two at the most, but then you're getting into autumn and winter, which means much less business for us anyway.'

'Why? It doesn't have to. You just need a new angle for those seasons. Try to attract the ski crowd for a twin-centre "snow and vino" trip, or maybe you could run courses on making ice wine or something.'

'I'm willing to try anything, and it's frustrating to see Mamma and Dad want to give up, but before now they were the ones who were trying and putting so much effort into the business, while I was being the stubborn, miserable son, so I don't think my protests hold much weight.'

'You've definitely changed your tune. It's nice to see you so pro-*Merlot*.'

'I don't know. I still think that sometimes the relationships that come from a holiday like this can bring false hope. Maybe they don't last. Perhaps people change their minds too easily.' He was choosing his words carefully, looking into the distance, and then he wrapped me up like I was a soft toy and pressed his face against my slightly squished head. 'That's why, until now, I stay away from you siren women. But despite my hang-ups, I just don't want to lose my family business.'

'You won't. We'll figure this out. I'm very clever, and remarkably good at all things marketing. Just give me tonight to sleep on it and we'll have a plan by morning.'

He smiled, but looked unconvinced. 'A great day for both of us, yes?'

'There have been parts that haven't been too bad.'

'Now that's true. Can we forget about the rest?'

'Gladly.'

'Do you want to stay here again tonight?' he asked, his question loaded.

'You know I'd like to, but I think I need a little beauty sleep. Lots to recharge, lots to think about.'

'All right. If you get cold in the night you know where to find me.'

♥

Before dawn had broken in Italy I was sitting up in bed, hair pulled out of my eyes, iPad in one hand and notepad in the other. I was overflowing with ideas to keep *You Had Me at Merlot*, and ultimately Bella Notte, in business. As for my job, I was trying to push that to the back of my mind. Why give over my holiday time to thinking about them? I would bet a million pounds they weren't thinking about us when they were on their corporate man-retreats, guffawing at seedy jokes and comparing willies.

I was nearly spilling over with bitterness, which is why I was trying to keep the lid firmly on.

Like a child on Christmas Day, I kept looking at the clock to see if it was an acceptable time to go and find Jamie yet. I knew he got up early, but heading over when it was still dark would seem a bit booty-call. And I know it's not a booty call if you're said person's girl-friend, but I still wasn't sure how I felt about that yet. That musing was in another jar with the lid on, though this one I kept opening and having a peek into.

Eventually the sky began to ombré to a sunflower

yellow and I leapt up, threw on some shorts and my *Ciao Bella* T-shirt and quietly left the main house. I was halfway down the hill, walking between rows of vines with fat, dewy grapes dangling on both sides, when Enzo came hurtling over to me. He circled me with excitement, stepping on my feet, warm tongue licking my bare legs, hair shedding all over the place. By the time we'd given each other a proper welcome I looked up to see Jamie coming towards me.

'*Buongiorno*, sunshine! I could definitely get used to your face being the first I see in the morning. Hey, nice T-shirt.'

'Thanks, some sleazy Italian gave it to me.'

'Can I get you a coffee?'

'Do you need to start work?'

'No, that can wait.' Again I felt a pang of envy – that I'd never felt before this holiday – towards people who are their own boss.

'Then coffee would be *perfetto*, thank you.'

I followed him into his house, my eyes drifting to the crumpled sheets on his bed, and the wall that my back had become acquainted with yesterday. I smiled.

As the kettle boiled, Jamie treated me to a good-morning kiss. His mouth already tasted of espresso, which just made me want mine more.

'How are you feeling this morning?' he asked.

'I'm feeling good, excited. I have lots to talk to you about, about this place.'

'Do you want to talk any more about your work problem? I'm happy to try and help.'

'No thanks, it's way easier to push my problems aside than deal with them. Let's focus on Bella Notte for now, if that's okay?'

'Okay, if you're sure?'

'Yes.' We took our coffees outside where the rising sun could see us, and sat at his bistro table. 'I have a question.'

'Shit.'

'What?'

'Go ahead.'

'What's wrong?'

'Nothing. Shit – ask me.'

'Do you mean "shoot"?'

'Oops, yes! Sorry. Go ahead, shoot, ask your question.'

'Right. You can say no, and I don't for one second want to come across as meddling, but I've come up with quite a lot of ideas on how to rev up business for *You Had Me at Merlot*, and Bella Notte wines as a whole. Do you want to hear them?'

'Absolutely!'

'You're sure you don't think I'm sticking my nose in?'

'No, I love your nose. Please, tell me your ideas.' He leant forward with interest.

'First of all, let's talk quick wins. Back at the main house are close to thirty people, all with their own lives, their own circles of friends and family, their own contacts lists, their own Facebook friends and Twitter followers, whatever. Imagine if each one of them could spread the word, share a link, send an email to even a hundred people – that's three thousand more sets of eyes that'll see this thing called *You Had Me At Merlot Holidays*. Or that'll consider ordering some Bella Notte wine. What I want is to have a quick chat to them all, and see what they'd be willing to do to help.'

'I don't know. They're on holiday – I don't feel right asking them to stop and be an advertising campaign for us.'

'That's why *I'm* going to ask, not you. Everyone is having a great time, they're not going to want to see you go under. I need you to allow me to let them know that the company's in trouble, though. And if they don't want to help, then so be it. We'll do it without them.'

Jamie nodded. 'So we'd be asking them to tell people it's good fun, and that they should book?'

'Yes. But first – like first thing this morning – I want you and Laurie to have a quick look at your website, because Laurie is the most amazing photographer and your photos on there are a little ... well, they don't do the winery justice.'

'Hey, I took those photos!'

'Then it makes all your other talents seem that much more special, doesn't it?'

Jamie laughed. 'Understood.'

'Now, how viable is it for you to give away a free bottle of wine with each booking, just for a short period?'

'Absolutely, that would be no problem.'

'Brilliant. We need to act fast to bring in the business before any deals are made with the supermarkets. What I'm thinking is that we say anyone who books within the next two weeks gets sent a free bottle of wine.'

'Consider it done.'

'But if you book within a week you get a free case.'

'A whole case?'

'You see, a bottle's a nice incentive, but it looks rubbish against a whole case. If you give people two weeks to mull it over, I'm not saying they wouldn't book eventually, but that initial excitement will give way to day to day life, like work or chores, or weekend plans. If people know that if they leave it a few more days they only get one bottle, rather than six, they'll be more inclined to just go for it and book up as soon as possible. No one likes to feel they just missed out on a freebie.'

'You're sneaky, I love it. Okay, I think we can make that work.'

'I'm so glad. Then, I'm going to hit George.'

'That's a little bit harsh.'

'Figuratively. He's the one with the big bucks and the links to America. I don't know what he could do for us yet, but I think he could be an absolute star.'

'He'll never help – I stole his girl.'

'I have a feeling he's pretty resilient. Are you ready for part two?'

'Let me top up your coffee.' He went back inside and I leaned back in my seat. I was revved up, bubbling with thoughts and plans and ideas. This was the feeling I had – used to have – at work. Bella Notte wasn't going under on my shift.

'Part two,' I said, jumping straight in when Jamie returned, 'is about getting people in over the winter. You're going to have a lot more insider knowledge than I am about events, but I think you should totally try to cash in on all the festivals Tuscany holds throughout the year, like Carnevale in February. Make sure you put a write-up about each one on your website, and offer wine-and-festival holiday combinations. Give them a reason to pick that week, and it'll also keep the reviews on TripAdvisor and suchlike fresh and full of new, interesting details.'

'This is waaaay too much work. I'm going back to bed, are you coming?'

I laughed, but that did sound achingly appealing. 'Don't tempt me, we have too much to do. Maybe later ... Also, I was reading about the hot springs, and I definitely think you need to strike some kind of deal with them. Exclusive use for three nights of the holiday or something. If I knew I could sit on a snowy Tuscan hill, neck-deep in a hot spring, holding a glass of one of your reds, I'd be back in a shot.'

'Now you're the one tempting me.'

I was determined to keep my mind focused, as much as it wanted to drift off into a little fantasy of smooching in a hot tub, and oops! We forgot swimming costumes! 'Anyway ... Finally, all of Bella Notte wines are delicious, but I get that out here there's masses of competition. However, your chilli wine is original, and *phenomenal*.'

'You're just saying that because it helped you get me into bed.'

'That's partially it.' He really needed to stop talking about bed. 'Um, I was thinking we should go to some local restaurants, you could even take it to some in Florence too, and see if you can get them to put it on their menus. I think it would be a great way to put your name out there a bit more, and once people try it they'll love it and be all "I've got to go to the Bella

Notte website and order some of that – ooo, that white wine sounds nice too." You see? What? Why are you looking at me like that?'

'I was just thinking how smart you are. You're very good at this. Your mind is just ... amazing.'

'That's a nice thing to say.' I blushed.

'It's true. Intelligent, beautiful, fun, likes wine ... I'm so angry that England gets to have you back in a few days.'

'Is it really just a few days?'

'Four more. Then you leave the day after that.'

'Oh no.' I wasn't ready; that seemed too soon.

'We'll make the most of it though, right?'

I nodded, and shook away the sadness. There was no point in wasting a second of the middle by moping about the end.

'But there's one problem.'

'What?'

'There's this really indecisive girl who hasn't decided if she'll be my girlfriend yet. So how do I thank her properly for all of this?'

'You mull that over and let me know if you come up with anything. I need to go and wake up Laurie, and she'll be grumpy as hell if you're there too, to see her bed-head. Can you meet us in the lounge in about half an hour?'

♡

Laurie and Jamie sat huddled in front of the guest computer in the lounge, poring over the Bella Notte and *You Had Me at Merlot* website.

'I don't mean to be a bitch, but it sucks.' Laurie yawned.

'What a bitch.' Jamie shook his head, a smile playing on his lips.

'I like the ideas behind the photos, but they just look too much like snapshots. They don't go – pop – *wow I want to go there*. I have some beautiful sunrise and sunset shots I've already taken which I'm going to give to you to replace the banners, and today I'll take as many as I can of people genuinely enjoying themselves, not this posed stuff, and we can update the other photos this evening. Oh, and I need you to stop using Comic Sans immediately. Please change that.'

'Yes, boss. You don't mind doing this today? I don't want to stop you enjoying your holiday.'

'Well, don't tell your parents, or any future clients – in fact, I'm reluctant to even admit this to Elle' – she cast me a look – 'but I could do with a short break from thinking about boys and love and kissing. It's exhausting, and I'm a little bored of myself.'

A little while later, the group had gathered in the lounge, waiting for the morning's activity to start, which was a cookery lesson from Sebastian – making authentic pasta and marinara sauce from scratch.

'Can I have a quick word with you all?' I asked, feeling a bit like I was about to make a presentation. The guests quietened and dragged their flirt-tastic selves apart. 'I'd like to ask a teeny-tiny, totally cheeky favour from everyone. You're all having a good time, aren't you?' When this was met with some yeses, some hell-yeses, and some dreamy eyes turning to gaze into each other, I told them as quickly and succinctly as I could about the problem and my potential solutions, hoping I didn't come across as a grovelling holiday rep.

'So, in conclusion, anything you can do would be great. Laurie's going to take some gorgeous, flattering, natural photos of you all today – please let her know if you don't want to be included – and then the website will be looking beautiful by the time any of your friends clicks through. And don't forget to mention the wine offer.'

'I'll put it on Facebook. I'll say the men are bloody hot,' said Vicky. 'Can you get me a picture of Jamie without a top on?'

'I don't know about that,' I laughed.

'I'm just going to tell everyone it's like an all-you-can-chug wine buffet,' added Jane, and the two ladies squeezed their phones out of the pockets of their uber-tight shorts and started tapping away.

Before long, people were piping up all around the room with thoughts and ideas, with names they could contact, mailing lists who'd be interested and local dating services that might want to get involved. I was pleased with the response, but this was only step one.

'Morning, love machines,' cried a grinning Sebastian, emerging from the kitchen already dusted to the elbows in flour. He betrayed no evidence of his business crumbling around him, determined to show his guests the best time he could. 'Who's ready to make some nosh?'

We followed him into the kitchen where we were divided into men and women and told that Sofia would be stopping by at lunchtime to taste-test all the sauces, and declare which sex had created the most tantalising tastes. 'It's not about just following the recipe, it's about adding the spices, giving it richness, making something that would make a loved one say *mmmmm*.'

An hour later I was stirring my watery pot of tomatoes and seriously considering swapping pans with Vicky, whose sauce looked thick and deep red, and who was merrily lobbing in handfuls of basil leaves while humming 'That's Amore' to herself.

'Psst, Donna,' I said, leaning over the counter and coming very close to getting my hair caught in the pasta machine.

She looked up, cheeks covered in flour. '*Sì?*'

'You must have a lot of rich friends, right?'

Donna threw her head back and laughed happily; a sound I realised I hadn't heard from her in a long time. 'Thank you for not walking on eggshells around me any more, Elle.'

'Was it that obvious?'

'Like you were standing to attention every time I was around. I thought you must have felt I was this total cow.'

'I did get a little bit paranoid that you might fire me if I let my professional guard down.'

'Being professional doesn't mean not being fun. Don't confuse the two. And no one worth worrying about would ever judge your behaviour on holiday as if it's some kind of reflection on how well you do your job. Besides, if this is you with your guard down, you have nothing to worry about. You're fun, relaxed, easy-going, thoughtful, very intelligent and with a sharp head on your shoulders.'

'Whoa . . . I'm going to take that as a verbal agreement of a pay rise.'

'Can I ask what's made you change around me? Because it is a big change. Is it because we finally learnt something real about each other, outside our thoughts on market trends?'

'Actually it's because I realised I don't give a crap.'

'Fair enough.'

'By that I mean, when you told me about Andreas it was like a big dark cloud rolled in. I got angry as hell, and then after me stomping about for a while it blew away and I actually felt lighter, like the weight of worrying, or of constantly thinking about work, lifted as well. And I guess I thought, Donna's always been a legend, but I no longer feel like I have to do everything right around you. Because right now, if you fired me, I wouldn't care. I just want to treat you like a friend and not a managing director.'

'That's very honest of you.'

'I'm sure I'll regret it – sometimes on this holiday I wonder if my body's ever actually had long enough to properly sober up. I reckon about two days after I get home the last of the alcohol will pass and I'll wonder what the heck I was thinking to tell you I didn't care if you fired me!'

'Well don't worry, I'm not going to fire you. Unless you decide you want me to. Now, what is it we can squeeze out of my rich friends?'

She didn't take much persuading. Donna was on board with spreading the word far and wide among London's media types about this fabulous wine direct from a vineyard in Italy, and how they should all buy it by the caseload, otherwise they'd be the absolute laughing stock of everyone from Soho House to Chelsea and all who were made there.

♡

'Hi, George,' I said gently, sneaking over to the opposition and leaning against the counter next to him as he fed another sheet of raw pasta through the machine and watched it split into strands of tagliatelle on the other side.

'Hi, baby,' he said with a little sadness. He didn't look up, just kept his eyes down and on the pasta.

'How's it going?'

'It's okay. My marinara's great – pretty spicy.'

'Just like you?'

'Just like me. So you really prefer that kid over me?'

'Jamie? I kind of like him.'

'What's he got that I haven't?'

'Better jokes.'

'Impossible. I really woulda liked to take you back to Florida, you know. I wasn't joking about that. You would have loved it: all that sunshine, all that freedom. All those different flavours of M&Ms that you don't get in England.'

'I'm just not really housewife material. I think we both know I would have annoyed you.'

'You got me wrong, honey. I wouldn't expect you to be a housewife; I'd want you to do whatever you wanted to do.' He paused, and squished a pasta strand between his fingers. 'And if you wanted to do me, that'd be A-okay.'

I chuckled. He never changed. 'Tell me, have you always been a bachelor?'

'No, I was married for forty-one years.' Wow, I hadn't been expecting that. 'Married my childhood sweetheart. And was she a sweetheart ... The cleverest head on the warmest body. Blew my mind with her intelligence. I wouldn't have anything of what I have today without her as we built my business from scratch; she was always the scaffolding, the architect, the rain cover when things looked tough. I loved the hell out of her.'

'What happened?' I asked, afraid of the answer.

'Stupid goddamn breast cancer, of course. Shittiest disease. What a nasty little trick that is of nature to play on women. But before she passed she told me ... She said I could mourn all I wanted, she couldn't stop that, but the minute I felt like I might be able to make it through a day I had to get the hell on with my life. She told me to love again, as much as I could, choosing anyone that made me think and made me smile.'

At this point, I was quite literally crying into his marinara sauce, leaving little salty droplets on the surface. 'She sounds amazing,' I sniffled. 'What was her name?'

'It was Ellen.' He met my eyes and shrugged, a half-smile on his lips. 'Kinda like your name. You remind me a little of her.'

'I had no idea. I'm sorry, George.'

'Shush, and thank you. You're a sweet girl. I hope he makes you happy. For all of five minutes, then I hope you come back to me. Now, I'm guessing you came over here wondering if I was going to do anything to help save this place.'

'Am I horrible?'

'No, the opposite.'

'You don't have to do anything, I shouldn't even be asking, I was just going to say that if there was anyone you thought you could reach out to . . .' I trailed off, feeling a little awkward.

'Ellen would've really liked this place, you know, and although I think you're a two-timing floozy . . .' He crinkled his eyes at me, '. . . I'm impressed with what you're doing to support this family. I'll spread the word to start with, then see what else I can do more long-term. You have my word, baby.'

♡

Although my marinara sauce was definitely the weakest link on the women's team, Vicky's had Sofia in culinary heaven and she won it for us. This meant the gents had to be dessert chefs for the night, and while the women were left free to spend the afternoon at leisure the men were confined to the kitchen.

I just wanted to get back to Jamie, which I'll admit made me cringe at the contrast between my scepticism about this whole holiday and how I was behaving now. But he was like my other half this trip, and my only other half for a long time had been Laurie. I was ready for more him-time.

For the remainder of the day Jamie and I were insep-arable, glued together planning, brainstorming and researching in the sunny courtyard in front of his house. It wasn't all work, work, work; we had fairly regular coffee-and-kissing breaks too.

It was on one of these breaks, when we'd come up for air, that Jamie brought me a cappuccino, even though it was totally frowned upon in Italy to drink one of these in the afternoon.

'Here you go.' He placed it on the table in front of me and I leant over it, breathing in the aroma.

'I know you're seriously considering sending me straight home for this crime, but you guys just make the best cappuccinos here. I'm drinking them morning, noon and night. I don't want to regret not making the most of it when I go home.'

That was a more poignant comment than I intended. I looked up at Jamie.

'Any more thoughts on what you might do when you're back?'

I shook my head. 'That just seems way too big, and hard, a problem to even start thinking about. This – saving the vineyard – has obvious, doable answers. But my future ... Do I brush the problem to the side and carry on working there? Maybe things will change by the time I've got further with my career. Or do I just find a new job? Urgh – all options seem horrible to me right now.'

'I think you should come here and be Bella Notte's marketing manager. I'm amazed by you.' If only he was serious, because right now that seemed like the perfect solution.

'I would love to. I'm going to be sad to leave Bella Notte – it feels like home.'

'Imagine if you lived in here with me.'

'In here? I don't know, I like the bathtub up in my bedroom.'

'I'll get you a bathtub. Where would you want it to go?'

'It needs to be by a window: I like relaxing back and seeing you at work in the vineyard.'

'You do? Do you see me when you take a bath up there now?'

'Why do you think I'm always so clean?'

He pulled his chair closer to mine and rested his hands on my legs. 'What else could we do to this place to persuade you to live here?'

'I'd like a little more colour on the walls. Some sea-green, some lemon.'

'No problem.'

'Shouldn't we fight over the decor?'

'Why?'

'Because isn't that what people do? You say you think a red sofa would be nice, I wrinkle my nose and find some weak excuse not to have it because I'm thinking there's no way in hell, then I suggest lilac on the walls and you say beige and I say, "Sorry I didn't realise only you lived here," and we both end up with pistachio green, which neither of us like, but we tolerate it to save an argument?'

'Is that really what couples do? I thought we could just put little parts of both of us around the place.'

'Next you'll be telling me we wouldn't have to be sewn together at the hip.'

'If you were my girlfriend, you could paint what you liked, do what you liked, be who you liked, as long as you stay as amazing as you are.'

'What if I got fat?'

'What if you did? You're still you. I'd take it as a compliment to Italian cuisine!'

'What if I didn't shave my legs?'

'I don't shave mine, so I can't complain.'

'What if I wanted you to leave the house for a while so I could learn dance routines from YouTube?'

'As long as you didn't need me to be your backing dancer, I'd be out of there.'

'And what if I did?'

'If that's what it takes for you to agree to be my girlfriend, I'll get my leg-warmers.'

This girlfriend thing. It was all in jest, just a bit of fun. All this talk about decorating his house and spending years together was just silly, schmaltzy stuff. We lived in different countries, for crying out loud. But despite that, I'd never wanted to be someone's girlfriend this much, and it scared me. I couldn't fall in love, my heart didn't even know what that was. It would very possibly have a heart attack.

Jamie leant forward, his dark eyes twinkling as they

looked into mine, that smile playing across his stubbled face. 'I'm just saying, if loving is what you think you might now want – and to me you've opened up a lot since I first ran into you in the hall a week ago – I'm here. Make me your man.'

♡

I demurred from staying at Jamie's again that night, and as I lay awake in my room I wondered what I was waiting for, why I was holding back. The clock was ticking on this holiday, and I felt closer to Jamie than I had with any man for a long time. It was time to give in to myself and stop being so stubborn, stop hanging on to these cynical feelings I'd harboured when we first boarded the plane. It was okay to fall for someone, even if I'd told people I wouldn't in a million years. Even if I'd told myself.

I rolled onto my side and punched my pillow. Hurry up, morning.

♡

Thanks to my sleepless night, I ended up snoozing a fair way into the morning, and when I woke up Laurie was not only in my room, but spooning me.

'What are you doing here?' I asked, bleary-eyed.

She blinked awake. 'I stayed in Jon's room last night, then came back this morning, but came in the wrong room – you should lock your door, by the way. I saw you snoozing and it looked comfortable. I didn't get a lot of sleep.'

'Me neither.'

'Was Jamie here?' She sat bolt upright and peeped under the covers.

'No, my brain was just whirring. What are we all doing today?'

'Nothing until this afternoon, then it's some activity to do with ... something. Can you believe we have to leave in just three nights?'

'Is that it?' I sat up too, and craned my neck to look out the window. There he was, in the distance, working away.

'He's a hottie. And I think he's really good for you.' Laurie snuggled back down under the covers.

♥

'No, you need to really punch towards the ground. Like, one-two-three HEAD TOSS four-five-six.'

'Am I doing spaghetti arms, like they go on about on *Strictly Come Dancing*?'

'Yes, you need more sass.' There was a knock on

my bedroom door, interrupting the 'Single Ladies' dance workshop I was holding for Laurie. 'Come in,' I called.

Donna popped her head around the corner. 'I just wondered if anyone fancied going for a jog?'

'Donna! Christ, no!'

'We're already on the chilli wine and homemade chocolate – you should join us instead of this running nonsense,' said Laurie, one hand clutching her wine glass and the other in the air, waving about her lack of ring on it.

'I just thought a bit of exercise would be good.'

'We're working out too. Elle's teaching me some Beyoncé. Join us!'

Half an hour later and we were all wearing heels and gyrating fiercely with mouthfuls of chocolate. There was another knock at the door.

'This is why it took me eight years to learn: bloody life kept getting in the way.' I tottered to the door and opened it to see Jamie standing there, holding his iPad and grinning like he was the one lucky enough to be dancing to Beyoncé in the middle of the day. 'Hello! Come on in, I'm just giving these ladies a try of a certain future-award-winning chilli wine.'

'You are? What do you think?'

'I hear Elle got a fiancé just from drinking a few glasses, so this bottle's mine,' said Laurie.

'Let me know when you run out and I'll get you some more. As much as you like. Ladies, guess what?'

'What?' I asked.

'We've had eighteen new bookings since yesterday. Can you believe it? And several orders for cases of wine from London. This is thanks to you guys.' He turned to me. 'Thanks to you, mainly.'

'That's brilliant!'

'I'm just amazed by you. Have I mentioned that? How come you're this nice to me?' he asked quietly, while the others edged closer so they could hear him better.

'I don't know. I think I might like you a little bit. I think I might just want to make sure you're happy.'

I was vaguely aware of Donna and Laurie softly humming 'Kiss the Girl' from *The Little Mermaid*.

We studied one another's faces for a moment, and I swear my whole body was blushing under my clothes; there was certainly some kind of heat radiating between us. I couldn't wait to climb back on to him, and it was a nice, unfamiliar feeling to think he felt the same. Jamie took a deep breath and bent down to give me a small, sweet kiss. 'Will you come over later and let me cook for you?'

I nodded. I didn't think I'd be sleeping back here tonight.

♥

I hovered outside Jamie's house in the setting sun for probably close to ten minutes. Just leaning against the wall, soundless, trying to play down the significance in my own mind about what this evening held.

It really wasn't that big a deal. People have sex all the time. There were people having sex right now around the world, maybe even elsewhere in Tuscany, somewhere on those hills that I was looking at. In fact, maybe someone else was doing it right here at the vineyard. They would have just shown their bodies to each other for the first time as well. We were all in the same naked boat.

And it can't have changed; the fundamentals, I mean. There may be new trends and fashions I'm not quite up to speed with, but the overall beginning, middle and end weren't rocket science.

But biology was only part of the worry. What about the chemistry? What if he didn't fancy me? I look kind of awkward without my clothes on. I look more like I'm about to go dancing around Stonehenge at midnight than like a Victoria's Secret model.

And what if I became utterly overwhelmed and made cringeworthy noises and Enzo started barking, or what if I burst into tears at the end? Maybe this was all just not worth it. My mind was taking some battering with all these what-ifs, but my body held out, staying strong and not running away.

An aroma wafted out through Jamie's kitchen window, seeping into my consciousness. I smelt rosemary, wine, olives, and my stomach growled in appreciation. Before I knew it, my feet had led me to the door, and I knocked and walked in.

'Finally.' Jamie grinned, putting the pot he'd been holding next to the window back on the stove. 'I thought you were never coming in.'

How embarrassing. I accepted a (large) glass of wine and pulled up a seat to watch him cook.

'What are we having?'

'*Pollo alla cacciatora.* It's a chicken stew made with herbs and olives and tomatoes and Chianti. I didn't think you'd had enough wine this holiday.'

'It sounds delicious.' My stomach growled again.

'That was a hungry noise. Here, nibble on these. There's no reason a starter shouldn't be eaten while we're still preparing the main.' He laid out a platter of antipasti in front of me, with thin folds of Parma ham, slices of cheeses, breadsticks, baby artichokes and marinated aubergine chunks. I tucked in.

'Did you teach your dad to cook, or did he teach you?'

'Actually my grandmother taught us all – it's quite stereotypically Italian, hey? We could all make the basics, but when we started *You Had Me at Merlot* she came over, told us our cooking was awful and made us prepare her recipes over and over until we got them right.'

'She did a good job – your dad makes amazing food, and this looks so good I want to eat it right from the pan, ready or not.'

'Thank you! Do you cook?'

'No, I don't really have time. And as you can tell, I'm a little impatient; I don't usually wait for things to be properly cooked before I'm stuffing them in.' I made myself sound so attractive.

'Do I need to distract you this evening, to keep you busy while we're waiting?' He turned to me and folded his arms, a smile playing across his face and a tea towel slung over his shoulder.

I couldn't think of a clever, saucy comeback off the top of my head, so instead raised my eyebrows and pursed my lips, which probably made me look more matron than temptress.

Jamie crossed the small kitchen and reached down to cup my face, his fingers causing shivers as they brushed against the back of my neck. He kissed me, and I sank into him. This man . . .

'You know,' he said, parting from me to go and stir the pot. 'I really don't want to stop kissing you.'

'But you don't want to ruin dinner.' Priorities.

'I don't just mean now, I mean in general. I don't want you to leave. And I really would like to call you my girlfriend – I'm not teasing.'

I drank some wine. This was it: was I ready to be a girlfriend, even with all this geography in between us? I think I was. I had to be brave; if the past few days had taught me anything it was not to let life pass me by like a scaredy cat.

'I think . . . ' I said.

'Yes?'

'That it might be quite nice . . . '

'What?'

'Tobeyourgirlfriendplease.'

'Did I hear that right? Did you say you'd be my girlfriend?'

'If you're sure you want me to be.'

'Of course I do!'

It was going to be very embarrassing telling the ladies that I had a boyfriend – it made me feel about fourteen years old. It annoyed me to think they'd be all '*We knew you wanted a boyfriend reeeeally*', not understanding the circumstances that had led me here. I didn't want to talk about it because it made me squirm, so instead

I got up and shushed him with a kiss. He tasted delicious, and I hungrily ran my hands up his back and into his hair. This man was mine now; I could explore this neck, this face, this hair with freedom.

He swung me around so happily it lifted me off my feet, and then placed me back down at the table. 'I hate to break apart from you, but dinner's ready.'

Knowing what was to follow dinner, even though it was unspoken, meant we ate in nervous near-silence, rushing the scrumptious meal, eager to get back into one another's personal space. I looked around the little house, my eyes falling on a pretty stained-glass panel in the corner of one of the windows, above a comfy chair. I was about to ask him about it when he ran a hand along my thigh, startling me.

'Would you like more wine?'

'Sure.' But before he could get up to reach for the bottle I clamped my hand down on his, pressing it to my leg, not wanting him to take it away. He leaned over and kissed me again, tenderly, and when I finally took my hand off his he moved it ever so slightly higher.

'I can't remember how to do sex!' I squeaked, immediately throwing a hand over my untrustworthy mouth. How come I got lumped with being the least sexy girl in the world?

'I bet that's not true. Shall we do a test?'

'Yes! No! What do you want to do?'

'Well ...' He looked around the room, his hand still burning on my thigh. 'Part of me wants to finish off where we left off at that wall. Another part of me wants to put you back in my bed, where you looked so beautiful the other morning.'

My mouth was dry and I reached for my wine, a big old Nervous Nellie. 'Maybe we could have some dessert first?'

'Sure. I have some frozen grapes and chocolate.'

'Yes please.' Okay, I really needed to be more confident. There was no way I was coming off as a bombshell with all this quivering.

Sexy, confident, provocative. I could be those things. I placed a frozen grape into my mouth and bit down slowly, my teeth bared, only for it to shoot straight out and hit him on the shoulder.

'God, sorry.'

'No problem.'

I should face facts that I really couldn't be those things. This time I ate one like a normal person, and when I bit in the sweetness burst around my mouth.

'Follow it with a bit of chocolate,' he said.

I did, and the sensation was similar to that with the chilli wine, but this time rather than fire and mellowness there was sweetness and cream. I took my time munching on several more of each, putting off the inevitable even though part of me found the wait excruciating.

'All right, if I see you make that "yummy" face one more time when you eat that chocolate, I'm going to be jealous.' Jamie grinned and pushed it aside, replacing it with his lips, which I gladly accepted. If there's one thing in the world I'd exchange chocolate for, I now knew what it was.

'You're more yummy than chocolate,' I said through the minute gaps between our mouths.

'So are you.'

'*Mmmmm* – ooo!' Jamie lifted me from my chair and carried me to the bed where he sat down, placing me on his lap, his head level with my neck. My breasts were heaving – like *actually* heaving – as if I was some kind of extra on *The Tudors*.

'Speak Italian to me,' I breathed.

'Um, *buenosero, gelato, linguine alla carbonara . . .*'

'That's not quite what I meant.'

'I'm trying to think of words you know, otherwise you won't know what I'm saying, and that's rude,' he said sliding down the straps of my dress and trailing kisses along my shoulders beside my bra straps.

'It doesn't matter if I know it; it's just hot when you speak Italian.'

'It is?'

'Oh yes.'

'*Stringiamci a coorte, siam pronti alla morte—*'

'Hang on,' I said, just as he was about to pull down a bra strap and all hell (well, my left breast) was about to break loose. '*Morte*? Isn't that "die"? What are you saying?'

'I couldn't think of anything, I'm a little distracted by a very, very *bella* woman right now. Fine, no more Italian national anthem for you.' He lifted me effortlessly off him and turned us around until I was lying on the bed and his body was above mine. He pulled my dress lower and then kept going, trying to slide it off over my hips. Unfortunately there wasn't a lot of stretch at the top of the dress, and I don't have the waifiest of hips, so the whole process came to a halt and had to be reversed, with Jamie shuffling the dress back up and lifting it over my head instead.

And then there I was, exposed in just my underwear, which was the prettiest underwear I'd packed, since I hadn't planned on this kind of thing happening. It was bright and colourful, but not matching, and the turquoise lace of the knickers was a little thready if you looked closely, which I hoped he didn't because it wasn't even dark yet and I did *not* need his head down there. One thing at a time.

He ran his fingers down over my stomach, a smile on his face, then met my eyes with a smile. 'You're beautiful. I'm the luckiest man in the world to have had you walk onto my vineyard.'

I unbuttoned his shirt, and pressed my face against his tanned, sunkissed chest, and added kisses of my own. I felt like I wanted to say something about how beautiful he was, or about how much he'd changed me already, but in a good way, but I couldn't put it into words. So when he placed his hand under my head, and brought my face up to meet his, I tried to say it all in a kiss.

He sensed I was still a little nervous so he removed his underwear first, and I resisted the urge to try to lighten the mood with a theatrical gasp. I took off my own, and our skin pressed together, warm against warm.

Dusk turned to darkness as the night rolled in, and we took our time, never getting tired, pulling sheets and blankets over us as cold air seeped through the windows, topping up the wine, snacking on a little more chocolate, murmuring compliments, anecdotes and jokes to each other. Occasionally one of us would fall into a light nap, but stir to find the other lying awake, patiently. And the night would continue.

♥

In the morning, I once again awakened dribbling on Jamie's chest. This time I wasn't wearing my clothes, so I made use of his toasty body, snuggling against him. We curled into each other for as long as possible, but Jamie had to get on with some work, and though I would have happily lazed about in his bed all day, I got up and dragged myself back to the main house.

Unfortunately, as if I cared right now, I missed the group, who all seemed to have disappeared for some activity or other. I hadn't meant to keep skipping out on these, but after the activities I took part in during the night, a little rest and relaxation would be a good thing.

I went straight to my bath and lowered my weary, flushed body into the warm water, with the windows wide open to allow in some cool air.

I looked down at myself. Although I'd shared my body last night, I felt closer and more connected to it this morning than I had in a long time. It put up with a lot of sitting at a cramped desk, and then being made to take late-night gym sessions when it was tired already. It deserved to be caressed and appreciated.

Perhaps I really should quit my stupid job and move out here. I could spend my days outdoors in the sunshine, taking coffee breaks whenever I wanted, making my own hours. I imagined waking in the morning over at Jamie's, throwing on whatever I wanted and then taking my laptop out into fresh air and working with a view like this, rather than with a view of another office block from inside an air-conditioned building.

Was that freedom? Was that real independence? I'd always been adamant that these things were the benefits – the prizes, even – of being single. But perhaps that wasn't the only way you got them. Not being tied to an office, not living your life based on someone else's timetable, performance evaluation, tightly controlled holiday allowance ... That sounded pretty free and independent to me. I thought maybe that could be quite a happy life.

After my bath, there was one more thing I'd thought of that might be helpful to save Bella Notte. The battery on my iPad was completely dead so I took myself down to the lounge, grabbed a great big cappuccino and plate of biscotti, and settled down in front of the guest computer.

My plan was to go through the TripAdvisor reviews for *You Had Me at Merlot Holidays* and make a note of everything people liked and didn't like, and see if there was anything workable.

Crikey, these biscotti were good. I read the first review, a glowing recommendation from an elderly woman from Oklahoma, who not only had a great time, but mentioned that she kissed not one but two men. I felt my heart flutter with pride when Jamie's name jumped out at me from the page: *I don't remember if he's a gardener or what, but that kid Jamie is one hell of a looker!*

There was nothing the woman didn't like, but I noted down that she seemed particularly keen on the authentic Italian food. Maybe we could advertise that more. I say 'we'; I mean 'they'. I didn't live here yet.

The next couple of reviews were from men, both fairly happy customers bar one of them complaining that his friend had more free wine in his room than he did.

The fourth review was by another man, who was indifferent about the whole holiday. He stated that he'd had a nice time, but no romance had been formed. He ended the review with a slightly snide comment, which I read several times over: *One can't help but wonder if the son of the owners is a hindrance rather than an asset. It's a demoralising thing to pay for a holiday like this only to find you're competing with the charms of a so-called 'Italian Stallion'.*

Who'd called Jamie an Italian Stallion? I felt bad for him, this personal attack on the internet for all to see.

One review caught my eye. It was one line. *Thanks Jamie, for making this trip unforgettable ;)* What did that mean?

I scrolled down the page. There were an awful lot of mentions of Jamie from women: *If you need some real romance, bypass the tourists, ladies, and spend a little quality time with Jamie* and *I wasn't planning on meeting anyone, I just went along with a group of girlfriends, but then out came their son . . .*

My mouth dried, the coffee sat untouched. I read review after review, all here in black and white, focusing on and re-reading anything which nodded towards Jamie. I felt like I was snooping, but I couldn't look away.

I made the trip for me.

I honestly didn't think holiday romance was even possible until I met someone. Not a traveller, but the man who makes the wine.

One word: Jamie.

My friends all met people they've stayed in touch with on this vacation, but I think I hit the jackpot with Sofia and Sebastian's son, Jamie. We got on immediately, love really IS in the air at Bella Notte. And yes, I got my money's worth . . .

I couldn't believe it. I must be getting the wrong end of the stick. But I couldn't help feeling queasy. Was this the real Jamie? I wasn't just another notch on the client-based bedpost . . . was I? It couldn't be that Jamie was just *You Had Me at Merlot*'s unique selling point, to be rolled out to their most jaded of customers . . . could he?

And then I saw the photo. It topped a one-paragraph review titled *Time of my Life*, and showed a pretty woman beaming at the camera, sun-rays pouring in from the left. The vineyard stretched out behind her. It was the perfect photo to advertise why you should want to come to Bella Notte to find your one true love. Because wrapped around her, holding her close and kissing her cheek like they were on honeymoon, was Jamie.

I opened the review, and read it with trepidation.

How could I not give this place five stars? It did everything it promised, and more. I met a man, J, who I'll never forget. Though I don't deserve him, he made me forget about any worries or nerves I had and gave me the best weeks of my life. There's no greater place than Italy for amore, and Bella Notte is as romantic as they come. You Had Me at Merlot had me at hello. I hope that one day I'll go back – I miss my seat by the stained-glass window. R xxx

That window – the window that was inside Jamie's house. There was no doubt that 'R' and he had had a thing together. I knew it was in the past – everyone has a past – but I couldn't help feeling empty, exposed and betrayed. I thought he 'didn't mix with the guests'. I thought he wasn't interested in the *You Had Me at Merlot* side of things. But it seemed to me that he'd been pretty involved all along.

I made the photo larger, their faces filling the screen. They looked so happy, and I hated this girl for it. I hated all these women. Because they'd opened my eyes to how false this whole thing was, right when I'd needed to believe in something.

I didn't hear someone entering the lounge behind me. Not until a suitcase thudded to the floor and the smell of coconut shampoo wafted over my shoulder.

'Hey, that's my review!'

My breathing slowed. I didn't want to look around because this couldn't be happening. But how could I not? And there she was, 'R', leaning over me looking at the computer like the photograph come to life. Her hair was shorter, and she was a little less tanned, but the smile was the same – full of happiness, excitement, hope.

She stepped back and picked up her suitcase again. 'I love that photo. It was the best day. Don't suppose you've seen Jamie around, have you?'

Part Four

'Um . . . ' I shut my eyes and rubbed my forehead with both hands. My brain was struggling to keep up, to know how to defuse this surreal situation. To understand how this girl – who a moment ago was a rival inside a computer screen, but who was now here in real life – fitted into the puzzle of me and Jamie. To know if I should tell her where he was, or take her to him, or get rid of her now. Maybe she'd be gone when I opened my eyes.

Unfortunately not.

'Oh I'm sorry. *Parla inglese?*' she asked, again flashing me the smile that caused me to ache when I thought of how Jamie might feel when he saw it.

'Yes.' I tried to bide my time by slowly shutting down the computer, shuffling about and making small talk. 'Do you want a coffee?'

'No thanks, I'm just ready to crash out, take a shower.'

'Shall I find Sofia, then, and ask if there's a room available?' I knew the answer, and I was torturing myself by making her say it.

'No, that's okay. I've got somewhere.'

'With a shower?'

'Yep.'

I couldn't let her leave the room. If she went to Jamie's house she'd be naked in his shower. 'So ... What brings you here?'

'I've been looking at that photo too and, well, as you see there's a very good, tall, hunky reason why I came back.'

'You both look ... very pleased with yourselves,' I rasped.

'We were. I can't wait to see him again. I'm Rachel.'

'Hi.'

'What's your name?'

'Elle.'

'Do you work here?'

'No, I'm a guest.' I wanted to tell her I was also Jamie's new girlfriend. But those reviews had left a black cloud of worry in my Italian sky. Did I still count as a girlfriend if every couple of weeks he was meeting new partners? Would the end of the holiday be the end of us? Perhaps he wooed every woman into girlfriend status, in which case I was out.

'Oh okay, you probably don't know much about Jamie then. No problem, I'll just head straight to his house and wait for him there if he's out working.'

She turned towards the door and I stood helplessly, watching her go. I needed to be there, I needed to see his reaction when he saw her.

'Wait!' I ran out of the house after her, squinting in the bright sunlight. She looked at me with a slightly strained smile. 'I think I know where he is.'

'Fantastic.' I made us walk at an excruciatingly slow pace from outhouse to outhouse, all of which I knew he wouldn't be in. She was obviously wearing a carefully chosen reunion outfit, and all this trekking, while lugging her suitcase, was definitely wearing her patience thin. Eventually she plonked down her suitcase. 'You know what: I'm going to go to his house directly.'

'But—'

'I'm sorry. I'm grateful for your help, but I've travelled a long way and I really just want to see my man now.'

She picked up her suitcase and started off down the hill, making a beeline for Jamie's. I ran after her. 'He's your man?' I said, with more bitterness than I'd intended.

'Yep.' She wasn't stopping.

'When did you last see him?'

'It's been a while; we've got a lot of time to make up for.'

'But how do you know he'll want to see you?'

'Um, okay, I can find my own way from here, *thank you*.'

I ran past her and blocked her path, standing between her and her happiness. 'Look, there's something—'

'Elle?' I heard Jamie call out across the vineyard, and I turned. There he was, my man, or so I'd thought, under the Tuscan sun, shirt sleeves rolled up, hair a mess and smiling at me with happy tenderness. I felt a lump in my throat. It wasn't about us any more, it was about her and those other women; I should never have got involved.

He tilted his head and we gazed at one another for a moment. I think it would be the last time he looked at me like that, and the last time anyone might look at me like that for another long time. This romance stuff was too hard.

With a shaking breath I stepped to the side, and I watched as his expression flickered from happiness to confusion to realisation, and then to shock as Rachel dropped her suitcase and pelted past me, throwing herself into Jamie's arms.

He never took his eyes off me.

But he didn't stop her.

'I'm back, baby,' Rachel was saying, pressing against him and kissing his cheek. Her suitcase tipped over and knocked me hard on the ankle, but I didn't flinch.

Jamie extracted himself and dragged his eyes from my face to hers. 'What . . . how come?'

'Because you asked me to come back, and I missed you.' She snuggled against him, holding her face up to his for a kiss but he held her away, staring at his hands upon her arms as if she were the last thing in the world he'd expected to hold. He looked at me, utterly torn.

'Do you want to go inside? I'll bring in your things,' he said to her, and she trotted happily down to his house.

I kicked the suitcase towards Jamie as he approached. 'Elle—'

'Surprise delivery! Look who showed up.'

'She's an ex-girlfriend.'

'Yeah, you seem to have a lot of those.'

'Huh?' He tried to take my hand but I balled it into a fist.

'Not that having ex-girlfriends matters, but lying to me about it – how do you think I feel?'

'What are you talking about?'

'I've read the reviews on TripAdvisor, and it sounds like you got a new girlfriend with every batch of guests. *"If you need romance, spend a little quality time with*

245

Jamie." "I got my money's worth with Jamie." "I miss my seat by the fucking stained-glass window."'

'I didn't—'

'You can't tell me it's not true, when one of them is now standing in your house. Probably taking her clothes off as we speak. In your *house*.' Where we'd been.

'But I don't know why she's here,' he whispered, his voice shaking. He tried again to hold my hands and this time I let him, waiting and hoping for a better explanation, but nothing came.

I snatched back my hands. 'Maybe you better find out. Look, last night was obviously a big mistake – you clearly have some unfinished business.'

'I don't. I haven't seen her in a long time.'

'Then why didn't you stop her, or tell her who I was, or *anything* other than sending her into your home?' He had no answer; he just looked towards the house pathetically. It was clear now, and unmistakable. He'd made his decision, and *I* was the one he needed to ask to leave. I nodded and backed away. 'I'm taking it back, everything. Go ahead, go to her, you're free.'

'Elle, wait. I don't understand how I should be feeling right now. I don't know what to say. Do you want to come inside with me?'

'*No*.' Although maybe that would have been a good

idea. I wanted to hear his side, but right now I was smarting with shame and humiliation.

'How can you be so cold?'

'How can you make me think you like me? I'm just part of a silly game.'

I turned my back on his protests and walked back up the hill, pleading with myself not to look back. At the very top I couldn't fight it any more and turned, hoping to still see him watching me. He'd gone; presumably he was in there with her now. Why hadn't he followed me? What was wrong with me?

Finding love was as pointless as I'd thought. And my dream job had turned out to be just that – a dream – and dreams are as pointless as love, because they're all just smokescreens for reality. I walked back into the main house, where all was still quiet. I guessed everyone else was still off pretending they would have fancied each other this much if they'd met in the real world, and hadn't simply been forced together by alcohol.

'Hi, baby,' said a voice from the corner. I looked over to see George sitting in a window seat with an expensive-looking laptop in front of him.

I resisted the urge to snap at him; he didn't deserve it, however foul my mood. 'Hi. What are you doing here? Why aren't you out on the activity?'

'I had a little work problem to sort out, shouldn't take long. What about you? What are you doing?'

'I don't know.' I really didn't. I certainly wasn't about to look at any more TripAdvisor gems – I didn't want Bella Notte to go under, but I think I'd given them enough of my free help.

'You look sad, baby. Where's Jamie?'

'I don't know.' *With Rachel, reuniting, speaking Italian nothings to her.* I hoped she could smell me on him. I hoped she stopped to question if he'd been with anyone else. I hoped that a niggle of doubt had crept in, and she couldn't look at him without wondering.

George, watching all this play out on my face, eventually closed his laptop and beckoned me over, but I shook my head and stayed where I was.

'Baby, I'm an old man and I told you about my dead wife. You can't not come and talk to me now: it's against the laws of polite society.'

'You're not old. You're not even retired.'

'When you own your own company I'm not sure you ever really retire.'

I sat down next to him and stared glumly out the window. 'Do you like owning your own company?'

'What's not to like?'

'Constantly working.'

'But if you love it, it's your life.'

'Only if you're at the top, though, I guess.'

'I think my employees are pretty happy.'

'Well. All good things come to an end.'

'Okay, this isn't you; who's this miserable, jaded girl? I wouldn't have the hots for you if you were really like this.'

I shrugged. 'Maybe this is the real me. Maybe being miserable would suit me, like a silent-movie star.'

'Bullshit.'

'You're bullshit.'

'I think you should join me in a little contraband and get whatever's bothering you off your chest.'

'What do you mean?'

George glanced around the empty room and then pulled from his laptop case a small bottle of limoncello and a shot glass. 'Sometimes you just gotta drink something that isn't wine, you know?'

I chuckled, and accepted a shot of the syrupy, highlighter-yellow liquid. It burned my mouth but slid down like an elixir. George refilled the glass and drank it himself, then filled it a third time and pushed the glass back to me.

'You're not too bad, George.'

'High praise indeed.'

'I mean, I feel I know way more than I should about your penis, but I think beneath all that bravado there's a good soul.'

'Well, if you want to know more about the little sergeant, you know where he'll be. But for now, why don't you tell me what's wrong? Did that kid do something to hurt you?'

'I really don't know what's going on, but Jamie's girlfriend apparently just showed up, and I think I'm just one in a long string of them. Maybe I'm better off now.'

'There's a girlfriend?'

'An ex-girlfriend, apparently, but she's here and with him now, and he wasn't exactly pushing her back into a taxi.'

'Where does that leave you?'

I shrugged.

'Do you want me to kill him? I've got friends, you know. I can jet them straight over here.'

I gulped the fiery limoncello. 'Thanks, but I don't think hiring a hit-man is the best option. I just want to be away from here, and away from London, and away from everyone I know.'

'Donna told me about your job – it sounds like a real class act.'

'She did?'

'You sound surprised.'

'I didn't think she was opening up to many people. And I didn't know you two were really friends.'

'I have a lot of respect for that girl. She didn't deserve that treatment, and neither do you.'

'But where do I go from here?'

'I don't know. Does your career start and end with one company?'

'No.'

'Then screw 'em. Take some time out.'

I rubbed my face with vigour, unintentionally pulling out four eyelashes. 'I'm a bit of a lost lamb right now, sorry.'

'Don't apologise; that's okay. Can I plant a little idea in your head?'

'Why not?'

George fiddled with the limoncello glass, his leathery hands shaking slightly, but whether it was with age, nerves, or ODing on Viagra I wasn't sure. 'Why don't you come and spend the summer with me, in Florida?'

'George, I—'

'I know, I know, you don't want to sleep with me and I wouldn't ask you to. But it might be good for you, and I'd sure like the company. You'd make an old man pretty happy.'

I'd never been loved. I'd never not had a goal. Even when I'd realised I might need to quit my job I'd plastered over it by making rash plans to be of use here – but I couldn't do that now. And here was a man offering me love, and a place to escape to, so maybe I should just stop resisting and fall in with everyone else I knew: settle down, live in an actual house, be part of a couple. If you can't beat them, join them. It was pretty tempting.

He was being sweet, sweeter than I deserved.

'I'll think about it,' I said with a sigh.

'You will?'

'I'll think about coming to Florida. It could be good.'

'What?' Laurie's voice screeched out behind me.

I turned, and there she was, standing in the doorway.

'*What* did you just say about Florida?'

'I'm thinking of taking George up on his offer and moving to Florida – for the summer, to begin with.'

Laurie marched over and grabbed me, dragging me towards the stairs. I smiled weakly at George, who was beaming. Laurie didn't stop until we were inside my room with the door closed.

'What the hell is going on? What have I missed? Where does Jamie fit into this?'

'He doesn't.' I filled her in on everything that had happened over the last twenty-four hours: the night with Jamie, the thoughts I'd had about moving out here and making this my new career, then the TripAdvisor reviews and finally Rachel.

Laurie hugged me hard. 'I'm sorry.'

'I just want to escape, Laurie. I don't want to have to think any more. I want to take the easy option.'

'But shacking up with an old pervert is *so* not the easy option!'

'He's not that bad.'

She pulled back, examined me and rapped her knuckles on my forehead, which hurt quite a lot. 'Hello? How utterly sloshed are you?'

'Ow, not even a little bit.'

'Then this has to be a joke, yes?'

'No.'

'*Yes it is.*'

'Laurie, it isn't. It's not for definite yet, but it's tempting. He'd take care of me, and maybe we'd be happy.'

'Oh bleurgh,' said Laurie. 'You have never been one to want someone to take care of you, or just want to give it all up to get married, so snap out of it. So this one job's turned out to be shit and *potentially* things have gone down the plughole with your new man. Welcome to that part of life where you get kicked in the fanny; it happens to everyone.'

'Wow. Have you ever thought of writing poetry?'

'I'm not trivialising it, I'm just saying that a couple of glitches doesn't mean you should give up on your career or your love life.'

I picked at my fingernails and digested her words.

'Stop being a bloody drama queen.' Laurie grinned, and I cracked a guilty smile. 'Look: I want to go to the Wizarding World of Harry Potter at Universal Studios as much as the next person, but you cannot move to Florida and live with George.'

'Yes I can. I can do whatever I want,' I sulked.

'All right, you have your crazy head on right now – moving to Florida with George, no less – so you're going to have to stay in here for a while, and I'm going to do some digging.'

'Digging for what?'

'Anything. Have a bath.'

'I had a bath a couple of hours ago.'

'Have another one. It's back to your tiny shower soon, so make the most of it.'

'In Florida I might have my own bathroom with a huge Jacuzzi.'

'Yes, with your sugar daddy sat in the other end of it. Stop this. I'll be back in a while. You're not to leave unless it's to tell George that Florida is off.'

'You're annoying.'

'You're annoying! See you soon, and don't leave this room.' She stopped at the door and turned back to give me a thumbs-up. 'And by the way, top work on losing your virginity!'

She was right – about George, I mean. I looked at myself in the mirror. I didn't just want to get married or have someone to look after me. I didn't *need* a man in my life so I shouldn't be leading him on. Now I had to tell him no, and hurt his feelings. How did I let myself get into all this mess? What was wrong with me? I curled up on top of the bidet and had a good cry, which felt about as pathetic as it sounds.

♡

Mid-afternoon, as I was scrolling aimlessly through celebrity gossip on my iPad, revelling in anything that described someone having a worse day than me, I got a knock on the door.

I heaved myself up and slouched over, feeling sorry for myself. On the other side was George, and I cursed myself for not checking the spy hole.

'Elle, why don't you come downstairs so we can talk about Florida?'

'Not right now. I'm not allowed to leave my room.'

'Who says?'

'Laurie.'

'Right ... why?'

'Because she's bossy. Listen, about Florida—'

'Shh, I won't hear another word from you until you've

listened to me. I've got something important to say, but I'd really rather do this downstairs.'

'Why?'

'Because I need to speak with Donna too, and while I may come off as a hot piece of ass, I don't want to be seen going into a bedroom with two young ladies.'

I nodded and pulled my dressing gown, which I'd put on over my clothes, tighter around myself. We walked to Donna's room together.

'She might be out enjoying herself,' I said glumly.

'No, I saw her come upstairs a short while ago,' George replied. I cast him a look. 'I haven't been watching her, I just noticed!'

Donna answered the door wearing her workout gear. 'Hi, you two! I was just about to try going for a run again, but I got distracted by this hilarious Italian TV show. Come and have a look.' I followed her into the room but George stayed demurely in the doorway. 'I have no idea what's going on, but these people have to stay on this mechanical surfboard as long as possible, while all these other people just laugh and laugh and laugh. It's been going on for nearly eight minutes so far. George, come and see this.'

'No thank you.'

'Why?'

'I'll wait out here.'

I dragged my attention from the TV and shrugged at Donna. 'I don't know why he's turned into this Good Christian Gentleman all of a sudden, but he wants to talk to us both, downstairs.'

Donna raised her eyebrows. 'Okay ... let me just change out of my running stuff and George, we'll meet you down there. Elle, you stay with me a minute.' She closed the door and came back over, peering at me. 'You've been crying.'

'Only a bit. Is it obvious?'

'Only a bit. What's happened? Are you still stressing about work?'

'No. Well, that's probably mixed in there, but ... please don't think any less of me ... but Jamie's ex-girlfriend just arrived.'

'Oh bugger.'

'Yep.'

'Was that better or worse than when I arrived?' she smiled.

'Much worse. I didn't cry about you being here, just had a mild heart attack.'

'What did he do?'

'Invited her in for a catch-up.' That wasn't really fair. 'I'm sorry – boyfriend troubles seem so insignificant to the ones you have.'

'Don't be silly. Exes are just as evil as corporate

wankers. Don't tell anyone I called them that; best to maintain an air of don't-give-a-fuckness. Now, are they back together?'

'I don't know – this all happened this morning, then Laurie banished me to my room, so for all I know they could be rolling about in the vines right now.'

'I doubt it, but let's go downstairs together, just in case of any nasty surprises.'

Donna changed into some lovely expensive-looking 'loungewear', which in my books would mean three-year-old tracky-bs and an ancient Foo Fighters tour T-shirt, but in her case it meant soft grey yoga pants and a dusky pink cashmere waterfall cardigan.

As we reached the bottom of the stairs I peeped around the corner, nearly as fearful about seeing Laurie as I was about seeing Jamie and Rachel smooching on the sofas. But there was just George, surrounded by paperwork, and curled on another sofa across the room were Annette and Pierre, sucking face.

'So, George, what is this about?' asked Donna, no nonsense, as she sat down. I perched next to her, nervous about having to let George down after I got his hopes up.

'All right,' he said, pushing the papers aside and removing his glasses. He leaned forward and fixed Donna with a businesslike stare. 'I want you to work for me.'

'Pardon?'

'I want you to move to Florida and work at my company. I have a vice-president position that's become available and I'd like you to fill it.'

Donna looked around the room in confusion and then refocused on George. 'You do realise I'm not a twenty-something in a pinstripe mini-skirt, right?'

'Of course I do. I don't want a twenty-something being my VP, I want someone with experience and brains. You're a smart woman – a smart *person* – and your agency are being dumbasses. I want to poach you before they realise this, or before someone else gets a hold of you.'

'George, I can't just move to the US . . .'

'It'll be a change, I get that, but it'll be more than that step-up you wanted. I'll pay you double what you're on now.'

'Why?'

'Because you have drive, and from the sounds of it you will be fully committed to your job and give it your all.'

'You don't know anything about my work ethic.'

'We just spent a week and half together. I know I was a little preoccupied with this one for a while' – he cocked his thumb at me – 'but in the last couple of days you and I have gotten to know each other.'

This was news to me. I glanced at Donna.

'Not in that way,' she said quickly. 'As friends. It turns out we have a little in common—'

'Country music!' George interrupted, and Donna cringed.

'—and he's actually a pretty good drinking partner.'

George continued: 'Don, I've seen how you are with teamwork. I've heard honest feelings from you about your job. I've even seen how you act around one of your employees. I really don't think I now need to ask you to take an interview.'

'But I did the stupidest thing, I accepted this—'

'Shh,' I nudged. I couldn't quite get my head around what was happening, but I didn't want Donna talking herself down and screwing this up. I didn't want to lose her, but this sounded like it could be just what she needed.

'So you came on a singles' vacation? So did I! How about I even write a clause in your contract to say we may never mention how we met to anyone else?'

Donna sat back in the seat, overwhelmed. 'I just . . .'

'Here's the job description. It's a little outdated, because our current VP has been with us for five years, but she's moving to Alaska, of all damn places. I've scribbled a few extra responsibilities and some changes on the top, but I can update this for you properly if you're interested.' He handed her a card. 'And this is the name of the president – she's unbelievable. You can give her a call if you have any questions you don't feel comfortable asking me.'

'So your current VP and president are both women?' asked Donna. I craned my neck to read the job description over her shoulder.

'I can't do anything about the fact that it's a man who's CEO, because it's me, and I'm not ready to quit yet. But yes. Now, I'm not saying I wouldn't hire a man if you rejected the offer; I just want to hire the best person, period.'

'Well this is very interesting.'

'Now you.' He turned to me and I gulped. 'I think you're great, and you know that. But I know you're smart, and you're headstrong, and that head of yours isn't in the right place at the moment. I'd love for you to come to Florida with me, for pleasure or for work, and therefore I'm leaving the offer open. When you've figured things out for yourself, if you decide you need a change of pace and want to work for me there'll be a place for you. If you decide you want a couple of weeks away from all that London fog, or from the arms of a certain Italian, should that work out, you come over for a visit.'

For crying out loud, that set me off again. I furiously blinked back the tears. 'Thank you,' I sniffled.

'I'm going to go and get some of those magic tear-mopping biscotti,' said Donna with a smile, heading to the kitchen. George gathered up the paperwork and looked at me fondly.

'You think about it, baby. I can just see you living in the Sunshine State.'

'I will. Thanks, George, it's an amazing offer.'

He walked away, and as I turned to watch him go I came face to face with Jamie, who'd come to a halt, mid-walk.

'You're going to Florida now?' He looked stricken. What right did he have to look stricken?

'Maybe I will.'

'Well I'm so glad you didn't waste any time, and that *You Had Me at Merlot Holidays* found a partner for you.'

'And the same for you. Who would have thought we'd both end up happy at the end of this trip?'

'He won't make you happy, you know.'

'I'll be just fine – you obviously don't know anything about me. Now, where's your girlfriend?'

'She's . . . at my house, I guess. I've been out working all afternoon.'

The disdain in his face was back, and it seemed to be directed at me. How dare he? I'm just one of many to him, but he gets all stroppy if I want a life after him?

He walked away, and so did I.

The sun dipped behind the hills, and the vineyard was cast in early-evening shade. I gazed, chin resting on windowsill, at the little house beyond the vines. I'd been staring at it for a long time now, watching for any signs of life, any twitching of curtains, movements of bodies behind windows, a naked butt cheek pressed against the glass. But they were giving nothing away. Jamie and Rachel were obviously cocooned against the world, just the two of them, being all tender and love-makingy in his bed. Urgh.

Just as I was about to attempt to pull myself back from the window his door opened and she stormed out (fully clothed, hurrah!). I sprang to attention, watching with unblinking eyes and holding my breath, as if I might be able to hear their conversation without that noise.

Rachel began striding towards the house and Jamie followed after her, grabbing her by the hand and spinning her back around. She wrenched her hand away, they both said some things with manic gesticulations and then she pointed up to the main house. I ducked my head, waited a very short moment and slowly rose again.

She was making a big deal of wiping her eyes and

shaking her shoulders, while he stood near by looking helpless. I wished, *wished*, I could hear what they were saying. Especially when what happened next happened.

Perhaps I blinked and missed something. Perhaps I can't remember because I'm blocking it out like post-traumatic stress. But one minute they looked like they were fighting, and the next he'd pulled her into him, strong hands on her arms and his face pressing against hers, kissing her like he couldn't stop the emotion pouring out any longer.

But it should have been me. It *was* me, and I'd been replaced, and I could never have it back. I was doing fine on my own before him, but now without him I felt broken and cast aside and how was I going to find the strength to come back from that? How had I even allowed myself to get to that place to begin with?

Jamie and Rachel broke apart. He stepped away from her and turned his head towards the main house. Rachel smoothed her hair. Jamie held out his arm and she led the way back into his home, and all I was left with was another closed door and a gentle water-feature of tears.

♡

I was the Queen of the Miseryguts. I ate a pizza dinner on my own, in my room, while I tried to figure out what to do with my life, and simultaneously tried not to think about it by channel-surfing Italian TV. I was chowing into my final slice when there was a swift knock on my door and in barged Laurie.

'Elle,' she said, grabbing my hand and chucking the pizza back onto the plate. She pulled me up and wiped my mouth with the back of her hand. 'I've just been talking to Sofia, and I think there's something you need to hear.'

She dragged me to the kitchen, where Sofia sat at the table wringing her hands. When we entered she leapt up and pulled me into a hug. 'Elle, I saw Rachel outside Jamie's house. I'm so sorry she's come back.'

'It's okay. I know he's your son, but I think I had a lucky escape – I didn't realise how involved he'd been with previous guests.'

'But he wasn't. You mustn't believe that.'

'I read reviews from countless women saying how Jamie was amazing, and romantic, and made this trip for them.'

'No, those aren't what they seem. Jamie is very attractive, and the female guests fall over themselves to get him to notice them, but he hates it. He hates being viewed like a piece of meat – I know he does, so he always stays away as much as possible. And I've had more than one complaint from male guests about how even when he's barely around he is overshadowing them.'

'But Sofia, he's your *son*. He probably does a lot more than he tells you about.'

'Do boys ever really get away with things and think no one notices? Us women notice *everything*. All those other girls had to admire him from a distance, whether they liked it or not.'

'It's true,' said Laurie. 'I spent some time on TripAdvisor this afternoon, writing comments on all the reviews those women left, asking whether they actually hooked up—'

'What is "hooked up"?' Sofia interrupted.

Laurie tried to think of a mum-friendly way of putting it. 'It means, if they ever kissed him ... or whatever.'

'Oh. Oh! Carry on.'

'So, quite a few of them have replied, and what Sofia's saying is right. Listen to this.' She pulled her phone out of her pocket and scrolled. '"*OMG, Jamie! He was such a hottie. All looking but no touching, unfortunately. Still, worth every penny.*"'

I crinkled my nose. That was rather a degrading thing to say. If it was true, I wasn't surprised Jamie didn't like how he was viewed by some of the women. But he can't have hated it that much – as proven by *her*, who was busy doing God knows what in his house with him right now. He was still involved with someone else, end of.

Laurie continued. 'Then there's this one from that guy who was moaning about Jamie being here. "*It wasn't his fault really, he kept a polite distance, but the way some of the women would stare and refer to him as the Italian Stallion made one feel quite inadequate.*" And there's more, if you want to see them. They all just thought he was yummy to look at; nothing actually happened. They were all just pervs.'

Sofia nodded. 'The only woman who he has ever developed something with since we started *You Had Me at Merlot* was Rachel.'

'Because Rachel is so special,' I said snidely, then looked at my hands, ashamed.

'She was to him ... once. He liked her very much; she brought him out of his shell and made him very happy. She promised to return here, that they wouldn't break up.'

I didn't like hearing this. As pathetic as it was, as loathsome as I was acting, I didn't want to think that she was someone who could make him glow.

'Elle, stop looking like a smacked arse and listen to what happened next,' Laurie said, ever gentle.

'Rachel left with all these promises, and all this

267

love between them,' Sofia continued. 'And then she just disappeared. He never heard from her again. She wouldn't answer Jamie's emails or calls, she blocked him on Facebook – it was like she wanted to wipe him out of her life completely. The holiday was over and so were they, only she forgot to tell him that.'

'So she's a bitch. But she's back now, so I guess it's back on.'

'No,' Sofia disagreed. 'Because of that, she's not my favourite person, and there's no way in hell she's going to marry my son.'

'What? They're getting married?' It couldn't have happened so fast, even if it was no longer my business. Surely I wasn't *that* easily replaced, was I? Another flake fell off my heart.

'No, no, I'm just saying that they have no future. You do not break my son's heart and then just walk back in with your designer sunglasses.' Sofia stabbed the wooden table with a handy kitchen knife, making me jump and Laurie snigger. Italian mothers, hey? 'Anyway. This is why he has a barrier, this is why he met you and fell in love but was afraid to act on it, this is why he's hurt because he feels like you've switched your feelings to someone else – George – so quickly and this is why it's not easy for him to dismiss her so fast. He needs answers, and closure, even if he doesn't need *her* any more.'

I let out a whopping sigh. 'They were kissing.'

'Sometimes people do silly things when they're emotional,' observed Laurie.

'So what you're saying is that I need to stop being an idiot and give him the benefit of the doubt?'

'No,' said Sofia. 'I think you should not see things in black and in white. Humans don't do things perfectly, or behave in the best most obvious way they should, especially not silly boys. But I do think you need to find out what he's stalling for. If it's to try and decide between the two of you, you say goodbye – you're not one of two dessert options, you're worth more than that. But if he's just finding it in himself to say goodbye to her, you should let him. Whether you like it or not, he was affected by her once.'

I nodded, and Sofia looked between Laurie and me, then stood up.

'I can see from Laurie's face she has a scheme, and I don't think I'd better know what it is. I'll see you both later.'

'You have a scheme?' I asked Laurie when Sofia had left.

She passed me some biscotti. 'I do. We're going to spy on Jamie.'

I pulled at Laurie's arm as we snuck closer to Jamie's house. 'I don't want to do this,' I whispered. The vineyard was completely dark, and we were crunching our way down between the vines. My legs were covered in scratches because apparently I am unable to follow a straight line unless I can see it.

'Yes you do,' Laurie whispered back.

'What if they're having sex?'

She stopped and faced me, and I bashed into her. 'If they are, it'll be rubbish for you. But at least you'll know.' I nodded, and after a moment Laurie said into the darkness, 'Do you agree?'

'Yes.' We trekked on, and I held my breath as we reached the house. I placed my hands against the cold stone wall as we felt our way around until we were crouching under an open window. Lights were glowing from inside, but there was no noise.

I wished more than anything that I had a periscope with me. Sometimes I was so underprepared. Instead I raised myself higher, centimetre by centimetre, until I was peeping in through the glass. If they saw me now I was going to feel like such an idiot.

Rachel was sitting stiffly on his bed, arms folded, legs crossed, her suitcase still zipped up. I almost audibly sighed with relief. Then Jamie walked right past the window holding cups of coffee and I fell backwards into Laurie, who thankfully caught me with no more than a stifled grunt. We both sat on the dirt with our backs to the wall, as silent as mice, praying neither of them came to look out of the window to see what the noise was.

Suddenly we heard Rachel's voice. 'Why won't Enzo come over here to me?'

'He hasn't seen you in a long time.'

'Are we going to go over this again? I told you I was sorry for not getting back to you. I know it's been a long time, but I'm here now. I don't know why you can't forgive me.'

'I don't think I want to, Rachel. It's just not—'

'I thought you'd be happy to see me, and we'd just go back to how we were.'

'We can't.'

'Jamie, I'm not going to do it to you again.'

We heard Jamie cross the room away from her again. 'I just don't understand why you did it in the first place. How did you think it was better to disappear completely rather than write back to one email saying you needed time, or that you didn't want to be with me any more?'

'I didn't want to hurt you. I thought that if I just drifted away it would be easier.'

'*How?* Easier for *who*? You! We were so close while

you were here; maybe we got too close, maybe I was too full on, but to suddenly have nothing . . . I didn't know if you were married, or dead.'

My heart went out to him, even though I was trying to keep it firmly in place. Clearly Rachel had played with his emotions in a way that still affected him, that made him wary and worried. But I had to keep reminding myself that it wasn't over until the fat lady sang. Or at least until the skinny cow left.

Rachel sighed. 'I'm sorry. *Again*, I'm sorry. But I don't get you; you write me all these sappy emails, you tell me you love me and you want to see me again and then when you do I get the cold shoulder.'

'But that was months ago. Things have changed.'

'They haven't changed that much. You still want to kiss me.'

Laurie squeezed my hand, and I could feel her pitying eyes on my face.

'That shouldn't have happened.'

'Of course it should have. Trust your feelings, Jay.'

'I just wanted to see, for a moment, if what we had could be brought back. But it couldn't.'

'Yes it *could*. Why are you so defeatist? Why don't you kiss me again—'

'I don't want to kiss you.'

'Why?'

'It was a mistake, an impulse reaction to something. I want to kiss someone else.'

Laurie tugged my hand and pointed at me with excitement.

'Who?' We now heard Rachel stamping across the room.

'I had no heart left for a long time because of you, but now I've met someone else, and she's genuine, and funny and fiery and confusing as hell, but I like her. And now she might be moving to America and it's my fault.'

'If she's moving to America then she's not very serious about you. She's moving five thousand miles away and I'm standing five feet away. It's an easy decision.'

No it's not, no it's not. I didn't know how I felt about Jamie right now, but I knew I didn't want him to choose her.

'It's not a decision, though: it's not like I'm trying to choose Rachel or Elle. I know it would be her, whether you're here or not, because it took a long time to move on and I finally have. If she goes I'm alone again – not back in love with you.'

'But I was here first. You can't just forget me.'

'I can't forget you, but I can get over you.'

'No you can't.'

'*Yes he can,*' I whispered furiously to Laurie.

'Yes I can. I'm sorry you came all this way. Here's an idea: maybe you should have called.'

I clamped a hand over my mouth to stop from giggling.

'Very funny,' Rachel spat. 'Well I hope – if she stays – she can make you as happy as you and I were together.'

'I think she can.'

Rachel appeared at the window above and leaned out, staring ahead; we flattened our backs against the wall and peeped upwards for an unadulterated view of her flaring nostrils. She composed herself, and then ducked back inside. 'How about one last night together?' she asked, smooth as silk.

Enzo growled, and I might have a little bit too.

'No.'

'Come on, she's not here.'

'Yes she is.'

Shit. Laurie and I gripped each other.

'What do you mean? Is she one of the guests? Hang on – don't tell me she's that dopey chick who brought me down here to you earlier.'

I was going to break her sunglasses at the first opportunity I had. 'Dopey chick' . . . that bitch.

'Don't say that, and yes – that was her.'

'She was stalking you, you know, scrolling through pictures of us on TripAdvisor when I first got here.'

'She didn't mean to be stalking me; she's been help-ing me with something. I'd be nothing without her right now. And I'm hers now, even if she doesn't want ... ' He trailed off. Here was a man staying loyal to me even when he thought I was running away. I'd have to be very careful with that heart of his, if I chose not to run.

'Well good luck with that, she seems like a psycho.'

Laurie balled her hands into fists and I had to hold her down to stop her from leaping through the window.

'Do not call her a psycho. You don't know her and I don't even want to hear you talking about her. This side of you ... you're not the person I was so in love with before. You're making this pretty easy.'

Rachel's distinctive footsteps stomped back and forth. 'She's not here *right* now and I am, so she can't be that special.'

'Okay, enough. I'm going to go and find a room up at the house. You can sleep in here tonight and I'll take you back to the airport tomorrow.'

'Forget it; I don't want to stay here, in your little love-nest. I'll go up to the house.'

'Whatever you want.'

The front door opened and then closed with a slam, and Rachel, plus suitcase, strode past us into the dark. It might take her a while to struggle up that hill in all this blackness, so I guess we had to stay put.

Inside, the bed creaked with someone sitting on it. Enzo's paws padded across the room and there was a *thud* as he leapt up and joined Jamie on the bed. 'Enzo,' Jamie said softly. 'I don't want her to go to Florida.' Enzo woofed, and Jamie crossed the room and came to a stop near the window but didn't lean out. 'No, Enzo, she's not a psycho stalker, she wouldn't have heard any of that. But in case she did, I hope she believes that I'm sorry if this whole situation hurt her. And I hope she'll talk to me when she's ready.'

Busted.

♡

A long time later, Laurie and I were back in my room, bathing our scratched legs in the good old bidet. Jamie had waited a while by the window, but I didn't know what to say so everyone just stayed silent and pretended it wasn't happening. Eventually, Laurie and I scuttled off.

'How do you feel after all that?' asked Laurie.

'Confused. Happy. A bit worried.'

'What about? He's ended it with her – finally. He's all yours.'

'You might kill me for saying this—'

'Oh for crying out loud, have you fallen for George now?'

'No, of course not. But my brain is ... tangled.'

'Why?'

'I guess I just need to do some serious thinking. Because if I want him back I can't do what she did to him. I can't change my mind once the holiday romance vibe has worn off and I'm back in London, with Italy seeming a million miles of effort away.'

'But you're nothing like her; I don't think you'd do that.'

'I don't think I would either, but I have a lot of decisions to make and I don't want to leave it until I get home. What if one decision impacts on something else?' I put my head in my hands and groaned.

'It's late, you were up all last night bonking, today you've met an arch-rival, you've agreed and also declined to move to Florida, and you've eavesdropped on two people while sat in the dirt. Get some sleep, and tomorrow we'll go somewhere you can clear your head and get some perspective.'

'Where? And we weren't bonking all night, by the way.'

'Let's take a couple of those Vespas out. We'll go for a ride, visit some more of this Tuscan countryside. Girls' trip.'

'No way, it's our last full day: you need to make the most of it with Jon.'

'No I don't.'

'Yes you do, I'm not letting you miss out on time with him just for me to have a moan.'

'Are you kidding me? You took a whole holiday for me; the least I can do is take a day for you.'

'But—'

'God, shut up. Shall we ask Donna? We don't have to – maybe you need to talk candidly about work and your awful bosses.'

'No we should, that'd be nice for her.'

'Is that a yes?'

I yawned. 'Yes.'

'Do you want me to stay over tonight?'

'No, stop creeping into my bed.'

♥

'Do you have one in turquoise?' asked Laurie, surveying the line of dirt-speckled Vespas the following morning.

'How's this one, madam?' Sebastian said, rolling forward a pale blue number.

'That will do nicely. Do you have a pink one for my friend Donna? She only likes pink.'

Donna, not a tremendously 'pink' person, laughed.

'Let me see what I have out back.' Off he went, and Laurie turned to me.

'How are you doing? Not going to fall off your Vespa because you can't see a thing through your tears, are you?'

'No, I'm okay – no more tears. I'm looking forward to clearing my head, having a day with you ladies, seeing a little more of this place and *her* being gone by the time I get back.'

Sebastian reappeared holding a pink ribbon, which he tied with a flourish to a gleaming black Vespa. 'How's this, Donna? Fit for the boss?'

'It's perfect, thank you.' She took it from him and proudly wheeled it out of the way.

'Bella Ella, which of these floats your boat?'

I chose a yellow one because it reminded me of the honey-hued white wine I'd drunk on the first night here.

'All right, ladies, anyone got any clue how to ride one of these?'

'I do,' said Donna, and we all looked at her in surprise. Well I never. 'Follow my lead, girls.'

After a few practice runs, several tippings-off, a helmet swap and much cackling from all of us, we were ready to go.

'Do you know where you're going?' asked Sebastian.

'Nope,' I replied. 'No idea at all. We're going to see

where the road takes us. We have GPS on my phone, so we'll find our way back before dusk.'

'Make sure you do: it's going to be a cracking dinner tonight – a proper Italian feast.'

We were waving goodbye when I spotted Jamie heading towards the main house. He stopped and looked over, a cautious smile playing on his lips. My heart caught in my throat but I couldn't help a smile spreading over my own face when I thought about what he'd said last night, how he'd defended me, and us. I gave him a light wave, and relief washed over him. We needed to talk – properly, not indirectly through an open window – but I felt brighter.

We zoomed away from Bella Notte, me squealing, Laurie yelling swear words and Donna whooping with joy. The balmy breeze stroked our faces as Tuscany opened out before us, a patchwork of cypress trees, vines and medieval villages on rolling hills.

For a while we followed dusty roads this way and that, taking whichever diversions appealed as we got to them. We came to a gradual stop near the top of a hill, where we removed our helmets, shook out our hot helmet-hair and took a seat under the shade of a tree.

I took a deep, clean breath. I really, *really* loved Italy. Not just because of Jamie – I actually felt like this was home. Like if it didn't work out with him I would still have to come back here.

'I don't want to go home,' I said.

'We sorted you out that quickly? Come on then, Donna, I guess that's us done for the day.'

I laughed. 'No, I still have thinking to do; this is just one thing I'm very sure about. I'm not sure what's going to happen with Jamie, long term, but the thought of living here makes me ... excited.' The girls were quiet for a moment while I gathered my thoughts. 'I guess if I don't continue things with him I couldn't live *here* – it would be too strange – but Italy's a big place. It could be a bit of an adventure, you know? Living in another country for a while.'

They nodded, and Donna started slathering on the sun cream, saying, 'Let's start from the beginning. So, what is it we're helping you figure out today? And I'm not your managing director right now, I'm just your friend, even if I am on the hottest Vespa.'

'In that case, one thing is definitely the job situation. I don't think I want to keep working there, Donna.'

'I understand that, but I do feel bad. I shouldn't have told you about my problems because it's now impacting your career. The whole glass ceiling thing might all change for the better some time soon.'

I shrugged. 'Even if it does, it just feels tainted now,

but I'm glad you told me. I think my time there has run its course.'

'So you're definitely going to leave?'

I stared at the view for a while, and Donna and Laurie remained quiet. Eventually I said, 'Yes, I'm going to leave. Who knows what I'm going to do, though.'

'If you choose to go to another company I'll write you a sparkling reference,' said Donna.

'Me too,' Laurie chimed in.

'What about you?' I asked Donna. 'Are you going to see it out, or are you going to take George's offer and swan off to Sunshine Land?'

'Unfortunately, that's like asking if I'm going to hold on far longer than I'm wanted, or give them what they want. Neither fills me with joy. But at least if I leave with somewhere else to go, somewhere better, that'd give me some sense of victory.'

'It does sound way better,' I said. 'Laurie, George's office is this huge glass building with views of South Beach in Miami. And Donna would be vice-president.'

'You know, I've always wanted to take a holiday to Miami. Is there any chance you're still considering that job offer, Elle?'

'Asks the woman who practically locked me in my room to stop me agreeing yesterday.'

'That was when I thought you were going to be his child bride.'

'What do you think I should do?' Donna asked me. My managing director was asking me for career advice. It felt nice.

'I think you should go for it. If it's awful, come home. You'll never be happy if you stay at the agency, anyway.'

'I think you might be right. I'm not going to give up my career, just maybe give up that company.'

'Just rolling things back to the present, does anyone want to go there?' asked Laurie, pointing to a town in the distance with several stone towers poking up into sky.

I shielded my eyes and squinted. 'I think that might be San Gimignano.'

'Oh that's famous,' said Donna. 'That's the medieval city isn't it? The walled one? From *Assassin's Creed II*? Yes, let's go there.'

This woman was full of surprises. And with that we dusted ourselves off, climbed back on the Vespas and took off.

♥

We explored every corner of the town, which didn't take long, and ended up in its main square, surrounded on all sides by houses and towers three, four, five storeys tall. We set up camp for a while at a bustling café, at an outdoor table where we could people-watch – and it was about time for a gelato fix.

'So. Do you think you could actually pack up your life and move here?' asked Laurie when our orders came. 'I'd miss you.'

'I'd miss you too, I'd miss everyone. I don't know – maybe I should stay in London.'

'No, if it's what you want to do you have to do it. Especially if you're going to leave one job anyway – it would be the perfect time. I'll miss you, but I'd also like free holidays to Italia.'

'But what about my parents? I don't want to be too far from my mum and dad.'

'Can I offer you a little advice?' interjected Donna. 'About moving away from your parents?'

'Go ahead, the more advice the better.'

'I have a daughter, as I think you know, and since the divorce I've kept her as close as possible. She's been not only my family, but my escape from work, my best friend, my everything. But when I think what she's missed out on because of me it breaks my heart. She had the opportunity to study abroad for a year, in New York, but she never even told me about it – just turned it down – and I know it's because she didn't think she could leave me. I clipped her wings as I was scared of being on my own, and now it doesn't feel good. It's my biggest regret. Trust me, your mum would hate to think she was the one holding you back.'

'I have an idea,' said Laurie. 'How old is your daughter now?'

'She's just finished university.'

'So prime gap-year age?'

'I guess so, though she's just been job-hunting.'

'If you go to Florida, maybe you could take her with you. You'd be giving her the adventure you think she's missed out on, but neither of you would be lonely.'

Donna lapsed into silence, stirring her melting gelato.

'It was just a thought,' said Laurie.

'It's a really good thought, I like it. It had crossed my mind as soon as the offer was on the table, but I was thinking more from the angle of "could I leave her", or "should I stay?", rather than would she want to uproot and come too. Now I think about it, I reckon she'd like it.'

Our conversation lulled for a while, and I thought about what it would be like to live here in Italy. Would I become fluent? How often would I fly home? Would it be the biggest mistake I'd ever make, or the best thing I could have ever done?

'I am the most humongous bitch in the world!' I

suddenly cried. 'This has all been about me. Laurie, I haven't asked you how you're feeling about Jon. Are you going to see him again after we've gone home?'

'I'd like to . . . ' she said.

'But?'

'Okay, you're not allowed to murder me in my sleep for saying this, because I *know* this whole thing was my idea, but I think I'd quite like to just take it slowly and not rush into anything. Maybe be on my own a little bit.'

'Who reversed our brains?'

'I know! It's just that I do really like Jon, and I would like us to see each other again, but I might just see if it happens organically.'

'Does this mean you'll go back to dating in London?'

'Not ... aggressively. I liked the concept of this holiday, of meeting people with similar interests and getting to know each other. Back in London I think I might just put myself out there a bit more – but not in an attempt to find love, just to get some hobbies of my own. Maybe I'll meet some new people, maybe I won't.'

Donna nodded. 'Sometimes it's nice to go and do these things you think you should only do on a date on your own, or with friends.' We all nodded at our combined wisdom. 'So what happened to Marco? Did you ditch him?'

'Yeah, there was no spark.'

I snapped my fingers at a memory. 'And what happened with Pierre – yesterday I saw him sucking face with Annette, of all people. I thought she was dead-set on Marco. She's like a dominatrix to Pierre, surely?'

Laurie coloured a deep red.

'What is that look for?'

'Nothing.'

I put down my gelato spoon (for all of five seconds). 'Laurie, you tell us this instant or we'll eat your ice cream.'

'Fine. But you can't breathe a word to anyone.'

Donna and I nodded. Except we might as well have shaken our heads because I had a feeling I was about to hear a story that would be repeated for years to come.

Laurie sighed, then ordered more gelato all round. 'The other evening I got a call to my room. It was Pierre, sounding a bit … husky. He asked if I could come and help him right away.'

'We have phones in our room? Sorry, not important.' I waved her on.

'First I just thought maybe he'd broken something and needed help, so I went over there, then as I was about to knock on his door I wondered if it was something more like he'd put a wine bottle up his bottom and it had got stuck there – and you can't miss that, it would be hilarious. So I knocked, he called me in, and ...'

'And?'

'I don't even want to say it.'

'*Say it!*'

Laurie squirmed. 'He was crouched on the floor, in little PVC shorts and this collary-strappy thing, and he'd tied his wrists to the bedpost.'

Donna and I gawped at her. 'TELL US MORE!'

'Well, I didn't know what to think, so I asked him who did it to him, and he said ...' She fanned herself. 'He said he did it to himself, because he needed to be punished, and I should give him a good *spanking*.'

Donna covered her eyes, I covered my ears, Laurie covered her mouth.

'Did you do it?' I whispered.

'No!' she cried. 'I told him to put his clothes on and stop being so silly, but that just spurred him on.'

'I think by this point I would have thwacked him one just for putting you in that position,' said Donna, gulping down some Sicilian lemonade and fanning herself.

'Then it got awkward,' said Laurie.

'*Then* it got awkward?' I cried.

'I think the penny dropped that I wasn't into all this stuff.'

'Why was the penny ever ... picked up?'

'I have no idea. I've asked myself the same thing. Maybe I was a little treat 'em mean, keep 'em keen to the three of them for a few days, but if he thinks that means a girl is a dominatrix I think he needs to do a little more research.'

'What did he say?'

'He got really flustered and tried to wriggle out of the hand ties and I tried to help, then he toppled over and one of his balls fell out.'

Donna was laughing so hard she knocked her gelato to the ground; then, after taking a moment to mourn it, her giggling fit started up again. To think that only two weeks ago I was terrified of upsetting this woman. Now I know she drives Vespas, plays video games and finds balls hilarious. She was so *normal*. Was I allowed to be friends outside work with my director?

'I just grabbed his nail clippers, snipped the ties, said a polite goodbye and legged it,' Laurie was saying. 'And I've avoided him ever since. Now you're saying he's hooked up with Annette, and frankly it makes perfect sense.'

'Pierre ... who would have thought it. I can't wait to tell Jamie.' My face fell. He would find it hilarious, but would we laugh together in the same way we had before?

Laurie and Donna glanced at each other. 'Would now be a good time to dissect the Jamie situation?' Laurie asked. 'Did you think any more about him during the night?'

'Just drifting thoughts, no conclusions. I like him so much, and it's clear he likes me too. It was all a misunderstanding, but I'm nervous about living up to this perfect girlfriend role.'

'What do you mean? Why would you need to be perfect?' asked Donna.

'I just wouldn't want to be the one to hurt him again, if things didn't work out.'

'You're not Rachel, though; you wouldn't do what she did,' said Laurie. 'And hang on, why so convinced it wouldn't work out?'

I shrugged. 'Just thinking of the worst case scenario, I guess. Donna, do you want another ice cream?' She shook her head, and Laurie narrowed her eyes at me; she wasn't done with me yet. 'In that case, does anyone mind if we split up and meet again in an hour or so?' I was keen to get off the Jamie topic. I still didn't have the answers – I just needed a little more time.

♥

I left the girls, and left the tourists, and walked until I found a secluded bench high on the hill, shaded by trees. I sat down and relished the peace and quiet.

I'd been on my own for a long time and I still con-sidered that a good thing, even if things were changing now. I knew myself so well, and I knew that if I needed to make some decisions, the best person to help me with that was myself.

It was so relaxing here, like all my worries were drift-ing away, even despite everything that was going on. I think I was ready to make a change to my life. Would it be as big a change as coming here? I didn't know – I'm not sure I could make that decision without going home first. But these ten days away had opened my eyes to not only all the fun, all the life, I was missing out on, but also to how my career could grow and blossom in a million different directions.

Jamie. What would become of me and Jamie? This time yesterday I thought it was over, but now the ball was in my court and I felt that it wouldn't be over unless I decided it should be. But there was no real reason we couldn't at least try to make it work – either long-distance or if I did end up moving to Italy. And with a deep breath I decided I needed to stop fannying about and plunge into this big love pool everyone's always harping on about.

'Live a little, Elle,' I told myself.

By the time I met Laurie and Donna again I felt refreshed, like someone had rinsed my mind with that lovely Garnier cleansing water.

'You look happy,' Laurie commented as we strapped on our helmets.

'I feel very happy. I think I'm going to try and make it work with Jamie.'

She beamed and leant over to high-five me, almost toppling from her Vespa. We then rode a short distance away from the town and parked up at a pretty lookout at the top of a vineyard, to survey the horizon and choose our final stopping point of the day.

'What about that place?' asked Donna as she and I climbed off our scooters, pointing to what appeared to be a crumbling monastery not too far away.

Laurie was still seated on her Vespa, muttering something, when all of a sudden there was a piercing scream and she sped off at top speed, her feet dangling wildly out to the sides, her scooter cutting right through the vines while she bumped and squealed her way over the soil.

'*LAURIE!*' I shouted and took off after her, as if I'd be able to chase down a Vespa. 'Jump off!'

She answered me with another trilling scream, the scooter shook manically and then they crashed head-first into a hedge. Laurie's bottom and a spinning bike wheel was all I could see when I reached them.

'Laurie, Laurie, can you hear me?' I pulled at her knickers, the only thing within reach.

'Owww,' she warbled from inside the hedge. 'Get off, these are expensive knickers.'

She shuffled out and collapsed to the ground, shaking. Her face and body were covered in tiny scratches, her dress somehow tucked into her bra, her shoes gone. She started crying, deep, breathy tears.

I reached into the hedge and turned the key in ignition, and the Vespa was silenced. I wrapped my arms gently around Laurie and stroked her hair. 'Shhh, it's okay, you're okay. Are you hurt?'

'M'ankle.' She pointed down and tried to flex it, which caused a fresh bucket of tears. 'Ow, m'anklehurts.'

Donna reached us, talking a million miles an hour on her phone. 'Your ankle hurts?' she asked. Laurie nodded and wiped her nose on my shoulder. Donna hung up. 'That was Sofia: Sebastian's going to drive out and meet us immediately. Do you need an ambulance?'

'No. Just a make-up artist and a driving lesson – oh, and some sand to stick my face into.' The shock was dying down, and her breath was gradually slowing.

'What happened?' I asked.

'I don't know. I guess I just got a bit cocky and made a mistake, started it in gear or something. Then I panicked and I couldn't remember how to stop, and my life was flashing before my eyes. Well, some fields were at any rate. Oh God, how bad is the scooter?'

'I'm sure it's fine, don't worry about that.'

'But I'm going to have to buy them a new Vespa. I'm such an idiot. Why do I do these stupid things?' Suddenly she sucked in her breath and grabbed my arms. 'How's my face? Did my Botox burst?'

'No, you look fine.'

'You had Botox? Why?' said Donna, crouching next to us.

'Because I'm determined to ruin everything about this holiday. Donna, did you see my knickers?'

'Only from a distance.'

'I'm sorry.'

'Why?'

'Because they're a bit slutty, they say "Slut" on them.'

'I didn't notice.'

'Then I'm so glad I told you.'

I smoothed her hair out of her face. 'Do you want to try standing up? You don't have to. You don't have to do anything.'

Laurie nodded and grabbed my hand. Donna and I took an elbow each and lifted her carefully. She squeezed her eyes shut as she tried to put weight down on her foot, and kept them closed as she took a wincing hobble forward.

'It hurts like crap, but I think I can walk.'

'Are you sure? If you need to go to hospital, or just rest—'

'No, I'm sure it'll be fine. I might just get one of those stretchy bandage hoo-hahs, and lay off the high heels until we're home.'

'Well, let's sit you back down for now until Sebastian gets here,' I said. Poor Laurie. 'But if you decide you don't want to travel tomorrow that's okay, we can stay as long as you need.'

'You just want more time with Signor Jamie,' said Laurie, mopping her mascara-streaked face with a wad of leaves.

'That's not true.' Except it was, and I'm the worst friend ever.

Donna went back up the hill to collect the remaining two Vespas, and somehow managed to come back clasping a large bottle of limoncello as well – who knows where she acquired that from. She poured a capful and handed it to Laurie. 'Drink up.'

'We're all going to have to have one hell of a detox after this holiday,' I said, helping myself to a swig.

'I think I need a holiday after this holiday,' said Laurie.

Donna looked out at the view from our little spot tucked in by a hedge, halfway down a field. Sitting there with bare, dust-covered legs, make-up free and swigging from a bottle of booze, she was a far cry from the woman who'd sat stiffly in the meeting room correcting me on *Mayor* Boris Johnson. 'It's been fun. I didn't think it would be, but it has. Thanks to you two.'

'Thanks to us?' asked Laurie. 'Are we your *amores*, Donna?'

'No, I'm no closer to finding an *amore*, but then I never had any intention of doing so. But what a miserable old cow I was when I first got here.' She giggled and put her face in her hands. 'Can you believe that entrance I made?'

I laughed. 'It was quite dramatic.'

'"*HOW DO I OPEN THIS BASTARD DOOR?*"' Laurie imitated, and Donna snorted into her limoncello.

♡

'What's for dinner tonight?' asked Laurie about half an hour later, as she studied her swollen ankle.

I yawned and sat up from where I'd been dozing in the sunshine. My stomach growled. 'Good question. I hope there's Chinese food.'

Donna laughed then stood up, a bit wobbly. 'Is that them?' She pointed to the horizon, where a large pickup truck was bumping its way over the vineyard.

I jumped up and waved, my skin and clothes now sprinkled with dust, sweat and sploshes of limoncello. The truck pulled to a gentle halt as close as it could come and out hopped two figures, who ran like they were in a Lucozade advert towards us.

'Laurie, it's Jon,' cried Donna.

I smiled, my heart beating faster. 'And Jamie.'

When they reached us they tried to pretend they weren't utterly puffed out, and Jamie mopped his brow with the bottom of his shirt, lifting it to reveal that lovely, taut stomach. 'Yum,' I accidently said out loud.

'Laurie!'

'Jon!' They exclaimed at each other melodramatically, and Jon dropped to her side while she tried to angle her cankle in a way that was more flattering.

'What happened? Are you okay?' asked Jamie, looking me over in panic and spinning me around to check all sides.

'I'm fine.' I couldn't help but chuckle. I looked him in the eye and tried to convey how I was sorry, how I wanted to talk to him, how I wanted to be with him, and how I wished everyone else wasn't around right now.

'I'm fine too, if anyone cares,' said Donna, between slurps from the limoncello bottle.

I explained what had happened, my mouth dry and

acutely aware of Jamie watching me. 'Laurie just lost control briefly and ended up in that hedge.' I was *not* to start giggling now. 'It wasn't funny at all. She's hurt her ankle pretty badly.'

Jamie caught my eye again, an amused twinkle in his, and turned to Laurie. 'Do you need to go to hospital?'

'No, I'll be very brave.' Jon was stroking her hair and cooing over her. I think she'd be suitably soothed with a couple of hours of TLC from him.

Jamie nodded and leaned into the hedge to yank out the Vespa. It looked fine, other than a broken headlight with a twig spiking out of it.

'Sorry, Jamie, I'll pay for any damage.'

'No you won't, this is nothing. Best not to drive it back, though; we'll put it in the truck. We do have one problem, however.'

'What's that?' hiccupped Donna.

'Neither of you two can ride your Vespas back because you've been drinking.'

I was mortified – I hadn't even thought about it. Donna mulled over the problem then started laughing, which was no help.

'And we can't fit five people and three Vespas in that truck.'

'I could walk back,' I said meekly, which started Laurie off laughing.

'How about this: Jon, do you think you can drive the truck back to the house? Would you feel comfortable with that?'

'Sure.'

'Then you take Laurie and Donna, and we'll put two of the scooters in the back, then I'll drive the third back with Elle riding pillion.' He looked at me. 'Are *you* comfortable with *that*?'

I gulped. I didn't know where we stood right now, or really how things were between us, but was I comfortable wrapping myself around a delicious man as he rides me around the Italian countryside, so to speak? Yes.

The gents made a show of lifting the Vespas to the truck with one arm, while we gathered up our scattered belongings, including Laurie's runaway shoes, and helped her down onto the road. When she was settled into the truck as comfortably as could be expected, and she'd given me the most almighty, unsubtle wink, off they went, Jon driving slowly and carefully.

Jamie and I walked back up to my Vespa. I didn't quite know what to say to him, so breathed a sigh of relief when he broke the ice.

'Do you want to hear something that makes me the most evil man on the planet?'

'Always.'

'When Donna called about the accident my mother

didn't catch everything she was saying and she didn't know who'd actually been on the Vespa, we just knew it was you or Laurie. When we got here and I saw it was Laurie, well ...' He peeped at me through his eyelashes. 'I was relieved it wasn't you.'

I shook my head. 'I can't believe you were glad my friend got hurt. What a sicko.'

'I wasn't glad, I just – oh, you're joking?'

'I'm joking. Now, you can't judge me for this, because I don't mean to sound like a massive bitch, but ...'

'Always a promising start to a sentence.'

'After it happened – when I saw she wasn't, like, dead or anything – a little tiny part of was excited that we might have to stay a few more days. You know, in case she couldn't walk or something.'

'So you're saying, in a way, you were glad your friend got hurt?'

'It's worse than that; *I'm* worse than that. When she got up with no more than a hobble I was actually a tad disappointed.'

Jamie laughed. 'Wow, I never knew what an awful person you are.'

'But I hide it well, that's what really matters. And it all comes from a place of good – I just thought you and I needed a little extra time.' I held my breath.

Jamie was silent, contemplative as he gave the Vespa

a check over. He then handed me my helmet, jumped on and patted the back for me to climb aboard, giving me a warm smile as he did so.

♥

We didn't say a word to each other all the way home. I just curled around Jamie, rested my cheek against his back and watched Tuscany whoosh past, the late-afternoon sunshine washing the hills with gold. My breathing coordinated with his and occasionally I would look up and catch a glimpse of the back of his neck, tanned a deep brown from all his days spent outdoors. One time he looked to his left and caught me, flashing a quick smile that made me snuggle in closer as if nothing was disjointed between us.

♥

Jamie dropped me outside the main house.

'Can I see you later?' I asked.

'Definitely. I'll be at dinner tonight, and then maybe you can come back to mine and we can talk.'

'And drink cappuccinos and eat chocolate?'

He smiled. 'I'd like that a lot.'

'Me too.'

'Me too. See you soon, Elle.' He touched my upper arm, his fingers sending an electric shock down the back of my spine, and just like that he left, trundling off to put the Vespa away. I think I had my man back. I don't think he ever stopped being mine.

I walked back into the main house, dragging my hands through my greasy hair. Hot Italian sun and bike helmets do not mix well. And I walked straight into Rachel.

She was leaning against the wall, her suitcase by her feet and her face the picture of pissed off.

'You're still here?' I blurted. Well, she did call me a dopey psycho, so we were obviously beyond niceties.

She scowled at me. 'Yes, I'm still here. The first flight out is eleven o'clock tonight. I've been hanging around all bloody day.'

I shrugged and moved past her to go up the stairs. 'Have a good journey.'

'Looks like you just did.'

'The best.'

'Everything you've done with him I'm sure I did first, sweetheart.'

I bristled. 'I'm going to have a bath.'

'Yeah, I think that would be a good idea.'

I stopped and turned to her. 'I'm sorry you wasted your time coming out here.'

'It wasn't a waste. The whole trip has been very interesting.' She looked me up and down and raised her eyebrows.

'But all that money you spent, all that time, and he didn't want you.'

Her eyes narrowed. 'You win some, you lose some. Better that I find out his tastes have changed now.' She slipped on her shades, as if to announce the conversation was over.

'I know in your mind you're much cooler than me, much prettier, much more alluring, but maybe this whole experience will make you realise you can't treat people like toys. If you do, people get tired of you, and even if you looked like ... Dannii Minogue he wouldn't want you back.' *Dannii Minogue?* Where did she come from?

Rachel sighed and turned away from me. I waited a moment for a response, before giving up and ascending the stairs. I was nearly at the top when I heard her again.

'I'm not a horrible girl, you know. We're probably pretty similar.'

'No, we're not. I wouldn't make a promise, then break it, then waltz back in when I think it's better timing for me.'

'So you never made a mistake, never needed time to think? Well congratulations to you. You win.'

A taxi honked outside and Rachel picked up her bag and left, without another glance in my direction.

♡

As I bathed and dressed for our final dinner, I thought a lot about Rachel, and whether I'd been too harsh. The girl was smarting and lashing out, but I wondered if it was possible that any one of us would have done the same in her position. To those who knew Jamie at the time, or for me, knowing him now, we could tell he'd been heartbroken – it was as if his girlfriend had died and he was suddenly never to speak to her again.

But what had been her side, her reasons? Perhaps she really did leave here hoping to make it work, not knowing how to do so and then giving up, thinking it would be easier to just let things slide away. And then one day she realised she'd been wrong, and she wanted him back. The hopes she must have had before coming here, the scenarios she must have played in her head, all of happy reunions and long-missed kisses. Then she arrives, and not only does he turn her down but he's found a replacement and they seem happy, and she has to live with that.

It was a thinker. I guess it takes a lot for us as humans to realise, truly, that we're not in the right, because it's rare we do something wrong with no motivation – even if that motivation comes from revenge, which comes from hurt, or because we're afraid of something. Everyone has their reasons for acting the way they do, even if others can't understand it.

But then what do I know, because I'm always right.

♡

After everyone had gathered in the wine-tasting room that night Sofia proudly led us on a final sunset walk through the vineyard to one of the wine cellars, in which she'd laid a long, thick oak table with a beautiful centrepiece of fairy lights and entwined twigs, and wine-toned roses.

There were no set places; everyone slotted in next to the person they had the most connection with. Jamie had yet to arrive and I didn't know if he had a special seat near Sofia and Sebastian, so for me that meant Laurie on one side and Donna on the other. I'm sure lots of the other guests must have assumed Donna and I were lesbians.

We were also sitting across from Pierre, which meant that none of us could look directly ahead for fear of catching his eye and imagining his ball. Or in Laurie's case, remembering it in all its glory.

'I am so sad that it's our final meal together,' Sofia announced once we were all seated. 'Please eat as much as you can and drink as much as you can and laugh as much as you can.'

Jamie arrived, looking handsome in a deep red shirt, his stubble trimmed back, and I met his eye. A grin spread across his face and he took a seat further down the table, raising a glass of wine to me.

Dinner was luxurious, relaxed, with flowing wine and flowing chatter – so much more comfortable than the stiff meet-and-greet that we'd had the first night. I'm the first to admit I'd been very cynical about singles' holidays, but looking at the happy faces around me, and all these new people I'd met and how they'd changed me, I saw how beneficial they could be. And I didn't want *You Had Me at Merlot* to have to end.

Plate after plate of every Italian dish imaginable came out, all cooked by Sebastian but brought in by hired waiters. We had shavings of ham direct from Parma, bulbous local olives, crisped basil leaves, olive oil-soaked mozzarella, those delicious bruschetta, flatbreads, braised rabbit stew, cannelloni, gnocchi, risotto, miniature pizzas … The list went on. Usually, if I'm nervous my appetite goes out of the window, but there wasn't a thing on the table that my mouth didn't beg to sample.

Until I saw Annette slap Pierre's hand as he reached for a stalk of prosciutto-wrapped asparagus and he visibly jumped with excitement. Then I decided I could do without one of them.

Jamie slipped out of the dinner before dessert, thanking everyone for coming and saying he'd see everyone in the morning. He turned back as he was walking out, and met my eye across the crowded room. I nodded.

'Go and party like it's 1999,' whispered Laurie.

'We just need to talk.'

'*Bullshit*,' she coughed.

'But after all that talking ... '

'That's my girl!' She practically pushed me up and out of my seat, and with a gushing thanks to our hosts I left.

I made my way through the vineyard, taking my time, looking at the stars, until I reached Jamie's house. I shouldn't be so nervous – we were going to be okay. With a deep breath, I knocked on his door.

'Hi.'

'*Buonasera*,' he said, standing there with his shirt untucked, a few buttons undone. I felt like a tornado of emotions whipped up inside me as I looked at him and all I could think was *I don't want to not be around you*. 'So, are you all packed for Florida?'

'I'm not going to Florida.'

He smiled. 'I know; George spoke to me earlier. He threatened me, actually.'

'What did he say?'

'That if I mistreated you again, or if any other girls suddenly show up with suitcases and kisses, he'd not only offer you the biggest, most high-paying job in the States that you couldn't refuse, but he'd also buy a supermarket just so he could buy out Bella Notte.'

'Wow . . . how high-paying I wonder?'

Jamie laughed and led me inside, his hand on my back causing butterflies. I sat at his table and the conversation dried up for a while as we both ate his homemade chocolate.

After a lifetime he pushed the crumbs aside and reached across to me. 'I'm sorry about Rachel. I hadn't seen her in a long time – it was kind of a shock.'

'I get it.'

'No, I hate myself. You're – at least you were – my girlfriend, and she isn't, and I don't know what I was thinking not sending her straight away.'

'I was pretty angry.'

'I know.'

'But I'm sorry for taking things too far and yelling at you so quickly.'

'You don't have to apologise.'

'Of course I do,' I said. 'I jumped to conclusions and screeched at you without even giving you a chance to explain. My emotions have been pretty high over the last week, what with work, and you.'

'I made your emotions high?'

'In a good way. An unexpected – but good – way. I think you opened my eyes to the prospect of a new adventure, and then suddenly it felt like it was all ripped away.'

'I still should have been a bit more open with you. It's just, I felt like our time here was so limited, so precious, that I didn't want to waste it dragging up all these miserable old memories.'

I popped in another piece of chocolate. 'So we're both a bit silly.'

'Yes.'

'In that case, I have a question for you.'

'Go on.'

'Can I be your girlfriend again?'

Let's just take a moment to think about what a massive deal it was for me to say this. In the past two weeks I'd gone from not wanting a boyfriend, to finding someone in an unexpected place, to reluctantly agreeing to be a girlfriend, to asking someone outright if I can be their girlfriend. I was proud of myself. I never thought something boyfriend/girlfriend related could make me say that, but it was true.

Jamie stood up and walked around the table, stopping in front of me. He bent down, smiled that smile and before he had a chance to kiss me I tilted my head up and kissed him. Then the chair couldn't hold me any longer and I leapt up, squeezing myself into his arms, allowing his fingers to run through my hair and for mine to glide over his sculpted arms.

You can guess what happened next. Well, it was our last night.

It was at least witching hour when we lay in his bed, the window open and a soft breeze tickling our bodies. The moon was as bright white as a ball of mozzarella and it meant I could follow my fingers as they traced their way around his chest.

'So,' he said. 'Let's talk about my parents.'

'What a great idea.' I pulled the sheet over my naked breasts.

'I actually have a message from them that I promised I would pass on. They wanted to do it but I said no, she's my girl, I want to.'

A smile soaked over my face. My man.

'Do you know that, thanks to all of your marketing magic, *You Had Me at Merlot* has now had over forty new bookings? Just in the last couple of days. That's a huge rise, and it's because of you.'

'Really? That's so cool.'

'It's the coolest. We've held off the supermarkets, at least for now.'

'It's actually because of all of you, though. I just lent you a little brainpower.'

'No, we need you.'

'You do?'

'More than you know. So we would like to formally offer you a job.'

I sat up. 'What?'

'I'm not just saying this because George offered you one, and I'm not just saying this because I *totally* want you to stay, but we all know you'd be invaluable. We probably can't pay you your London salary, but it wouldn't be bad, especially if business keeps going like this, and you'd have free room and board. That means living with me, or in your own room with a bathtub.'

It was what I wanted, handed to me on a plate. I was so lucky. But this was still a huge decision and I didn't know if I could make it right now. I looked down at him, lying there, and imagined what it would be like to be next to him every night. I imagined it would be really good.

Would it be as good as it felt to live on my own, and have my independence? How could I make that decision, or know the answer to that?

'Can I get back to you on that?' I asked, afraid that

he'd have hurt feelings, or compare me to Rachel. But Jamie just laughed and pulled me back down.

'Of course you can. Nobody has to give an answer to a job offer in the middle of the night with no clothes on.'

With the knowledge that I had real, transferrable talent for marketing, I had options, I had love – or something on its way there – and I had a few hours left in this country, I settled in for my final *bella notte* in Italy.

♥

In the morning, there were many tears. New couples parted, new friends said goodbye, and one by one the people we'd become familiar with over the past ten days disappeared.

Donna held my face before she went and for a moment I thought she was going to kiss me. But she looked at me and said, 'If you stay at the agency, you do everything in your power to knock them off their pedestals.'

'Does that mean you're not coming back?' I felt a pang of sadness, for her situation and for the loss of a friend.

'I'll come back long enough to pack up my office and delete a few important files on the shared drive, but they won't want me to serve my notice. And I'd like to just take a few weeks to relax and sort out some things at my home before I go to Florida.'

'You're definitely taking the VP job?'

'Definitely, and my daughter hasn't sounded so happy in a long time; she can't wait to come with me.'

I squeezed her, hard. 'You send me an invite to you and George's wedding, won't you?' Donna laughed and stepped aside, so the man himself could get his greasy mitts all over me. 'I'm going to miss you, George, weirdly.'

'Imma miss you too, baby. My offer always stands.'

'The marriage offer?'

'The marriage, the job, the vacation – all the offers stand, just visit us once in a while, okay?' He hugged me, and whispered in my ear, 'I know Donna would appreciate it – she thinks a lot of you.'

Jon and Laurie were saying goodbye to each other as he was sharing a lift to Florence airport with George. He looked more broken than her, but I could tell she was sad. Sad, but strong, and I was proud of her for keeping it together while she murmured into his ear about what would happen next time they met.

I squeezed Sofia and Sebastian one after another, and then had a second helping of both. 'Thanks for an amazing holiday, it couldn't have been better.'

'It was okay was it, Bella?' asked Sebastian.

'It was okay.'

'Not too much of a wasted trip?'

'Leave her alone,' hissed Sofia. 'We want her to come back.'

So that just left Jamie. How could I leave Jamie? I couldn't; I couldn't do it. I was going to have to stay. How could I not be in those arms tonight, or next to that face again? But . . . how could I give up everything I know?

'I have to go home.' My voice shook as I said it.

He nodded, a forlorn shadow settling across his features. Then he shook his head and took my arms, holding them gently in his big hands and he looked down at me. 'No, you don't. Just stay with me.'

'I can't just stay.'

'You can't just go.'

'But I might come back.'

'Don't say "might".'

'I can't make you a promise right now, you need to understand that.' I reached up to his face. Would I be okay without it? I'd been okay without it for years before now, surely I could pull through? 'I need to sort my life out there, and make some decisions when I'm not intoxicated by all this delicious wine – and delicious you.' I smiled at him, the best I could through my tears.

'It's going to seem empty here without you now. There'll be no Bella at Bella Notte.'

'I'm going to seem empty too.'

'You will think about it, yes? It's a real job offer.'

'Is it just a job offer?'

'It's a real offer of . . . me.'

I knew it was. 'I will think about it, really seriously.'

The taxi pulled up and Laurie hobbled in, finally letting a few tears fall as Jon's car faded into the distance. Sebastian dutifully loaded all of our bags in while I clung to Jamie's shirt, tears dripping down my cheeks.

He wouldn't take his sad eyes off me. 'Please let me know how you are and what you're thinking. I don't want you to just not be here any more.'

'We'll talk all the time. You'll let me know how things are going here? And how Enzo is?' I felt frantic, afraid of these last moments. 'I hope it isn't goodbye.'

'It isn't,' he said firmly. 'You'll come back, this is your second home. You can't not come back home.'

My feet took me to the taxi though my heart hated them for every step. I needed to remember everything as beautiful, and as we pulled away, crunching over the dust, I forced a small smile to settle on my face. I wanted him to remember me smiling. With effort he smiled back, and as soon as the taxi descended the hill, and no amount of neck-craning could show me him again, I broke down.

I *couldn't* not come back home.

Epilogue

Two months later ...

The taxi crawled through the Tuscan countryside, the windows down, the air still warm though the sun was dipping earlier than I remembered.

As we carved up through the hills the emerald greens of summer had been painted over with bright oranges and reds, the colours of the roofs in Florence. The vines boasted fat purple grapes in such abundance it looked like they could topple over at any moment, and the violet haze I'd been promised was there.

I hadn't wanted Jamie to pick me up from the airport because I'd wanted to do this journey on my own, to see my new home turf by myself, and not as his guest.

I quit my job; I'd had a better offer and there was no contest really. After Donna had handed in her notice morale was noticeably down anyway, and ripples of why she'd left were permeating throughout the company, leaving bitter tastes in their wake. But for her that job was long gone; she was as over it as if it were a lucky break from a bad boyfriend, and whenever we spoke on the phone she sounded as bright as the Floridian sun she and her daughter were now living under. And George had more than stuck to his word, placing a rolling yearly order for a case of wine for each of his employees to complement their Christmas bonuses and booking corporate retreats to Bella Notte for the spring and autumn. Laurie had booked flights back to Italy in a month, and I had a sneaking suspicion that Jon might also be under instruction to do the same. Mum and Dad would be coming over in two weeks, and Mum's excitement was dazzling.

Who knew how long I'd be out here for? But with Jamie, sunshine, a challenging new job and *that* chilli wine, I was in no rush to run back.

My heart ping-ponged as the taxi made its way towards Bella Notte. I'd been away from Jamie for too long, and my skin was tingling at the thought of being back by his side. Does that make me co-dependent? Am I no longer the career-driven, modern woman I held myself up as?

As my new workplace came into view, the vineyard I was going to save, and not a partition, a keycode, a desk or a Tube train blocked my way, I'd never felt more independent.

And there he was. Jamie met me outside Bella Notte, his shirt crumpled, sleeves rolled up, messy hair and that lopsided grin. I jumped from the taxi before it had even come to a complete stop and ran to him.

'What took you so long?' he smiled at me.

'I really don't know.'

Jamie didn't *complete* me, but he complemented me. He was the chocolate to my chilli wine.

Acknowledgements

So. Have you all been as sloshed reading this as I was writing it? Just a couple of thank yous and I'll be out of your way. (Bear with me – this is as close as I'll get to a dramatic Oscar speech.)

Manpreet – in the paraphrased words of Britney Spears, blimey, we did it again with another book! Thanks for helping keep up this massive practical joke that I'm a real author, and for being all-round smashing in every way. Thanks to all the other Little, Brownies too – Hannah G, Marina, Thalia, Zoe, Clara, Rachel, Hannah W, Kate, Andy and Helena, to name but a few.

Hannah Ferguson, my beautiful-haired agent at Hardman & Swainson – thanks for all your lovely patience and advice, and for also nodding politely when I go off on some embarrassing tangent. You're the best in the biz. F-to-the-E-to-the-R-G-I-E-Girl you tasty.

Husband Phil – sorry this one *still* didn't contain any

dinosaurs or explosions. Thank you for reading it all for me anyway, and for being lovely and basically doing everything for me while I was glued to the laptop.

Emma – winner winner chicken dinner of the Sunlounger 2 short story competition – you are so clever! Thanks for all your help with this, and once we've moved into a luxury writing retreat together I'll return the favour, because you're going to be *famous*.

Mama G – thanks for setting the scene in Devon with the Italian Merlot and the Tuscany travel guide, and for concocting an elaborate story in a travel agents just to nab a few brochures for me. And Papa G – I'm really not rich yet, so stop telling everyone you're set up for life now. I might buy you bar of Cadbury's if you're lucky. Love you both heaps.

Thanks to Belinda Jones, an author who continually inspires me and without whom I'd probably still just be working on Sweet Valley fan fiction, and to all the new author and blogger friends I've made who are so bloody lovely! I'd love to name you all, but you know who you are and you're all Twitterati Glitterati. And big hugs, smooches and thanks for putting up with me to all my extended family, my friends, my holiday buddies and my work chums.

And thanks to YOU GUYS for reading: it's been a blast. Now go and get yourselves another glass of vino!

Six Summer Breaks to Take With Friends

You know in summer-anthem music videos people are always dancing on boats with their friends, all coloured sunglasses and perfect bodies? That could be you! No, really. Even the perfect body bit – because your bod is perfection no matter what shape, size or shade. Key criteria for a break with besties: a) space to talk, catch up, and laugh; b) plentiful food and drink to consume during the above. Whether your thing is dancing, culture, working up a sweat or lying on the beach, it's time to salute the sun and get some happy holidays booked up.

London, UK

A London city break is something that should be on every friendship group's bucket list – there's so much to do and see that you'll get caught up in the whirlwind of London life from the get-go, and the long summer days offer the perfect time to summer in the city. History buff? Take your pick – museums, galleries, the Tower of London, Shakespeare's Globe Theatre … All about the fun? Try Madame Tussauds, or my fave: the London Dungeon. Sports fan? Swim or bike in the Olympic Park, watch some balls whiz by in Wimbledon or jog through Hyde Park with your best lycraed-leg forward. Retail therapy your thang? Oxford Street, Covent Garden Market, and the Westfield malls are all waiting for you, doors flung wide open. And then end the days with city-view dinners up the Shard or lungfuls of laughs over half-price cocktails at Dirty Martini. Bliss!

Anywhere You Like, UK

Little can beat a good cottage holiday with your ladies – chuck way too much food in the car, create a cracking summer playlist (must include 'Mysterious Girl') and drive a hundred miles or so in any direction. Open rosé immediately upon entering your cottage and settle down for some well-deserved gal pal time. I'd always migrate towards Devon or Cornwall because I'm a beach bum who loves nothing more than a beer, a sunset and the sea, but the beauty of this break is you can take it wherever works out best for you. Within a couple of hours' drive from anywhere there's always going to be a pretty cottage just waiting to host your homemade margaritas and LOLs.

Paris, France

Paris, the city of love ... well you love your friends, right? Don't go thinking you can only explore this amazing city if you're with someone who likes to look at your rudey bits; non non non! Hop on the Eurostar and can-can your way around France's capital, like the belles you are. Treat yourselves to pricey patisserie treats and trips to the top of the Eiffel Tower, and ('cause I know you like books) be sure to drop by the Shakespeare and Company bookshop on the Left Bank, which is a wonderfully higgledy-piggledy maze of writings, and is a famed attraction for anyone who likes to get lost in literature. The Hotel Saint-Jacques near Notre Dame is a good base for exploring the city if you like a touch of 19th Century charm and ambience, Edith Piaf piped in the background, and burning off those croissants with a long walk along the Seine.

Greece

If ever there was a place to make all of you step off the plane, drop your bags, throw on the wide-brimmed hats and let out a collective *aaaahhhhhh* it would be Greece, with its warm air, blue skies and seas and beautiful coves and sands. Visit Zakynthos for the beaches and turtles, Mykonos for swanktastic hotels and spas, Santorini for stunning scenery or Rhodes for nightlife to keep you buzzing till dawn. But these niches aside, all the islands have a melting pot of fun, sun and culture, and delicious foooooooooood to keep you yumming from sunrise to sunset . . .

Las Vegas, USA

Vegas. Remember when Ross and Rachel got *married* in Vegas?! That was the best. But anyway, shotgun weddings aside, Vegas is a great place to go with friends. I know it seems like a really long way away and is mega-expensive, but WHO CARES ABOUT BEING SENSIBLE, VEGAS BABYYYYYYYYYYYY. Plus you can win all your dosh back at roulette; it's easy*. Las Vegas is the epitome of fun in the sun, so be sure you and your squad check out the pool parties, Britney's residency, Sky Bar at the Palms and (believe me) Matt Goss's cabaret show at Caesars Palace.

The author relinquishes all responsibility for funds lost whilst holidaying in Vegas.

East Coast, Australia

If you have at least two weeks, an adventurous friend and a pocketful of savings, head south to Australia's East Coast. Start with snapping crocs up in Queensland's Daintree National Park, followed by swimming with the fishes on the sparkling Barrier Reef, before moving down to the Whitsundays, Fraser Island, perhaps a trip inwards to an outback cattle ranch for good measure, Byron Bay and finally Sydney for a cold glass of wine in front of the Opera House. You'll stack up so many memories together that you'll be laughing your heads off over the photos for years to come (believe me, my friend and I spent six months doing this trip and more way back in 2002 and we still speak in awful Aussie accents to each other whenever we meet up ... it's *well* annoying for everyone else). Go for as long as you can and stop in as many places as possible. If you can spend the whole summer out there, you won't be disappointed, but a two week tasting menu will be enough to whet your appetite.

Recipe: Sun-Baked Summer Days

Hello, what's this? *yawn* Is that sunshine outside your window? Already? Even though your morning alarm has only just gone off, and it only feels like yesterday you were still slapping on your make-up in the dark and leaving the house in twelve woolly jumpers? *throws back curtains* It *is* the sun! It is! Summer is HERE! Time to whip up a batch of Vitamin D-drenched Sun-Baked Summer Days to relish throughout the season...

Preparation and cooking time: 3 months

Makes: Fun in the sun

- Start by turning the temperature up and putting the fan on cool.
- Soak yourself in sun for 1–12 weeks and add a large dollop of time off work.
- Splash in a waft of summer scents – coconut, salt water or the insides of paperbacks.
- Add a clink of ice cubes into your mojito.
- Pair with a summer playlist bursting with happy-making tunes.
- Reduce stress and worries until they've evaporated and then fold in plenty of relaxation.
- Whisk in a holiday until happiness and laughter is bubbling over.
- (Check to make sure skin is not burning, and rub in lashings of lotion if so)
- Mix shorts with kaftans as the sun dips for casual cosiness during a late afternoon walk on the beach.
- Barbecue all meals, if weather permits. Best enjoyed al fresco with plenty of friends.
- Allow body to rest for long periods overnight, preferably from sunset to sunrise.
- Incorporate ice cream and kissing where possible (too much is advised).

Method:

Combine ingredients together over summer months until the temperature has cooled, at which point apply a thick layer of woolly jumpers and endless memories.

Turn the page for an exclusive extract from *Mistletoe on 34th Street*, Lisa Dickenson's hilarious new novel.

Available in November 2016!

3 weeks, 4 days to Christmas

I grasped around, trying to find something to pull my tired body through the water yet again. So cold, so achy, such conflicting feelings as to whether it would be better to escape this hell or just die under the surface of this mud-churned lake. And I'd *paid* to do this? In *December*? I would give anything to be a chestnut roasting by an open fire right now.

Yes, dying was definitely preferable. Goodbye, world. But then a pair of hands pushed into the squash of my butt cheeks and I was propelled through the sludge, hippo-style.

Then finally, there was the wooden platform above me. I would live! My thigh muscles remembered they had a job to do and pushed me up out of the mud and into the wintery air, where the noise of a hundred other racers – grunts, groans, cheering, laughing, the odd person crying – filled my ears as the brown lake trickled out of them.

I wiped the mud from my eyes with an equally muddy arm, and stretched my arm back to pull out Kim, who broke the surface like Ariel the mermaid, whooping and pushing her dark curls out of her face. She slung a tiny bronzed arm around my shoulders and we trudged towards the river bank.

'How fun is this?' she cried just as I was about to say 'How awful is this?'

At that point an enormous fairy wing thwacked me in the back and I crumbled back towards the freezing water again, and for a second my final ever thought was nearly, *I'm going to die . . . who'll take my place on the stand in New York?*, but luckily Kim steadied me. The owner of the wing, a gigantic man who was also clad in a tinsel tutu, a headband and nothing else yelled, 'SORRY, LOVE,' as he picked up speed and ricocheted up the bank and off down the hill.

'Olivia, what's the rule?' Kim warned.

'No grumbling.'

'What happens if you grumble?'

'I have to sit by Jasmine at the Christmas party.' I caught my breath, finally reaching the riverbank. 'I'm not grumbling, I'm fine, this is great, I'm having the time of my life! Thank God she's not here though. Hey, where's Ian?'

Kim smirked. 'Helping Dee, back at the monkey bars.'

How sweet. 'Of course he is. And Scheana? I feel like I haven't seen her since the start?'

'Me neither.'

'I do have one grumble. Keep your gym pants on, it's not even really a grumble, think of it as a heartfelt request: can I come with you to Antigua the week after next? Can I lie on the beach and be so warm I'm almost too warm? I want to feel sweat again.'

We dug our fingertips in the mud-slide that was the riverbank and hauled ourselves up. I'd always fancied trying one of those Tough Muddy Survival events – it looked fun, like a challenge, a good morning of cama-raderie with friends, so when someone at work had said they were interested too I leapt in, face-first, and cajoled together a team to enter the Fearless Freeze 10k event on December the first. December the first? The 'Fearless Freeze'? I was definitely a massive plonker, and now my colleagues were scowling at me every time our muddy paths crossed. But that didn't matter, they'd get over it. The important thing was that the group of girls who were waiting to cheer us through the finish line would see us complete the event in one piece, strong and capable.

Urrrggghhh, I could not admit defeat, no matter how much I secretly wanted to.

Kim clawed her way to the top of the riverbank, shaking her head. 'No, New York's always so fun, you're going to have the best time.' We set off on a slow, tired jog. Just three kilometres and twelve obstacles to go. I was nearly there, ish.

'But New York is so cold . . . '

'HEY,' Kim scolded. 'What did we say?'

'No grumbling . . . Should we stop and wait for the others?'

'I think if we stop now we might turn into ice sculptures. Besides, the finance arseholes have already gone on ahead anyway.'

'OK. I will miss you though, and I hate Steve for taking you from me,' I said. 'I'm not grumbling, I'm just saying. And I don't hate Steve really.'

'I'll miss you too,' Kim sighed. 'This'll be the first year since starting at Girls of the World that I won't be doing New York. But I am kind of looking forward to three full weeks off.'

'This year has just been insane. As soon as I'm back from New York I'm not planning to talk to anyone for the whole of the Christmas break. Just me, TV, and jammies.'

On we ran, towards our fate: a fifty-foot wall, which we were expected to scale, that stood atop a hill in the distance. It was covered with people in brightly coloured, mud-soaked running tops, who were charging up and over, pulling up those behind and pushing on the bottoms of those in front. It looked eerily like a scene from *World War Z*.

Kim and I worked for Girls of the World, a foundation created to promote women's rights through educating and empowering school girls to be creative, be themselves, and be heard. I was part of a team of six led by the founder, Scheana, a fiercely confident woman with the most appealingly gung-ho attitude. Everyone at the foundation, men and women, wanted to be Scheana when they grew up. I couldn't get enough of my job – I got to meet and work with these young women – future CEOs, writers, scientists, artists, inventors, sports people – and learn from them, encourage them, give them an outlet, celebrate them in all their weird and wonderful ways. And it was lucky that I couldn't get enough because we hadn't stopped all year. The company had grown threefold in the past twelve months and we'd been breaking our backs to keep up and make sure not a single girl, school, society or hope was left behind. We had apps and contributors and sponsors and now, after years of attending conferences to spread the word about Girls of the World, our small UK foundation, we were finally hoping to branch out internationally too, starting with the USA.

A major, *major*, benefit of working at Girls of the World – aside from knowing without a doubt that you're on an equal pay scale – was the annual conferences, where similar organisations from around the world gathered to share thoughts, ideas, seminars and have amazing guest speakers. The rumour-mill was on overdrive this year about the potential for Emma Watson or Amal Clooney to put in an appearance at this year's New York do, the #IWasHereNYC event.

I loved spending conferences with Kim, who worked as an executive in the marketing department; she had such energy and enthusiasm that she could waltz into a school and convince a kid, on the brink of ditching her biology exam for a smoke with the boy from the upper sixth, to not only take the exam but also to chuck the boy and become such a badass biologist that it would make her want to help cure lung cancer. With, like, one speech. Kim was a miracle worker, our very own Derren Brown.

And now Evil Steve, who was actually really nice, was whisking my Kim away for a romantic Christmas break in the Caribbean, which she chose over a work trip with me. Sigh.

We reached the wall and I (being the giant in our relationship) crouched so Kim could stand on me and pull herself up to the first ledge.

'Remind me who's going this year?' she called back, reaching her arm down for me, while I flailed my legs about in the air until some bloke got fed up with being kicked in the knees and helped me over.

'Scheana, of course. Abigail.'

'The new girl?' Kim asked.

'Yep, she's pretty nervous. Our fave: Jasmine.'

'Oh lord, that'll be fun. How's she being with you now?'

'The same as she always is,' I said, sighing. 'I actually wish she was that cliché of a colleague who was after my job because at least there'd be some healthy competition to it, but she's actually just a cow for no reason.'

'True story.'

'And Dee and Ian are both going too.'

'Ahh, romantic!'

'I know, I'm really curious if this'll be the year they break and just admit they're seeing each other.'

'You never know,' Kim grunted over the next ledge. 'New York is pretty special around Christmas. The temptation of a snog on the Rockefeller ice rink could be just the nudge they need to come clean. John will be there to keep you company, won't he?' she asked, all innocent.

'Subtle. Yes he will be there, but nope, still not in love with him. And as I've said a million times if I haven't fallen in love with him yet, it's not going to suddenly happen.'

'Mmm-hmm,' Kim agreed, blatantly disagreeing. 'Have you seen much of him lately?'

'Not since the Amsterdam conference in September.' But I had dropped him an email this week to tell him I couldn't wait for a catch-up and to find out which flight he was on. And I really couldn't wait – like Kim, John was a good friend. Unlike Kim, he had a penis, which meant everyone who knew us couldn't wrap their heads around the 'just friends' part. John currently worked on the United Nations' HeForShe campaign, and we met a few years ago on the conference circuit after I saved myself from tripping over a poster stand by smacking his coffee cup out of his hand so I could grab it. *Selfless*. We try and catch up between work events by grabbing a drink or dinner. One time we even went on the Harry Potter studio tour together, but work has been so crazy this year that I've barely had a minute to myself, so I've been a crap friend and I haven't seen him as much as usual.

We reached the top ledge of the wall, (dear God, it must be nearly over), and took a breather, gazing back at the obstacles. Dee and Ian's heads bobbed about in the lake, and a couple of other colleagues were reaching the wall below us.

I looked up at the sky, heavy with bruised clouds and getting darker by the minute. 'Do you think there's a storm coming?' I asked Kim, who was leaning over the other side of the wall, contemplating the best way down.

'Shit-wise or weather-wise?' she called back.

'Weather-wise.'

'As long as it doesn't stop my flight to Antigua it can be a total whiteout this Christmas for all I care.'

And with that, the heavens opened and a blizzard to rival an arctic snowstorm swirled around us as we ran for our lives to complete this godforsaken race.

Just kidding, but it did start to pelt it down with rain. I could see the finish line in the distance and squinting through the drops I thought I could also see a group of teenage girls in orange Girls of the World raincoats and tinsel scarves. They were some of the girls I worked with, and they're the best. They grouped together a few months ago to make YouTube videos for us about getting involved in sports even if you don't feel good enough, and they've been big hits on our website. So I couldn't let them see me acting like my body wasn't capable of sliding through a few more mud patches and surviving a couple more bruises.

No grumbling, I told myself for the fortieth time that day.

It was over; we'd made it. We had survived. Kim and I were freezing, but my group of girls made coming across the finish line an unexpected joy. They called me a superhero, which wasn't true at all but I pretended I didn't hear and asked them to repeat it a couple of times anyway. They'd zoomed home quickly afterwards as they were drenched right through, and I was now thawing out under a heat lamp, cuddling a hot chocolate and wearing a Santa hat (whose Santa hat was this?) when I was brought back from my thoughts about how strong and brave I was by the sound of someone calling my name from outside the tent.

'Olivia! Over here. Down a bit.'

'Scheana, what happened?' I leapt up and rushed (hobbled) outside the tent, shaking the remaining water from my ears. My manager was lying, damp and bedraggled, on a stretcher. Two paramedics moved aside and tended to a dislocated shoulder while I spoke with Scheana. This place was a warzone. Sort of.

'I think I might have broken my leg,' said Scheana with a shrug. 'No biggie, but I think I'll be out of action for a while.'

'Bloody hell, where?'

'On one of the big log things.'

'But where on your leg?'

'Lower, I think.'

'Does it hurt?' I asked.

'Yep, loads, but I wanted to talk to you about work.'

'Now?' I shifted my weight and I'm sure I heard either my ice-crystalled T-shirt or my rib crack – was I starting to actually freeze?

'Just a quick thing. Well done on completing by the way, you did brilliantly, I'm so proud of you all.' Scheana reached out and squeezed my hand like a person on their deathbed. 'Urgh, you're glacial. I'll keep this quick. New York is two weeks today, and I'm not going to go.'

I must still have had a lot of water in my ears, because I couldn't be hearing this right. 'You're not going to what?'

'I'm not going to go. My leg won't be better. So I need someone to take over as head of Girls of the World. Temporarily. That person needs to represent the company in New York, try to push us forward. They'll need to be quick-thinking and a good problem solver, even with little resources. You have no idea how many little tasks befall a manager in the lead-up to a trip like this.'

'I'LL DO IT,' I said. 'Let me do it, I won't let you

down. Can I do it?' This was the break I wanted. I wasn't pleased that Scheana had snapped her leg, and I wasn't trying to poach her job, but Girls of the World was growing and we were hoping to expand into other countries within the next year. I wanted to be part of it. One day I wanted to be a director in this company.

'Are you sure? It's a big responsibility. You've had a busy year. Aren't you feeling burnt out?'

'No.' Yes.

'Because you don't know busy until you've been in charge of something like this.'

'I can do it. I've been to New York four years in a row and I want to be more involved. You focus on your recovery and I'll look after everything. I promise.' Ohmygod, could I do this? Yes, of course I could. Well, I had to.

'Good, I was hoping you'd say that. In that case, from now until the new year, you're the boss.'

And with that, the paramedics returned and wheeled Scheana away.

I went back to the tent and squeezed my bum back onto the bench under the heat lamp, in between a snoring woman and a man who looked close to throwing up. I was the boss . . .

Dee appeared, her long frame pink all over from the

severest of workouts. 'Um, did I just see Scheana on a stretcher?'

I nodded. 'She thinks she's broken her leg. She's OK though, she's gone off in an ambulance.' I knew Scheana wouldn't want her injury to overshadow our achievement so I added, 'She says well done to everyone. Look what we just did! That was hard work but we slayed those muddy hills and slippery bloody monkey bars.'

'What about those dangling electric wires?' said Ian, staggering over to us and putting his hand on Dee's back before quickly removing it. 'I nearly gave up at that point.'

'I welcomed that,' I said, like I thought I was some kind of Kray twin. Like a *boss*. 'The electric shocks warmed me up.'

'OK, folks,' Kim said, walking into the tent with a leaflet clutched in her hand. 'It says the tear gas used under that polythene obstacle wasn't real tear gas and it was totally safe. So you're not going to go blind, Olivia.'

I blinked a few times to make sure. 'OK, thanks. All right. I have something to tell you guys about Scheana and New York . . .'

2 weeks, 3 days to Christmas

I scrolled through the music on my iPhone – surely I had at least one Christmas track on here? Ah-ha! 'Let It Go' from *Frozen*; that counted. I stuck it on repeat and put my phone in the speaker dock just as my doorbell rang.

'Shit me, it's *freezing* out!' burst Kim, as I opened my front door to the sight of my friend – all pink nose and frostbitten fingers – peering out from a mummification of long woollen scarves.

She pushed me aside and unpeeled down to a moderate covering of two woollen jumper dresses, tights, snow boots and a hot water bottle. Kim was always cold, even in the summer, so December in the UK was her Everest.

'I'm not even sorry about choosing Antigua over you, any more,' she said, shaking out her curls. 'It's definitely true what they're saying; winter is coming.'

'Let it Jon Snow . . . ' I muttered with a smirk, leading Kim to the living room. She stopped short.

'I thought we were having a Christmas party?' she demanded. 'Where are your decorations?'

'It's only you and me.'

'I don't care! It's our annual Christmas get-together, you insisted we have it at your house, and you don't even have a tree. I'm sorry, are we homeless? Christmas isn't Christmas without a muthaflippin' Christmas tree.'

'You'll be in Antigua over Christmas – good luck finding a Christmas tree there!' I looked around my sparse maisonette. 'Besides, there are decorations.' I wafted an arm past a tea light candle on a side plate, and a bottle of Baileys.

'Urgh.' Kim started furiously wrapping herself back up in her four-hundred-foot scarf. 'First of all, Antigua will have a lot of Christmas trees, and second of all, we have to go and get you a Christmas tree. Now.'

'But—but—' I looked around. 'We can't go out now, the pizza's in the . . . freezer.'

Kim was already nose-deep in my hall cupboard,

where she emerged and lobbed an armful of coats my way. 'Dress warm, come on.'

'You're so hardy since we did the Fearless Freeze,' I muttered.

'I'm so hardy, Tom Hardy called and wants his name back.'

'You're so tough, you should marry Hilary Duff.'

'You're so weird, you should grow a beard.'

We stepped outside and the cold air hit me like a dry-ice bucket challenge. The dark street twinkled as wet pavements reflected the strings of Christmas lights between lamp-posts. I stamped my feet and blew into one clenched fist while I locked my door. 'Where exactly does one buy a Christmas tree at seven p.m. in the middle of London?'

'No idea,' said Kim, marching off down the street before whizzing around. 'Actually, of course I do. How do you feel about artificial trees?'

I shrugged, unsure what the right answer was.

'Shrug? That's all you give me? Your mother taught you better than that, lady. Always have an opinion, am I right? And *everyone* has opinion on real versus fake. Do you like them full and real and nice-smelling, or perfect and symmetrical and low-maintenance?'

'Are we still talking about trees?'

'Of course.'

'I think I prefer fake. Because I kill things.'

A passing teenage boy darted a look up at me, clutched his phone and ran away.

'Plants, I kill plants,' I clarified. 'And therefore probably trees.'

'Then answer me this,' said Kim, a big smile creeping onto her half-hidden face. 'What do you think of when I say "Christmas shopping"?'

'Oh!' I knew this. 'The scene in *Love Actually* with Rowan Atkinson and the necklace and the dried flowers and the cellophane.'

'Nope.'

'*Serendipity*? You know, when they meet over the last pair of gloves?'

'No, something not from a Christmas movie.'

'January sales?'

'What is wrong with you? John Lewis, of course!'

We reached the Tube station and within minutes we were squeezed among commuters and tourists, roasting like turkeys under all our layers.

Kim was still rabbiting. 'The snowman . . . ? The bear and the hare . . . ? The penguin . . . ? The man on the moon . . . ? Liv, you're killing me.'

'Oh, I remember the penguin advert! He wanted a girlfriend or something, right? But I don't recall the other three.'

'Well congratulations on being the most cold-hearted person in Britain. Have fun on your throne of stone.'

Just as I was beginning to really dislike the feeling of another passenger's roll of wrapping paper jabbing me in the eye, it was time to untangle from the Tubers and spill out onto soggy Oxford Street. It was still heaving at this time in the evening, with a mash-up of every Christmas song from *Now That's What I Call Christmas '94* booming from open shop fronts.

Kim marched us both up the street, weaving expertly like a Dickensian street urchin through the crowds while I bumped my way past the other shoppers and generally made everyone hate me. We stopped in front of John Lewis.

'Merry Christmas! Get in,' Kim commanded.

I'll admit it; John Lewis is lovely at Christmas. Immediately I wanted to buy the entire Scandinavian winter lodge-style fake living room just inside the entrance, from the faux-fur blankets to the log tea-light holders, to the snow-sprinkled reindeer ornaments. I was just reaching for a miniature frosted tree in a pot when Kim slapped my hand away.

'Nope. You need to think bigger. A Christmas tree is going to light up your whole apartment; nay – your life.'

Off we trotted, accepting some of the most wonderful

swag of the year from smiling sales assistants en route: a mini mince pie, a shot glass of Prosecco, and a spritz of the latest Philosophy festive scent. By the time we reached the winter wonderland that was the Christmas department, I was humming along to 'Something Stupid' like I was Nicola Kidman herself.

'How about this one?' I stopped at the first tree, an all-white creation whose spray-painted branches glistened with glittery faux-snow. I liked it.

Kim scrutinised. 'It's a bit ... blank.'

'I like it; it would go really well in my apartment.'

Kim gave me a pointed look which I ignored. 'You know it's only up for about a month, right? We're not shopping for one to coordinate with your curtains.'

'Nope, I like this one.'

I fingered the branches, willing myself to feel Christmassy. I squeezed my eyes shut for a moment, trying to tug back memories from my past of twinkling, traditional ... no. I fell short at the recollection of a Santa in board shorts passing out slices of watermelon. I opened my eyes and focused on the tree, which *was* pretty.

'I like the glitter, I like the fake snow, and I like the thought of buying those three-for-two baubles in red and covering it with them.'

'Like blood splatter on a white wall.'

'Oh. I'll get the gold ones then.'

'If that's what you want . . .' Kim caressed the fluffy branch of a gigantic fake-fir that looked as if it had been lopped down from beside Santa's house in Iceland.

'I want the white one; you don't own me.' My strange affinity with this blank, emotionless tree was something I could mull over with my therapist, Squidgy Rabbit the stuffed rabbit, sometime, but for now I smiled at my friend, who succumbed, and helped me pull the box out of the rack, giant-Jenga style.

Kim looked up at me halfway through the task. 'You will make time for Rockefeller, won't you?'

'Well—'

'That's one Christmas tree you aren't allowed to not care about.'

I pictured the towering red and green-lit tree in my mind, an icon of New York at Christmas, and Kim's favourite place in the world. 'I don't know, I'm sure I'll go past it . . .'

'Liv, you have to go, it's our place.'

'But you won't be there, so it won't be the same anyway. And I don't know if I'll really have time—'

'*Make* time. Please. I know you're one pair of finger-less gloves away from Ebenezer Scrooge but we've been on the New York trip together every year, and every year we go and see the Rockefeller Christmas tree together. This year you have to go for both of us.'

I looked down at my fingerless gloves. Was Kim right? Was I a Scrooge at Christmas? No, I had nothing against Christmas. I liked Christmas, it's just that I didn't really ... care about it. I'd watch a Christmas movie if it was on TV, and drink Baileys if it appeared in my hand, and exchange a couple of presents with my family sometime around the big day, depending on when they were all free to get together. But when you grew up in a family who escaped for two weeks of winter sun every Christmas, and were now spread out around the world, traditions and 'proper Christmases' were a bit off the radar.

Christmas to me was a very lovely, very welcome break from work, from my team and the pressures that come with any job. It was a time to catch up on sleep, and it was the milestone between September and March where I gave my legs a shave.

'I'll go to Rockefeller,' I said. 'I'll send you a photo. If I have time.'

'You're the boss this year, you'll have time.' Kim heaved the box out and, satisfied, trotted off towards the counter while I armed myself with gold baubles (and one box of the red) and a red reindeer to go on the top, because I'm not keen on fairies and the stars looked too prickly.

There was no getting away from it – I *was* the boss

this year. Which was exciting, but ... what had I got myself into?

On the Tube ride home, I trumped that passenger with the awkward rolls of wrapping paper from the previous journey, by forcing everyone to angle themselves around my Christmas tree box as if it were Baby Jesus himself.

'I love my Christmas tree,' I sighed, hugging the box. I'd show Kim Ebenezer Scrooge.

'Praise the lord!' she said, embracing me with one arm. 'And you promise you'll go and see Rockefeller?'

'Sure. This is my first ever Christmas tree, you know.'

Several eavesdropping passengers side-eyed me like I was mad.

'No way.'

'Seriously. We've never had a family Christmas at home, and I've never had one in my flat before.'

'Not even with Kevin?'

'Nope.' I looked away, the best I could, without staring straight into a stranger's set of boobies. It still smarted to think of him, even after all these years. 'We always had Christmas separately, and we never decorated because all the spare money went towards—'

'—the house fund.' Kim finished for me, putting a much-needed end to that little conversation. Kim thought for a while, whilst sucking on a complimentary John Lewis candy cane. 'New York is going to be really good for you, I think. This year, especially. You've never been the one making the decisions about the schedule and planning the itinerary. You've always been told you have to do this at this time, and be there at that time, and have dinner at Ristorante el Blandezvous while making small talk with delegates.'

'This isn't going to be any different – I still have to make sure everyone does the same job.'

'But *you're* in *charge*. You want to have a business meeting over hot chocolates at the top of the Empire State, you can do it. You want to hold a feminist rally on the Central Park ice rink: just book it, honey pie.'

I gulped. All I heard was 'business meeting', and suddenly the fear of everything being On Me hit me. I had to make sure Girls of the World's presence at the #IWasHereNYC conference was a success. Christmas would have to wait.

Back at the flat we decorated my tree, Kim dancing along to a particularly festive-themed episode of *Strictly Come Dancing* (she'd declared my one Christmas song as 'crap') while I found myself thinking about not wanting to think about Kevin.

Trickles of regret ran through me as I hung the gold

and red baubles. I shouldn't have spent this much on a fake tree. A little part of me bitterly thought that Kevin wouldn't be worrying about spending money on a Christmas tree. Well, he didn't need to save up again from scratch, did he?

I looked at my flat. It wasn't even *my* flat; getting out of rented accommodation seemed like such a faraway dream.

Luckily Kim trod on my toe at that point while cha-cha-ing backwards. 'What are you standing still for? It's Christmas, you're going to New York next week, *Strictly*'s on!' She saw my face and stopped. 'Are you OK?'

I stood back and observed the tree. It did look nice. 'I'm not sure I should have spent the money on this tree.'

'Don't start that again.'

'But—'

'Nope. You're in a good job; you're well behaved, like, *all* the time with your money. You can treat yourself once in a while; it's hardly going to make an inch of difference.'

'I'm not well behaved all the time. I like living wild. I ate a muffin for breakfast the other day, and it wasn't even the breakfast kind.'

'What kind was it?'

'Blueberry. They were reduced in Sainsbury's.'

'That's still the breakfast kind.'

I shrugged. 'Fine. Maybe I'll just move in with you and Steve. I'll be the spinster in your basement, the bitter old Miss Havisham in your granny flat. The fly in your ointment.'

'That's the Christmas spirit I was after,' Kim said, and twerked against me (I think she was trying to jive) until I snapped out of my bad mood.

Join the fun online with
Lisa Dickenson

🐦 @LisaWritesStuff
f /LisaWritesStuff

www.lisadickenson.com